ST. MARTIN'S

MINOTAUR
MYSTERIES

GET A CLUE!

Be the first to hear the latest mystery book news…

With the St. Martin's Minotaur monthly newsletter,
you'll learn about the hottest new Minotaur books,
receive advance excerpts from newly published works,
read exclusive original material from featured mystery
writers, and be able to enter to win free books!

Sign up on the Minotaur Web site at:
www.minotaurbooks.com

PRAISE FOR BOB MORRIS AND HIS MYSTERIES

JAMAICA ME DEAD

"[A] zany sophomore effort. . . . The tropical backdrop and Zack's wisecracking commentary make for another crackling whodunit for Morris."

—*Publishers Weekly*

"Good-natured . . . the Jamaica background the biggest plus."

—*Kirkus Reviews*

"A year-round summer read . . . thanks to smart, polished prose; an affable narrator; swift, straightforward plotting in bite-sized chapters; and fun, exotic setting."

—*Booklist*

"The splash that Morris made with last year's Edgar-nominated *Bahamarama* becomes a tidal surge with his highly entertaining second novel. Briskly paced . . . Morris joins the ranks of Florida authors such as James O. Born and Claire Matturro whose second novel is even stronger than the first."

—*South Florida Sun-Sentinel*

"*Bahamarama* is no fluke. While Morris can't be called the Carl Hiaasen of South Florida—there already is one—he comes closest to what fans of comedic mysteries are looking for when they hear that comparison."

—*The Flint Journal*

"A bumpy, tightly-wound ride, with enough cliff-hangers and red herrings to satisfy even the most jaded mystery buff."

—*Sarasota Herald-Tribune*

"Great characterizations, a thorough knowledge of his locales, plus an easy-breezy style that's hard to resist make Bob Morris's *Jamaica Me Dead* another must-read. A new mystery series that's smart, funny, and slightly off-kilter."

—*Bookloons*

MORE . . .

BAHAMARAMA

"I was wondering when Bob Morris would finally get around to writing a novel, and it was worth the wait. *Bahamarama* is sly, smart, cheerfully twisted, and very funny. Morris is a natural."
—Carl Hiaasen

"Bob Morris, a terrific writer and Florida boy, has created a marvelous tale that perfectly captures the nation's strangest state. Like Florida itself, *Bahamarama* is wild, weird, unpredictable, populated by exotic denizens—and funny as hell."
—Dave Barry

"Chasteen makes a fine hero, one who lives by his own rules . . . a highly enjoyable way to pass an afternoon."
—*Miami Herald*

"Morris captures the islands and local people well . . . a great bullets-and-beaches book to pack on your next trip."
—*Caribbean Travel & Life*

"This book stands out. It's a fun and engrossing read from an author who expertly knows the lay of the land and the sea."
—Michael Connelly

"Bob Morris is as tough and fast as Elmore Leonard."
—Randy Wayne White

BERMUDA SCHWARTZ

BOB MORRIS

St. Martin's Paperbacks

This is a work of fiction. All of the characters, organizations and events portrayed in this novel are either products of the author's imagination or are used fictitiously.

BERMUDA SCHWARTZ

Copyright © 2007 by Bob Morris.
Excerpt from *Dead Ahead* copyright © 2008 by Bob Morris.

Cover photo of ocean background © PhotoDisc.

ISBN: 0-312-99749-3
EAN: 978-0-312-99749-6

Printed in the United States of America

St. Martin's Press hardcover edition / February 2007
St. Martin's Paperbacks edition / January 2008

St. Martin's Paperbacks are published by St. Martin's Press, 175 Fifth Avenue, New York, NY 10010.

10 9 8 7 6 5 4 3 2 1

To the one and only Debbie

A long time ago—yet still I remember—
   that I was cut down from the edge of the timber,
and removed from my roots. Powerful fiends there held me off,
   for a spectacle to make, command me a criminal aloft.

—from "The Dream of the Rood"
Anonymous
C. A.D. 750

He knows he will die. No use fighting it now.

"Where is it, Ned?" his killer says.

The words sound far away, as if he were lying at the bottom of a well and someone was calling down to him.

It reminds him of when he was a boy. Three, maybe four. Delirious with fever. Meningitis.

His mother and sister stand by his bed.

"Is Neddie going to die?" his sister says.

"Shhh," his mother quiets her.

And then the sound of his sister crying.

He remembers how he pulled himself back to them, willed himself not to slip away, crawled out of that deep, dark well to where he belonged.

But now . . . there is nothing he can do.

"It's still down there, isn't it?" his killer says.

He doesn't try to answer. His body is shutting down. All that is left of him has retreated to a small safe place, a place beyond fear, beyond pain.

The boat engine idles. He can feel it throbbing through the deck, hear its low rumble. The sound is comforting.

It makes him think of Polly. Her and her yoga. How she talked him into practicing it with her.

It felt good to stretch, to sweat. And to watch Polly, so graceful, so beautiful.

What he couldn't handle was the part, at the very end of

a session, when they had cooled down, and Polly would fold her hands, as if in prayer, close her eyes, and start in with that "Om" business.

"You're supposed to chant with me," she would say. "It's the universal hum, our connection with the life force."

He would try, really he would.

"Ommmm . . ."

But it was too hippy-dippy for him. He would start laughing. And Polly, unable to help herself, would start laughing, too.

He loves her. Their time together has been so brief.

The rumble of the engine . . .

He tries to match its tone.

"Ommmm . . ."

"What's that, Ned?" his killer asks. "You trying to tell me something?"

He feels his killer close to him.

"Ommmm . . ."

"Sorry, Ned. You're not making any sense. But that's okay. I know what I need to know. And I think it's still down there. Else, why would you have come back, eh?"

He feels tightening in the ropes that bind his arms and legs.

"Up you go," his killer says.

He senses himself being lifted to the side of the boat.

And now—a touch of something against his ear, something cold, metallic.

"Sorry, Ned," his killer says. "This might sting a bit."

But the sting is brief, the blackness welcome.

He is dead before he hits the water.

1

Lunchtime at Ocean's Seafood—I'm eating a fried grouper sandwich and grappling with a major philosophical dilemma.

Barbara Pickering sits across the table from me. As usual, she is in tune with my innermost thoughts and desires.

"You are already contemplating a piece of the key lime pie, aren't you?" she says.

"Depends on what you mean by already."

"I mean, you are one bite into your rather large sandwich, there remains a rather small mountain of French fries to be consumed, plus that cupful of coleslaw, and yet there you are thinking about ordering the pie . . . already."

"It's good pie," I say. "They mix crushed peanuts with graham crackers for the crust. They use real lime juice in the filling, not the bottled stuff. Pie like that, there's a lot to contemplate."

Barbara smiles.

"I can read you like a book, Chasteen."

"Oh, really?" I put down my sandwich, lean across the table, and dial up my inner Clooney. "So what are you reading right now?"

Barbara feigns concentration, then surprise. She looks pretty cute doing it.

"Why you filthy, filthy man."

"Damn, you're good."

Barbara's cell phone rings. She looks at the caller ID.

"Oh my, it's Aunt Trula."

"The one in Bermuda?"

Barbara nods.

"The one who is richer than God?"

She nods again.

"Sorry, but I better take it."

No objection from me. I finish off the coleslaw while Barbara exchanges pleasantries with Aunt Trula.

"Why no, Titi, I haven't forgotten, it's your seventieth, isn't it? . . . Oh? That sounds lovely, just lovely . . . We'd be delighted . . ."

The two of them carry on. I eat my sandwich and take in the view outside.

Truth be told, the view from Ocean's is lousy. The Atlantic is nearly a mile away and the windows open on A-1-A as it slithers through Minorca Beach before dead-ending at Coronado National Seashore.

Just down the street from Ocean's sits a miniature golf course with a humongous pink plaster of paris gorilla as its centerpiece. Next to the golf course there's a strip mall anchored at one end by a chiropractor's office and at the other end by the Mane Event, which despite its name is a decent enough place to get a haircut.

In between you'll find Blue Cat Surf Shop, Barr's Bait and Tackle, the Wine Warehouse, and not one, but two real estate offices. This is, after all, Florida. By state law, the percentage of realtors must always be at a level three times that of any other so-called profession and there's not nearly enough room to store them all.

I finish the grouper sandwich and catch the eye of the curly-haired woman, Kim, who is working behind the counter. I mime my desperate need for pie and she delivers it.

Just as I am savoring the first bite, I hear Barbara say: "That sounds like a wonderful idea. I'm sure Zack can help you out. He's sitting right here."

Barbara hands me the phone. I look at it. Then I take another bite of the pie.

"Aunt Trula wants to speak with you."

"That would be rude," I say. "To the pie."

Barbara covers the phone with her hand.

"She's getting ready to celebrate her seventieth birthday," she whispers.

"We'll send flowers."

"It's not until April. She wants me to go early and help with the party."

"So, go."

"She wants you to go, too. She has a business proposition for you. She has offered to buy our tickets."

"She doesn't even know me."

"I've told her all about you."

"Including the part about how I can stand by the bed naked and flex my butt in time with my dazzling a cappella rendition of 'Chantilly Lace'?"

Barbara gives me that look she can give. She sticks out the phone. I take it.

"Hello there," I say.

I think I sound fairly chipper, at least for someone who has just been unwillingly separated from his dessert.

"Hello, Mr. Chasteen. It's a pleasure to meet you."

"And you."

We go on like that for a bit. And I manage to nibble at the pie without making loud swinish noises.

Aunt Trula speaks in a British accent. She sounds a lot like Barbara. Understandable. She is the younger sister of Barbara's mother. And ever since Barbara's mother passed away a few years ago, Barbara and Aunt Trula have become particularly close.

"I understand that you are a horticulturist, Mr. Chasteen."

"Nope, I just raise palm trees."

There is a brief silence while I suppose that Aunt Trula is considering whether she really wants to continue a conversation with someone who is more dirt farmer than title-holding functionary.

I take the opportunity to grab another bite of pie. And to consider Dorothy Parker. You can lead a whore to culture, but you can't make her . . .

"Think you can help me with a little landscaping project that I have in mind?" Aunt Trula says.

"I'll try."

"If one wished to plant one's backyard with palm trees that made a statement, then which palm trees would one choose?"

"Depends on what statement one was trying to make."

"That one had lived for seventy years and wished to celebrate it," says Aunt Trula. "Majesty, splendor, that sort of thing."

No self-esteem issues for her.

"Then I'd say you should go with *Bismarckia nobilis*. Better known as a Bismarck."

"Like that German chap, the one with the mustache, the first chancellor or whatever he was."

"Like him exactly. Otto von Bismarck. Had lots of things named after him, including a battleship that got sunk and a city in North Dakota. I think he'd be proudest of the palm trees."

"Tell me about them."

"Broad silvery fronds that fan out like a crown. Grow to about eighty feet tall. Real showstoppers."

"Do you raise Bismarck palms, Mr. Chasteen?"

"Matter of fact, I do. There's a large stand of them at the nursery, several dozen. My grandfather brought back the seed pods from Madagascar and planted them years ago, before I was even born. They're nearly full-grown. Just like me."

Another pause on Aunt Trula's end. She's a Brit. You'd think she'd appreciate my brilliant dry humor.

"Very well then," she says. "I would like eight of your very best Bismarcks delivered to me here in Bermuda—one for each of the decades in which I have lived. And one more for the decade yet ahead of me."

"Why cut yourself short? You might hit ninety. Or a hundred."

"I don't intend to," she says.

Before I can come up with a suitable response, Aunt Trula says: "So how much?"

"Well, it's not quite that simple," I say.

As palm trees go, Bismarcks are fairly cold hardy. So I'm not worried about their surviving winters in Bermuda, which, even though it is six hundred miles off the coast of North Carolina, enjoys the blessings of the Gulf Stream and gets no cooler than Minorca Beach.

Bismarcks are salt tolerant, so stiff sea breezes aren't a problem. And they're adaptable to a wide range of soil, so given a suitable pH range they can thrive in Bermuda's limestone marl.

The trouble comes with transplanting. Bismarcks don't take kindly to it. Once established somewhere, they prefer to stay put. Like too many people I know.

I spend several minutes explaining the downside to Aunt Trula.

"No buts, Mr. Chasteen. I want those Bismarcks. And I want them planted in my backyard in time for my party in April. How much?"

I come up with a price in my head. Then I double it. Because I don't really want to dig up eight specimen-quality Bismarck palms and ship them on a freighter to Bermuda. Especially if they are just going to die once they get there.

I tell Aunt Trula what it will cost her. It is hard to get the number out of my mouth without laughing.

"Splendid, Mr. Chasteen," says Aunt Trula. "What say I add another fifty percent for all your trouble?"

"Deal," I say.

But like always, I've underestimated the trouble part. And hauling palms to Bermuda is only the start of it.

2

Three months later, on an April afternoon eight days before Aunt Trula's big birthday bash, our plane touches down at Bermuda International.

The runway glistens from a midday rain. Barbara and I follow Boggy as we step onto the tarmac for the short walk to immigration and customs.

We are a dapper-looking bunch. Barbara is wearing something gray and silky from Eileen Fisher that manages to be casual and sexy and elegant all at once. I sport a brand-new blue blazer, nice khakis, and a relatively spot-free polo, all the better for impressing dear Aunt Trula. Even Boggy looks fairly dashing—this is Bermuda after all—in a white guayabera with baggy cargo pants and his best leather sandals.

Halfway to the terminal, Boggy stops dead in his tracks. We almost bump into him.

He slings his carry-on bag off his shoulder. It isn't really a bag so much as it is an old handwoven blanket into which he has stuck everything he thinks he might need in Bermuda then rolled up and fastened with bungee cords. He didn't check any luggage.

He reaches inside the bag and pulls out a leather pouch. He opens the pouch and takes from it two small, black, shiny stones. He sets down the bag and the pouch. Then he stretches out his arms, palms to the sky, a stone in each hand. He closes his eyes and sniffs the air.

Other passengers weave around us, staring at Boggy.

"Don't mind him," I tell them. "He thinks he's a Taino shaman."

Barbara gives me an elbow.

"Shhhh," she says.

She's far more tolerant of Boggy's ways than I am. Still, I am glad he has decided to join us.

Boggy oversaw the delicate business of getting the Bismarcks ready for the road. We couldn't just pluck them out of the ground and ship them off. They wouldn't have survived the shock.

Boggy nursed them along. He spent a couple of hours each day with them, gently digging and nipping away.

Eventually each of the Bismarcks was extracted from the loam at Chasteen Palm Nursery. Its root ball, about the size of a VW Bug, was wrapped in burlap. And its fronds were drawn together around the crown and tied with sisal rope.

We loaded them onto two tractor-trailers and hauled them to the port at Fernandina Beach. Cranes stacked them side by side aboard the freighter *Somers Isles* for their four-day trip to Bermuda.

An excruciating amount of paperwork was involved, mainly from the Bermuda Department of Agriculture, Fisheries and Parks, which wanted all sorts of guarantees that the palms were not infested with weevils and other vermin. As if anything coming out of Florida could make such a guarantee. We sprayed them with Dursban and hoped for the best.

The day before we were to fly out of Orlando, I got word from the shipping company that the Bismarcks had arrived and passed inspection. Aunt Trula had already paid the 33 percent import tax—even though I lowballed the value on the bill of lading, the levy still hit a low five figures—and the palms would be ready to plant once we got there.

But first, we have to go through immigration, get our bags, and clear customs, then get a taxi to Aunt Trula's. And here we are, still standing on the tarmac, while Boggy gets in touch with the freaking cosmos.

All the other passengers are long gone. The crew will soon be exiting the plane. They'll see Boggy standing there zoned out, in one of his trances—a short, round dark man with a braided ponytail that falls to the seat of his pants— and they'll call security. The authorities will lock us all up. You just don't screw around at airports these days.

I poke Boggy in the back.

"Move it, Mr. Mystic," I say.

He doesn't budge, doesn't even seem to notice that we are standing there. Barbara shoots me a dirty look.

"What?" I say. "He's just going to come out of it spouting some crap about having one of his visions. 'I see much darkness, Zachary.' Or 'The way ahead it is very gray, Zachary.' It's always something goddamn gloomy like that. It creeps me out."

"He's always right," says Barbara. "Exactly right."

I look at her.

"No, what he is, he's exactly vague."

"How can someone be exactly vague?" Barbara says. "That doesn't make sense."

"And that's what I'm saying. He talks mumbo-jumbo."

"Oh, really? And what about that time in Harbour Island? He knew the hurricane was going to turn and slice through the Bahamas."

"A lucky guess," I say. "Even monkeys and TV weathermen sometimes make them."

"What about last year, when you went down to Jamaica?"

"What about it?"

"Before you left, he predicted that everything was going to turn bad."

"No, he did not," I say. "I remember exactly what he told me. And what he told me was, 'It will not be quite so easy as you expect, Zachary.'"

Barbara makes a gesture with her hands and her shoulders that says, "So, there."

"No, no. That is not a prediction," I say. "That is horse flop. Because nothing is ever quite so easy as anyone expects.

And just because Boggy says it doesn't mean he's clued into the future more than anyone else."

Barbara does this thing with her eyebrows that says: "You're wasting your breath, pal."

Boggy lowers his hands, opens his eyes. He returns the stones to the pouch, the pouch to the bag.

When he turns to face us, he is smiling. Peculiar, since Boggy is generally pretty miserly with emotions and his smiles are rare indeed.

He says, "That which is planted here will grow strong."

Then he picks up his bag and walks toward the terminal.

As we follow him, Barbara says, "Now that wasn't so goddamn gloomy, was it?"

"Just more mumbo-jumbo," I say.

3

As promised, the Bismarcks are waiting in the backyard of Aunt Trula's house when we arrive.

It is some kind of house—a three-story Georgian affair with more rooms than I'll probably have a chance to see during the two weeks we plan to stay here.

And it is some kind of backyard—the length of a football field from the rear of the house to the bluffs overlooking the beach.

The whole place is called Cutfoot Estate. I figure there must once have been a Lord Cutfoot or an Admiral Cutfoot or a Rich Somebody Cutfoot who originally owned the property. I figure wrong.

"Named after Cutfoot Bay," explains Aunt Trula, with a nod to the ocean. "The rocks down there are quite vicious, like razors. They make the beach rather difficult to walk on."

After a pair of butlers haul away our bags—I am pretty sure we'll need detailed maps to find our rooms later—Aunt Trula whisks us off to a sunny terrace, where we sit having tea.

It is just the three of us—Barbara, Aunt Trula, and I—sipping cups of Earl Grey. Boggy has already joined Aunt Trula's chief gardener to inspect the Bismarcks.

A pretty young woman in a black-and-white maid's uniform serves us goodies from a silver tray—cucumber topped with a smidgen of salmon, watercress sandwiches, and other

dainty things that require you ingest them by large handfuls
if you wish to gain anything approaching sustenance. I am
hungry, my natural state, and I am trying hard not to make it
look as if I am foraging.

We watch Boggy as he moves from where the Bismarcks
lay on one side of the lawn. The chief gardener—a slender,
erect man named Cedric, outfitted in a khaki uniform—
follows Boggy, carrying a shovel. When they reach the general vicinity of where the palms are to be planted, Boggy
takes the shovel and starts digging a hole.

Aunt Trula wants the Bismarcks planted in a V-shape,
four on each side. They will start just beyond a big fountain
off the terrace, bordering beds of lilies and amaryllis and
opening onto the ocean.

The pretty young woman refills our cups and disappears
inside the house. Aunt Trula takes a sip of tea, puts down her
cup, and fixes her gaze on me.

She smiles. It is a thin, forced, I'm-still-sizing-you-up
smile. That's OK. I'm still sizing her up, too.

So far, she has pretty much met my expectations. Sturdy
and imperious, quite fit for almost seventy, her beauty still
rigorously intact. Dame Judi Dench was born to play her.

"I must tell you, Mr. Chasteen, I am rather disappointed
in those palm trees of yours."

It catches me off guard.

"Oh?"

That is all I can manage, but I ennunciate it nicely.

"They seem rather unsubstantial," says Aunt Trula.

"Well, that's probably because they're tied up and laying
on the ground. Wait until we get them planted, then I think
you'll like them just fine."

"I don't think so," she says. "They aren't as tall as you led
me to believe."

I look at Barbara. The way she wrinkles her eyebrows is
barely perceptible, but it conveys boundless sympathy. It
also conveys an unmistakable amusement. I am on my own
here. I forge ahead.

"It was never my intention to mislead you," I say. "Those

Bismarcks are at least sixty or seventy feet tall, and that's just about as tall as the species gets."

Aunt Trula makes a face.

"Disappointing," she says.

She reaches for one of the cucumber thingies. She removes the salmon from it and takes a small bite of cucumber, studying me while she chews.

"Don't worry," I say. "You're in luck."

"How's that?" says Aunt Trula.

"I brought a palm stretcher with me."

"A palm stretcher?"

"Uh-huh. We can hook it up and get another twenty feet out of each of those palms, no problem."

Aunt Trula considers me. She purses her lips while she does it.

"You are jesting," she says.

"I am," I say.

Aunt Trula says nothing. I get the distinct feeling that she is not someone who appreciates a good jesting.

I reach for the watercress sandwiches and dispatch with two of them in rapid order. Enough to fuel a hummingbird for maybe fifteen minutes.

Aunt Trula says, "My niece tells me that you were once an athlete, Mr. Chasteen. Football, was it?"

"It was."

"Rather a brutish sport, in my opinion."

"In mine, too."

It gets a raised eyebrow from Aunt Trula.

"Then why, Mr. Chasteen, did you play?"

"Because I'm a brute."

Barbara covers her mouth, stifling a laugh. Aunt Trula scrunches her lips some more, then unscrunches them to sip some tea.

We turn our attention back to the lawn. Boggy puts down the shovel. He kneels by the shallow hole he's dug and reaches into it.

"Your man there," says Aunt Trula. "What did you say his name is?"

I start to tell her that Boggy is neither my man, nor any-one else's. But I catch a look from Barbara. Behave, it says.

"His full name is Cachique Baugtanaxata," I say. "That's why we call him Boggy."

"And what is he exactly?"

"He's my associate," I say.

"No, no, I meant what *is* he?"

"Well, he's an aggravation sometimes, I can tell you that. A damn aggravation."

"Mr. Chasteen," she says, "I mean . . . where does he come from?"

I know what she means. I'm just not having any part of it.

"He's from Hispaniola," I finally say. "The Dominican Republic side."

"He doesn't look Hispanic."

"He's not."

"And he's not a Negro."

"No, he's not."

"And he's no Chinaman."

I don't reply to that.

"So what is he exactly?"

"He's Taino," I say.

"Tie what?"

"Taino. They lived in the Caribbean long before any Europeans made it there."

"Ah, I see," says Aunt Trula. "He's an Indian fellow."

"No," I say. "He's Taino. Indians are what the Europeans called them. Because they had their heads up their asses about where they were."

If I sound a little testy it's only because I am.

Cue, Barbara.

"Titi," she says, reaching for her aunt's arm, "why don't we take a stroll?"

"Splendid idea," says Aunt Trula. "I could use the fresh air."

And she gives me a smile even thinner than the one before.

4

I follow Barbara and Aunt Trula off the terrace. They go their way—to a gazebo on the bluff overlooking the ocean. And I go mine—to where Boggy and Cedric kneel by the hole in the lawn.

The two of them stand as I approach.

Boggy says, "There is a problem, Zachary."

"Yep, there is," I say. "It's called Aunt Trula. She's a pain in the ass."

Cedric looks away, biting back a smile.

Boggy picks up the shovel and pokes it in the hole. It only goes down a foot or so and then it hits something. Something that sounds like rock.

"That is the problem," says Boggy. "Limestone. We cannot dig a hole that will be deep enough for the palms."

"Well, so much for your prediction, huh?"

"What do you mean, Zachary?"

"I mean, that little scene back at the airport, where you held those stones in your hands and did your Taino-vision thing. You said what we planted here would grow strong."

"Yes, that is what I said."

"So this limestone thing is just a little bump in the road? We'll work around it? The palms will be all right?"

Boggy shrugs.

"About the palms, I do not know, Zachary. Maybe they live, maybe they die."

I just look at him. An aggravation, a damn aggravation.

"How much hole do we need for these palms?" Cedric asks.

"Five or six feet at least," I say. "The root balls need to be covered with soil or else the palms will die."

"Then we've got some hard digging ahead of us. I don't know that we have all the equipment here that we'll need. I better go make some calls."

"I'll go with you," Boggy says.

After the two of them have stepped away, I kneel beside the hole. I reach down and touch the limestone. Hard digging for sure.

We might be better served by dynamite. And, if not that, then at least some kind of big drill.

Which will mean renting heavy equipment, maybe paying for a couple of guys to help shovel out the rock and haul it away.

I'm thinking that these are turning out to be some very expensive palm trees when I hear Barbara shout: "Zack!"

She is standing in the gazebo with Aunt Trula, waving for me to come quick.

I set off on a run across the big back lawn. When I get to the gazebo, Barbara points to the water.

"Out there," she says. "I think it's . . ."

I look to where she is pointing. A wave washes over a finger of jagged rocks that juts out from the beach. Sea foam sprays everywhere. I can't see what she is pointing at.

"Darling, please," says Aunt Trula. "It's just a bag of garbage. Probably off one of the cruise ships. It happens now and then."

Then the wave washes out to reveal something hung up on the rocks, something black and misshapen, something that is no bag of garbage.

"Stay here," I tell Barbara and Aunt Trula.

I scramble down the side of the bluff, stripping off blazer, shirt, and shoes as I go.

There's no reason for me to hurry. Not if the object in the water turns out to be what I fear it is.

But pumped by the adrenaline of the moment, I hit the beach running, hurdle the first wave, and the next, and then land squarely atop a rock, one of those rocks that gave this particular beach its name.

Knives slash the sole of my right foot and I twist as I go down, trying to break the fall. And then knives are slashing my shoulder.

A wave rolls me over and I catch a glimpse of my foot, blood drizzling from the heel. I grab for my shoulder, feel the gash, figure it must be bleeding, too.

Another wave crashes in, and now the water is just deep enough for me to grab a stroke without scraping bottom. Then another and another.

I close in on the finger of rocks that juts out of the water. And I can make out what I'd been dreading to see.

The dead guy wears a black wet suit, a full-body one, with footies and a neoprene hood. He is hogtied, his arms and legs bound behind his back with a nylon rope that has hung up on the rocks.

Easy enough to forgive Aunt Trula for thinking she'd seen a bag of garbage. It is a neat little black bundle of death.

I tread water, trying to figure out the best way to approach this, how to get the body unsnagged without actually, you know, having to touch it.

I reach for the rope, manage to slip it off the rock. I get a good grip and sidestroke to shore, towing my grim cargo behind me.

And then another wave rolls in. It lifts the body, thrusts it forward. And suddenly I am face-to-face with the dead guy.

Only his is like no face I've ever seen, nor ever wish to see again.

It's his eyes. They are gone. Just two ugly holes where once eyes had been.

5

By the time I draw close to shore, Boggy is wading out to help me. Together we drag the body from the water and lay it on its side in the sand.

I grab my blazer, drape it over the guy's head, and shield us from his zombie stare.

Barbara and Aunt Trula have already gone inside the house to call the police. Boggy and I sit on the rocks and wait.

The cut on my foot is nasty, but it will heal without stitches. The scrapes on my shoulder sting worse than they look. No telling what all kind of marine bacteria is now crawling around under my skin.

Still, I'm way better off than the guy lying on the beach under my blazer. Boggy and I try not to look at him.

"It was not the fish," says Boggy.

"Not the fish what?"

"Not the fish that did that to his eyes."

"Why you think that?"

"Because he has not been dead so very long. The body, it is not swell up. His wet suit, it has no tears, no holes. The rest of him, it has not been eaten."

I taste something bitter at the back of my throat. I swallow hard and keep it down.

I look at the ocean. And I keep looking at the ocean until the team from the Bermuda Police Service arrives.

There are six of them, plus two EMTs, one of them carrying a fold-up stretcher as they make their way down the side of the bluff.

On their heels is a tall woman with a frizzy ponytail of black hair, her notepad at the ready. A newspaper reporter, I'm guessing. A photographer trails her. And following them is a TV news crew. The insignia on the camera says ZBM-TV and has the CBS logo. The guy carrying it stumbles as he comes down the bluff, catching himself just before his camera bites the sand.

The cop in charge of things introduces himself to Boggy and me as Chief Inspector Worley. He is fortyish, short, and slender.

"If you gentlemen don't mind staying right where you are, we'll take your statement shortly," he says in a deep voice that doesn't match his compact size.

Worley moves toward the body and squats beside it. He studies it for a moment before lifting the blazer.

He jerks his head away, lets go of the blazer.

"Goddamn," he mutters.

He pokes his chin at the reporters and photographers as they jockey for angles.

"Get them out of here," Worley tells one of his people.

An officer steps in and herds them away. The woman reporter who led the charge puts up an objection, but soon she is climbing back up the bluff with the rest of them, joining Barbara and Aunt Trula.

The rocks create a natural barrier and keep the few curiosity seekers on the beach at bay. But the blufftop provides a prime vantage point. It stretches for half a mile on either side of us, lined by stately compounds, some of them bigger even than Aunt Trula's. Already, there are dozens of people standing in tight little clumps along the bluff, pointing and taking turns with binoculars.

Worley lifts the blazer again. He studies the face longer this time. Then he lets the blazer drop and wipes his hand on his pants.

He stands and speaks with the other cops. One of them

squats down and peeks under the blazer. He gets up quickly. The others keep their distance.

I look up at the bluff. The TV cameraman has his lens trained on Barbara and Aunt Trula. The reporter he is teamed with stands off camera asking the two of them questions. Barbara has an arm around Aunt Trula's shoulders. Both of them seem to be handling everything just fine.

Worley steps over to where Boggy and I sit on the rocks.

"Show me where you found the body."

I point to the place.

"It was wedged between those rocks out there."

Worley flips open a cell phone and steps away, punching numbers. He speaks to someone on the phone, then closes it. He steps over to the five other cops and speaks to them.

When he is done, the cops split up. Two of them work one way along the shoreline, nudging clumps of seaweed with their shoes, poking around rocks. Another two go in the opposite direction, doing the same thing.

The fifth cop waves in the two EMTs. They unfold the stretcher as Worley makes his way back to us.

"You two together?"

Boggy and I nod.

"American?"

We both nod again.

"Passports?"

"Up at the house," I say.

"You're staying with Mrs. Ambister?"

It takes me a second. I only know her as Aunt Trula. I've never heard Barbara use her last name.

"Yes," I say. "We just got here this afternoon."

"Some welcome," Worley says.

The EMTs finish loading the body onto the stretcher and start moving toward the bluff. It will be a tricky climb.

Worley sees them and calls out: "Just put it down right there. Got a boat on the way. You can load him up in it."

He turns back to us, pulls out a notepad and a pen.

"OK," he says. "Tell me anything else I need to know."

There isn't much to tell. By the time I'm done, two

Boston Whalers have arrived and are idling several yards offshore. They are twenty-seven-footers, each bearing the logo of the Bermuda Police Service.

There are three people in each boat—a uniformed officer at the helm and two scuba divers, wet suits on but not zipped up all the way.

Worley steps to the edge of the water and hollers instructions. One of the boats moves out about a hundred yards. Moments later both sets of divers are in the water, working a grid, slowly and methodically closing in on each other.

There is nothing to do but sit and watch. I look up at the bluff. Barbara and Aunt Trula are no longer to be seen. But the crews from the newspaper and the TV station are still hanging around.

Worley climbs up the bluff and speaks to them for half an hour or so. By the time he comes back down to the beach it is starting to get dark. The divers have converged, but there is nothing to report. They get back on the boats.

Worley waves in one of the boats. The EMTs roll up their pants, wade out with the stretcher, and load it onto the boat.

The officer at the helm whips the wheel and gives the boat some gas.

Boggy and I watch the boat skitter away across the inky waves, heading to wherever it is they take dead bodies that wash ashore on the beaches of Bermuda.

6

It's not like you," Barbara says.

"Not like me what?"

"To let someone like Aunt Trula get under your skin."

Barbara lies in bed, multitasking, chatting with me as she reviews a stack of galleys for *Tropics* that she lugged with her on the plane. For her there's really no such thing as a total vacation.

I lean against a wall watching her. It beats hell out of ESPN any day.

Dinner was a couple of hours ago—breasts of chicken, iceberg salad with bottled dressing, nothing to get excited about.

"How many husbands did you tell me she'd been through?"

"Five. Uncle Taylor, my favorite, was the last."

"So, for Aunt Trula, marriage is a growth industry?"

Barbara levels a look at me.

"Please," she says, "she's the only family I've got."

"Sorry, guess I've got no complaints. Not compared to that poor bastard on the beach."

"The police have no idea who it might be?"

I shake my head.

"No identification on the body, but there's nothing unusual about that. The guy was in a wet suit. He'd obviously been diving. You don't carry your wallet when you're doing that."

Barbara returns her attention to the galleys. It's crunch week at Orb Communications, the magazine publishing company she owns. The next issue of *Tropics* is due to the printer in two days and, as always, the staff is scrambling to make deadline. Barbara has a 228-page issue to review before she can call it a night.

"You like this cover?" she says, holding up one of the page proofs.

A gorgeous tanned woman in a yellow bikini lounges on a raft in one of those ritzy infinity pools. A handsome tanned man wades toward her, carrying two pinkish umbrella drinks on a tray.

In the background, St. Lucia's dreamy twin peaks, the Pitons, soar over Soufrière Bay. The cover line reads: "10 Best Places for Romance."

I recognize the photograph, mainly because I had accompanied Barbara on the photo shoot just a few weeks earlier. It was taken at Anse Chastanet, the hillside resort owned by Barbara's friends, Nick and Karolyn Troubetzkoy.

"So what do you think?" says Barbara.

"The girl in the bikini and the guy with the drinks—they gonna do it in the pool?"

"I suppose that would be the subtext. The image is rather evocative. That's why I like it."

"We did it in that pool. That very night as I remember."

"Another reason why I like this particular shot," says Barbara.

"But you can't have a headline that says: 'Ten Best Places to Get Laid.' "

"No," Barbara says, nearly laughing. "That would be breaking ground that I'm not sure we want to break."

"You'd sell a helluva lot of copies."

"And lose a helluva lot of advertisers."

"Screw 'em."

"Screw the advertisers? Never," Barbara says. "That's blasphemy."

She lays the page proof across her lap, drums her fingers

on it. She looks at me as if she is getting ready to say something.

"You're getting ready to say something," I say.

"Yes, I am."

"So say it."

"It's a question, actually."

"So ask it."

"Okay, I will." She pauses. "How is your room?"

And the laugh she's been holding back breaks loose.

"Not funny," I say. "I mean, separate bedrooms? What's that all about?"

Barbara shakes her head.

"I don't know," she says. "I mean, this is Aunt Trula's home and she is entitled to make the rules. Still, I must say that the sleeping arrangements rather surprised me. When I stayed here before with Bryce . . ."

She stops, the mirth of a moment before suddenly gone.

Bryce was Bryce Gannon, Barbara's former fiancé. He's been dead going on two years. Barbara had split up with him long before that. Still, his death—his murder, actually—had been brutal and ugly and she had felt largely responsible for it.

"You can talk about Bryce. It doesn't bother me."

Barbara nods. She doesn't say anything.

"Do you mean to tell me that when you and Bryce stayed here, she let you share a room?"

Another nod from Barbara.

"And here I am stuck clear in another wing of the house? Good thing I dropped bread crumbs. I think I might find my way back."

Barbara smiles.

"So," she says. "What about Boggy?"

"Oh, Aunt Trula put him out in the servants' quarters."

Barbara's eyes go wide.

"Kidding," I say. "He's next door to me. He's already tucked in."

I lie down beside her on the bed, hold her close. We're a good fit, like spoons in a drawer.

Barbara lets out a big sigh.

"What was that for?"

"Oh, nothing really. Old memories, good times," she says. "It feels more like home here than anywhere else I know."

"More like home than back in Florida?"

Barbara touches my cheek, smiles.

"I can't help it, Zack. I was a little girl here. It was all horse-back riding and learning to swim and magnificent golden days with endless possibilities. I've always thought . . ."

She stops.

"You've always thought what?"

"I've always thought that if I was to get married then this is where it would be."

There are any number of things I could say at that moment. I don't say any of them.

I roll onto my back, stare at the ceiling.

We've been together four years. Exclusively. Of course, I spent almost two of those years in a federal prison for something I didn't do. So that time doesn't count.

Or maybe it does. Maybe it counts even more because we endured it. We have endured a lot.

I keep staring at the ceiling.

Barbara says, "That wasn't meant to be, you know, a hint or anything like that."

"I know."

"It just came out," she says.

"Things do."

There isn't much to see on the ceiling except maybe it could use some paint.

"Look at me," Barbara says.

I look.

"Is it just a girl thing?"

"Is what?"

"Dreaming of where you'll get married, how it will be? The music, the flowers, the dresses . . ."

"Definitely a girl thing. Because I have never once dreamed about dresses. Except whichever one you might be wearing and the quickest way to get you out of it."

She takes a swat at me.

"You," she says. "You know what I mean."

"I do," I say.

Barbara gets a funny look on her face.

I sputter: "I mean, I know what you mean. About thinking about getting married and all that. I don't mean 'I do' like '*I do*.' Not like that. But I've thought about it. In, you know, a general sense. Nothing specific or . . ."

She puts a finger on my lips.

"Shut up, please," she says. "I love you."

7

By noon the next day everything is proceeding about as well as one can reasonably expect.

On the palm-tree front, a backhoe crew has arrived to survey where the eight holes need to be dug. They have brought along an auger attachment and they figure it will chew through the limestone, no problem. Still, it will be slow going and take several days to complete the job. Boggy and Cedric the gardener are working with them and have everything under control.

On the Aunt Trula front, the caterer is due to arrive any minute. Aunt Trula wants Barbara to sit in and help finalize the menu for the big party.

And on the Zack front, I'm hurting. The cuts on my foot and shoulder are puffy and red and show every sign of imminent infection unless I keep dousing them with hydrogen peroxide.

That's OK because no one seems to need me for anything. I am Zack the Expendable. Not that I am feeling sorry for myself. There's something I need to do.

"I think I'll go visit my money," I tell Barbara.

"I'd almost forgotten about that," she says. "It's living here now, isn't it?"

"Yes. Richfield Bank in Hamilton."

"And you intend to just waltz into the bank and spend some quality time with your money?"

"Yeah, I think I'll ask them to put it in a big pile and let me roll around in it."

"Not bloody likely."

"No, bankers are funny like that. So I'll probably just introduce myself, check the place out, and put a face on whoever's in charge of things."

"Meaning, you'll be heading into Hamilton."

"I'll need a car. Think I can borrow Aunt Trula's?"

"Don't see why not," Barbara says. "I'll go ask her if you like."

"I like," I say.

One reason things have proceeded so well this morning is that Aunt Trula and I have avoided each other. She is in her study, attending to her affairs and preparing to meet the caterer. I am sitting in a little alcove off the kitchen where Barbara and I have just finished a late breakfast.

Barbara steps away. And I sit there thinking about my money.

It is a pretty good chunk of money, better than two million gringo dollars. I need not go into all the details of how it came my way. That's why it is now living in Bermuda, where they tend not to ask questions about the lineage of one's liquid assets.

It took me a couple of weeks to earn the money, through a venture in Jamaica that I entered with no thought of profit, only friendship. When the friendship sputtered—exploded was more like it—and profit presented itself, then who was I to ignore it?

I need not go into too many details, either, about the guy who paid me the money. His name is Freddie Arzghanian, and he is based in Montego Bay, where he oversees various enterprises throughout the Caribbean, most of them illegal.

Still, Freddie is, in his own way, a man of honor, and I earned the money he paid me without breaking any laws. At least no big ones. Or any that didn't need breaking in the first place.

Put it this way: There's nothing for me to hang my head about.

Freddie had advised me that my life would be a whole lot simpler if I set myself up as an IBC, an international business corporation, with headquarters in Bermuda. Sounded fine by me.

I didn't have any moral qualms about sheltering somewhat shady money from the sticky fingers of the IRS. By my ledger, the U.S. government was still working off the debt it owed me for the one year, nine months, and twenty-three days I'd spent in Baypoint Federal Prison Camp for something I didn't do. My time was expensive. They owed me a ton.

So I'd let Freddie handle the details. He connected me with a firm in Bermuda that had done all the legal stuff necessary to establish an IBC. I decided to call it Guamikeni Enterprises, a little joke between Boggy and myself.

"Guamikeni" is what Boggy calls me sometimes, when he's trying to be funny. It's a Taino word, meaning "Lord of land and sea." It's what the Taino called Christopher Columbus after they were there to greet him when he landed on San Salvador. Less than a century later, the Taino were no more, victims of twin European imports—disease and colonization.

So when Boggy, who claims against all proof to the contrary that he is the last living full-blooded Taino, calls me Guamikeni, it carries with it the insinuation that I could be responsible for his eventual demise. Taino humor is really twisted.

In any event, it was easy setting up Guamikeni Enterprises as an IBC. All I had done was sign some papers. And my money was now residing at Richfield Bank.

I hadn't touched it. I'd just let it sit. I know people who are smart with money and they would never just let it sit, but I wasn't particularly smart with money. Besides, it felt good knowing I had money I could just let sit if I wanted to.

8

Barbara returns from her mission to see Aunt Trula carrying a copy of the *Royal Gazette*. She hands me the paper and points to a boxed story at the bottom of the front page.

BODY FOUND ALONG CUTFOOT BAY, the headline reads.

There's a photo, not a very good one, showing Worley and the other policemen huddled on the beach, with the body just barely visible in the background.

The story is short. And it doesn't reveal anything I don't already know. The victim has yet to be publicly identified. Cause of death remains unknown. There is no mention of the victim's eyes and how they'd been mutilated.

The story quotes Worley as saying the police are "treating the incident as a possible homicide." Right. As if someone could hogtie himself and then commit suicide. After gouging out his own eyes.

I put the paper down.

"I asked Titi about her car," Barbara says. "She says she can't let you borrow it."

"Why am I not surprised by that?"

"It really has nothing to do with her, Zack. I'd forgotten, but they have some rather odd laws about cars here."

As Barbara explains, it all has to do with Bermuda's status as one of the most densely populated places on the planet. As a result, no household can own more than one car.

And foreign visitors are prohibited from obtaining a driver's license, which means they can neither rent cars nor borrow them from Bermudians.

"Which explains why all the tourists drive mopeds," I say.

"Exactly," says Barbara. "It also explains why King Edward Hospital is such a busy place. Something like forty tourist-on-moped accidents a week."

"That statistic courtesy of Aunt Trula?"

"No, right here," Barbara says, tapping the *Royal Gazette*. "There's a story about how the hospital is building a new orthopedic wing. Apparently it's boom time for broken bones in Bermuda, not something they advertise in the tourist brochures. Still, if you want to take your chances, Titi does have a couple of mopeds. She says you are welcome to borrow one of them."

"I told you she hated me."

"She doesn't hate you. It was just a prickly beginning," Barbara says. "Do you want to borrow a moped or not?"

"Guys like me don't do good on mopeds. Too much beef, not enough butt-rest. Plus, our knees stick out and wreak havoc with the aerodynamics," I say. "I think I'll pass."

"That's what I thought you'd say. So Titi went ahead and called for a driver. He'll take you wherever you need to go. And he'll be here any minute."

"That was nice of her."

Barbara smiles.

"She *is* nice. The two of you just got off on the wrong foot, that's all," Barbara says. "Once you've finished your business in Hamilton, she'd like you to join us for cocktails and dinner at the club."

"The club?"

"The Mid Ocean Club. It's down-island a bit, in Tucker's Town."

"Sounds uppity."

"Very uppity. Which is what makes it the institution that it is. Everyone who's anyone in Bermuda is a member, along with the likes of Ross Perot, Michael Bloomberg . . ."

"The mayor guy. New York, right?"

Barbara nods.

"Silvio Berlusconi . . ."

"Who's she?"

"He. Former prime minister of Italy, media baron," she says. "And, of course, Michael and Catherine."

"As in Douglas and Zeta-Jones?"

"As in."

"And you're on a first-name basis."

"Oh, but of course." She laughs. "Actually, I vaguely remember Michael bouncing me on his lap when I was a little girl. His mother was a Dill. They go way back here. She and Titi are friends."

"Well, I hope the Mid Ocean Club will let the likes of me through the door."

"On good looks alone," says Barbara.

"Still, I'll need to make myself presentable."

"In an old-line clubby kind of way."

"Which presents a problem," I say. "The last time I saw my blazer, it was taking a boat ride."

"You left it on that poor man's body yesterday?"

"Didn't seem right to take it off."

"And you don't have any intention of trying to get it back?"

"Would you?"

"Omigod, no. Just the thought . . ."

"I'll pick up a new one while I'm in Hamilton," I say.

"Try A. S. Cooper, on Front Street, right across from the ferry terminal. While you're there you can try on some Bermuda shorts."

A good thing she smirks when she says it.

"Do guys actually wear those things here?"

"Oh yes, they get quite outfitty with them. Socks that match the shorts, with suit coats to go with it. You'll see."

"I'll try not to snicker."

One of the butlers appears in the doorway to the alcove.

"Your car is here, sir," he says.

"Be right there," I tell him.

I get up from the table. I give Barbara a hug.

"Titi would like for you to meet us at six o'clock," she says. "And please, Zack, do give her another chance."

"You can count on me," I say. "I'm all about the three P's: punctual, properly attired, and polite as all hell."

"So pucker up," Barbara says.

And she kisses me good-bye.

9

The driver is fiftyish, a thickset guy almost as tall as me, with just a smudge of a mustache, a dab of gray against brown skin. He stands by a white minivan. A magnetic sign on the side of it reads: J.J.'S CAR SERVICE: TOURS, AIRPORT, DAILY/HOURLY.

He holds the sliding door open for me.

"I'll ride up front with you," I say.

I climb in and he climbs in and we are off.

"Are you J.J.?"

"Yes, sir," he says. "John Johnson."

I stick out a hand. He shakes it. I tell him where I need to go and how long I think I might need to be there.

"How much?"

J.J. shakes his head.

"Taken care of," he says.

"What you mean taken care of?"

"Mrs. Ambister, she's taking care of it."

"I'd rather handle it myself," I say.

J.J. cuts his eyes my way.

"Then you tell her that," he says.

J.J. and I are obviously on the same page regarding dear old Titi.

He turns onto the road to Hamilton.

"First time to Bermuda?"

"It is," I say.

"You want me to give the tour talk, or you want to ride in quiet?"

"The tour talk cost more?"

"Oh, I might add on a dollar or two."

"Which you will no doubt charge to Mrs. Ambister?"

J.J. nods.

"Talk away," I say.

On the twenty-minute drive to Hamilton, I get a crash course in all things Bermudian. How Bermuda is not just one island, as many think, but 120-some-odd islands, with the main dozen or so connected by bridges and causeways. How there were no indigenous people living here when the first settlers arrived, quite involuntarily, aboard the British ship *Sea Venture*, which crashed on the reefs in 1609 on its way to Jamestown, Virginia. And how there are thought to be at least another three hundred shipwrecks on the reefs encircling Bermuda, maybe even more.

We pull off near the Gibbs Hill Lighthouse and get out so J.J. can show me a roadside marker.

It reads:

On this spot her majesty Queen Elizabeth II paused for a while to admire the view. Wednesday the 24th of November 1953.

It's a nice view—a hillside filled with pretty houses sloping to Hamilton Harbour. If I had a Post-it Note I'd stick it on the marker with the message: "His Ownself Zack Chasteen admired it, too."

We get back in the car and I tune J.J. in and out, absorbed by the scenery. Sherbet-colored houses topped off by white-washed, terraced roofs. Hand-laid stone walls, pocket-size vegetable plots, manicured boxwood hedges, gardens wildly abloom. And a beguiling assortment of street names, each of which seems to suggest its own story: Controversy Lane, Buggy Whip Hill, Ducks Puddle Drive, Featherbed Alley, and, my favorite, Pie Crust Place.

It's as if Bermuda is populated by a happy tribe of really

well-to-do Hobbits, cozy and content and given only to the pursuit of pleasurable things. It is all just so goddamn charming.

And then, as we squeeze into a roundabout and merge with the traffic of downtown Hamilton, J.J. yanks me out of that happy reverie.

"So you saw the body, huh?"

I look at him.

He says, "I heard it was you found it and called the police."

"Yeah, something like that."

"That true about the eyes, how they'd been pulled out?"

"Where did you hear that? It wasn't in the paper."

"Small place. Everyone's heard by now," he says. "It true?"

"Yeah, the guy's eyes were gone."

J.J. lets out air, shakes his head.

"Man, oh man," he says. "Just like before."

"What do you mean like before?"

J.J. looks at me, then back at the road. He adjusts his hands on the wheel.

"Must have been six or seven years ago," he says. "They found two bodies, a couple of scuba divers, washed up like that one you found. Eyes in them were missing, too."

"Who were they?"

J.J. thinks about it.

"The way I remember, one of them was an Englishman. The other, I think he was American."

"And no one ever figured out who did it or what it was all about?"

J.J. shakes his head.

"Nah, I mean, there was all kinds of theories, some of them pretty wild, most of them having to do with how the two of them had stumbled across a shipwreck that no one seemed to know was out there. There was talk about treasure and all that sort of foolishness. But after a while nothing came of it and people stopped talking about it," he says. "But this what happened yesterday? It has got them talking again."

"What are people saying about it?"

J.J. shrugs.

"Same thing they've always said. Those dead men saw something they wasn't supposed to see. And that's what happened to them."

We drive the rest of the way in silence. We head down King Street to Front Street, pass the Cabinet Building to our right, the cruise ship docks on our left. There are two ships in port. They loom over Front Street, blocking our view of the harbor.

J.J. hangs a right on Parliament Street then a quick left on Reid Street. He pulls to a stop, points out the window to Richfield Bank, and says: "That's your place right there."

10

Ten minutes later, I am sitting across the desk from a young banker named Mr. Highsmith who has succeeded in turning my world upside down.

"There must be some mistake," I say.

"I assure you, Mr. Chasteen, Richfield Bank does not make such mistakes," says Mr. Highsmith. "Here, have a look for yourself."

He swivels his computer monitor so I can see the screen. It is full of columns and figures, but I am only interested in the bottom line.

I stare at the numbers, not wanting to believe what I see.

Then I look at Mr. Highsmith. That's how he introduced himself. Not Charles Highsmith or Robert Highsmith or Joe Highsmith, but Mr. Highsmith. Even though he is just a kid, barely out of his twenties.

He wears banker clothes—dark suit, white shirt, unremarkable tie.

I look back at the computer screen. Nothing has changed from the first time I looked at it. It is all there plain enough. A two, followed by three zeroes, then a decimal point and two more zeroes.

Two thousand dollars.

Mr. Highsmith says, "That's the minimum amount required to maintain an account such as yours."

"That's bullshit is what that is," I say. "Total bullshit."

I am not a quiet guy. My voice carries across the bank lobby. People sitting at nearby desks turn to look at us. Mr. Highsmith leans toward me and speaks low.

"Mr. Chasteen, please," he says. "Perhaps you'd like to discuss this with our manager."

"You bet your ass I would."

Mr. Highsmith steps away. I watch him walk across the lobby and disappear down a hallway.

I study the computer screen some more. The top of the page lists the name of my account and the account number. A few lines down is the date, seven months earlier, when the account was created. Alongside that a column shows my money was transferred to it. Two million dollars.

I click down the page. There are only a few lines of transactions against the account. Interest accrued, applied quarterly. Maintenance fees charged by Richfield Bank for all the hard work it has done letting my money sit around and collect interest.

My eyes land on the last transaction in the column. It is a withdrawal of two million dollars and change, dated two months earlier.

I keep staring, trying to make sense out of it. It is like staring at a plate of scrambled eggs and trying to find a Shakespeare sonnet in it. No sense at all.

"Mr. Chasteen."

I look up. Mr. Highsmith has returned.

"Mr. Bunson can see you," he says.

I follow him across the lobby and down a hallway and into a paneled office. Another man in a dark suit stands when we enter the room. He is closer to my age, with that air of assumed gravitas shared by bankers, funeral directors, and TV anchormen.

"I'm Mr. Bunson," he says.

"Mmm," I say.

Mr. Bunson motions me to a chair. I sit down. Mr. Highsmith stands behind me, near the door. All the better for calling in security should my outrage extend beyond another bullshit-shouting episode.

Mr. Bunson says, "Would you mind so very much if I were to look at your credentials, Mr. Chasteen?"

I hand him my passport and the papers that Richfield Bank had mailed to me in Florida after I'd opened the account. I had presented the same papers to Mr. Highsmith just a few minutes earlier, but Mr. Bunson gives them greater scrutiny.

He compares my passport photo to the studly individual sitting across the desk from him. The photo is a couple of years old. I've only gotten better looking.

He examines the signature on the bank papers. He holds it alongside the signature on the passport. My penmanship is lousy. Still, it is consistent.

Satisfied that I am indeed the one and only Zachary Taylor Chasteen, he slides the credentials back to me. I tuck them away.

Now it is Mr. Bunson's turn to study the computer screen on his desk. Which he does for the next several minutes.

Finally, he looks at me, smiling.

"Guamikeni Enterprises . . . am I pronouncing that correctly?"

"Close enough," I say.

"Interesting name."

"Mmmm," I say.

He probably wants me to explain it, but I'm not up for that. I just want to know about my money.

"What about my money?" I say.

Mr. Bunson shuffles in his chair. He clears his throat.

"After the most recent withdrawal, month before last, you are left with a balance of exactly two thousand dollars," says Mr. Bunson.

"That's what I tried to explain to young Mr. Highsmith," I say. "I didn't make a withdrawal month before last or any other month. I haven't made any withdrawals. I haven't touched that money. There's been a mistake."

There is more edge to my voice than I'd intended. Mr. Bunson pulls back, his eyes widening. It might also have something to do with the fact that I am pounding a fist on his desk.

I stop pounding. I sit back in my chair. I breathe deep breaths.

Mr. Bunson says, "There are four chartered banks in Bermuda, Mr. Chasteen. Between us we handle the accounts of nearly twenty thousand international corporations and countless thousands of IBCs like your own. One reason so many people choose to do offshore business here—we don't make mistakes."

"Then where's my money?"

"A simple explanation," says Mr. Bunson. "It most likely was withdrawn by the other signatory on your account."

"What other signatory?"

Mr. Bunson gives Mr. Highsmith a look. It is a look best described as "significant." I don't like the way this is going.

Mr. Highsmith punches at the computer keyboard, studies the screen. Then he looks at the papers on his desk.

"According to our records, the account for Guamikeni Enterprises lists two signatories—you and . . ." He flips through the papers, runs his finger down a page. "You and Mr. Trimmingham."

"I don't know anyone named Trimmingham."

Another look from Mr. Bunson to Mr. Highsmith, this one even more significant, as if Mr. Bunson has detected a noxious odor that my nostrils are not privy to.

"Mr. Brewster Trimmingham," says Mr. Bunson. "Of Trimmingham & Artemus International Management. They are the nominee for your account."

The name Trimmingham & Artemus rings a bell. It's the Bermuda-based firm I hired, upon Freddie Arzghanian's recommendation, to do the paperwork for my IBC. They charged me ten thousand dollars. It seemed pretty steep, but Freddie Arzghanian assured me it was money well spent.

Still, I have no specific recollection of a Brewster Trimmingham. And I certainly have no recollection of making anyone by that name a signatory on my account.

"So what you're saying is that Brewster Trimmingham withdrew the two million dollars?"

"No, Mr. Chasteen, what I'm saying is that a signatory of

your account made the withdrawal. Our records show that there are two signatories, you and Mr. Trimmingham. Therefore one or the other of you made the withdrawal. We have no way of telling."

"What do you mean you have no way of telling?"

Mr. Bunson heaves a sigh and continues, as if he is explaining all this to a three-year-old.

"Because, Mr. Chasteen, it was an electronic transfer of funds, made with a log-on, a password, and a PIN number. Either of the two signatories could have done it."

"But it wasn't me. I never created a log-on, a password, or a PIN number."

Mr. Bunson simultaneously shrugs and turns up his hands, the universal gesture for So-what-do-you-expect-me-to-do?

"Then I suggest you take that up with Mr. Trimmingham," he says.

11

Before ushering me out, Mr. Bunson is kind enough to provide me with an address for Trimmingham & Artemus. It is a few blocks away, on St. Anselm's Place.

When J.J. dropped me off at Richfield Bank I told him that I wouldn't need him for a couple of hours, until it was time for him to drive me to the Mid Ocean Club. So I start walking.

Downtown Hamilton is a nice place—nice shops, nice restaurants, nice people. But nice is not the featured attraction on my personal marquee, not right now. I trudge my way to St. Anselm's Place wholly oblivious to everything I pass.

I try to remember each and every contact I had with Trimmingham & Artemus. There were only two occasions: Once at Freddie Arzghanian's office in Montego Bay when I'd signed some papers that were then sent back to Bermuda for Trimmingham & Artemus to countersign. And again when I returned home to LaDonna and found some more papers waiting for me, along with an invoice in the amount of ten thousand dollars for the work Trimmingham & Artemus had done on my behalf.

Hindsight exists so we can see our own asses and give them a proper kick. And yeah, I probably should have had my attorney look over the papers. But I don't like the idea of too many people knowing my affairs. So I signed the papers and sent them off.

I'm not saying I went over everything line by line that Trimmingham & Artemus sent me, scrupulously parsing all meaning and nuance. But I read most of it. And I do not remember anything that gave Brewster Freaking Trimmingham the authority to withdraw money from my account.

Trimmingham & Artemus is in Suite 406 of a gray block building that houses lots of outfits with ampersands in their names. I get tired of waiting on the elevator and take the stairs.

By the time I get to the fourth floor I am breathing hard, more from boiling blood than exertion. The hall ahead of me is long, narrow, and deserted. A couple of dozen doors open onto it, all with small brass plaques bearing the names of businesses that sound much grander than their surroundings.

The plaque on Suite 406 reads TRIMMINGHAM & ARTEMUS INTERNATIONAL MANAGEMENT, LTD. I try the door. It is locked. I knock. No answer. I knock again, louder. Nothing. I beat hell out of the door. And then, just because it feels right, I kick it.

I hear something creak behind me. I turn around. A man peeks out from behind a door directly across the hall from 406.

"May I help you?" he says.

"I'm looking for Brewster Trimmingham."

The door inches open a bit. The man is middle-aged and wears one of those telephone headsets favored by people who are just so damn busy they can't be bothered.

He says, "You aren't likely to find him here."

"This is his office, isn't it?"

"Oh, yes, it's his office. But he's already come and gone. He picks up the mail about eleven each morning and then he's off."

"What about the rest of the staff?"

The man gets a big kick out of that.

"Good one," he says.

The door is open just enough for me to see inside the man's office. It is small and sparse. One desk, nothing on the walls.

"You know where I would find Trimmingham?"

The man eyes me.

"Are you an acquaintance of his?"

"Yeah," I say. "We go way back. I'm in Bermuda for a few days and thought I'd look him up, see how he's been doing."

The man thinks it over. I'm pretty sure he doesn't believe me. If I were him I wouldn't believe me. He looks at his watch.

"It's almost three o'clock," he says. "I'd try Benny's Lounge. It's up on Queen Street."

The man starts to close the door.

"Just one more thing," I say, nodding at the plaque on Suite 406. "Is there really an Artemus?"

The man grins a sly grin.

"That's another good one," he says.

12

Benny's Lounge is as elegant as its name implies—a faded sign on an unadorned door and nary a window opening onto Queen Street, all the better for avoiding prying eyes and anything that resembles the tourist trade.

Inside, the place is bigger than it appears from the street—a couple dozen stools around a horseshoe-shaped bar, seven or eight wooden tables, and a row of highbacked booths along the far wall. A hallway leads to the bathrooms and, at the end of it, a box sits wedged in the back door, a token nod to ventilation that isn't doing much good.

Benny's is crowded, the clientele mostly male. I find a seat at the bar. There is Tennants on tap. When the bartender comes around I order a pint.

"I'm looking for Brewster Trimmingham," I say.

The bartender is a fat-faced man with droopy lids that conceal most of his eyes. He nods to a corner booth by the hall. I turn in my stool, sip the Tennants, and study the man in the booth.

He does not fit my image of what a Brewster Trimmingham should look like. I am expecting someone like Bunson or Highsmith, the twerpy bankers. But Trimmingham is big—massive is more like it—his ample girth creating a snugness in the booth that borders on the uncomfortable.

He has the look of John Madden portraying a yachtie gone to seed: faded blue polo with the tail out, worn khakis, deck shoes without any socks. His hair is thick and gray, and his face blotched red, a testament more to drinking, it appears, than to time spent in the sun.

I sip the Tennants and watch Trimmingham some more.

He drinks from a glass that looks tiny in his big hand. He holds a cell phone to one ear. He finishes his call and promptly makes another.

I finish my Tennants and order a refill. Trimmingham keeps talking. He catches the bartender's eye and holds up his glass.

The bartender puts ice in a glass and fills it with gin, then the barest splash of tonic.

"I'll take that to him," I tell the bartender.

The bartender sets the glass down in front of me.

"Shall I put it on your tab?" he says.

"No," I say. "You shall not."

I walk the drink over to Trimmingham's booth. He spots me coming and keeps watching me as I sit down across from him. I slide the glass his way. He takes it, gives me a nod, and speaks into the phone.

"I'm telling you, it's one hell of an investment," he says. "You can probably sell them in a year for half again as much."

He listens. Then he says: "Believe me, I'd prefer to hold on to them myself, but I need to move the money into something else for a while. I'm coming to you first with this, but I need to move quickly, OK?"

He listens some more, says: "Right then, think it over. Cheers, now . . ."

He flips the phone shut, sets it down, and picks up his drink. He takes a long pull on the gin, studying me over the rim of the glass.

"Sorry, I'm not placing you."

"Zack Chasteen," I say.

I stick out my hand. Trimmingham shakes it and smiles, all hale and hearty. If my name means anything to him, he's covering it well.

"Brew Trimmingham," he says. "What can I do for you?"

Yeah, if my name were Brewster, I'd probably go by Brew, too. He tries to pull his hand away. I hold on to it.

"You can put two million dollars back into my account at Richfield Bank."

Trimmingham's face sags. His eyes dart around the bar, then back to me. He tries again to pull away, but I squeeze his hand tighter. I have a good grip, right where I can bear down with my thumb knuckle into the bone. I bear down. Trimmingham winces.

"For chrissake," he says. "I can explain."

"Then start doing it."

I let go of his hand. He rubs it, studying me.

He polishes off the rest of his drink and signals the bartender for another one. He doesn't ask if I want one. That in itself tells me everything I need to know about Brewster Trimmingham.

The bartender delivers the drink. Trimmingham sits back in the booth and sucks the top off it.

"So," he says, "how long have you known Freddie Arzghanian?"

"Doesn't matter," I say. "Talk to me about my money."

"You have to promise not to tell Freddie."

"Why? Are you screwing around with his money, too?"

Trimmingham shakes his head.

"I'm not that stupid. But I would prefer that Freddie didn't know anything about this. You have to promise me."

"I'm not promising you anything. And you've got about ten seconds to tell me something I want to hear or I'm going to the cops."

"I wasn't trying to cheat you."

"You're down to five seconds. Four, three . . ."

"You'll have your money back in a week. With interest. Let's say fifty thousand dollars' interest," says Trimmingham. "Is that something you want to hear?"

"It's a start."

Trimmingham slides out from the booth. It is a tight squeeze.

"Excuse me for a moment," he says. "I need to step down the hall to the men's room."

He turns to go. I stand, grab the back of his collar, and pull him back. I pull a little harder than necessary. Trimmingham loses his balance and falls onto the floor, overturning a nearby table.

It gets the attention of everyone in the place. The bartender starts our way, but I wave him off and help Trimmingham to his feet.

"Sit down," I tell him. "You're not going anywhere."

We settle back into the booth. Trimmingham studies me. I study him back. We're just a couple of real studious guys.

A smirk creeps onto Trimmingham's face.

"It won't do you any good to go to the police," he says. "I haven't done anything illegal."

"You stole two million dollars from my account."

He holds up a finger, wags it at me.

"Point of fact," he says, "as the legal and designated nominee of your account, and a signatory under the banking laws of Bermuda, I have full authority to transfer, withdraw, or deposit any funds . . ."

I grab his finger and bend it backward. I'm pretty sure I feel something crack.

Trimmingham lets out a yelp and yanks his hand away, clutching it against his chest. All eyes in the bar are once again on us.

"Arthritis," I tell everyone. "It flares up on him every now and then."

People go back to minding their own business. I go back to my little tête-à-tête with Trimmingham.

"Point of fact," I say. "You're going to be in a lot worse agony than you are right now unless you tell me exactly why you took my money."

"All right, all right, I'll tell you," he says. "See, this investment opportunity came along, a very good one. But I had to move fast. I was working on your behalf, of course, and fully intended to notify you once everything was complete, but . . ."

I stomp on his foot. I hit the bony top of his arch and I can tell that it stings. Trimmingham jolts his leg away and jostles the table. I manage to grab my beer, but Trimmingham's drink topples over before he can save all of it.

"Fuck all, that hurt," says Trimmingham.

"The truth, Trimmingham. Or else you aren't going to have many parts left that don't hurt."

He looks away, jiggling the ice that remains in his glass.

"The truth is, I'm in a bit of a jam, OK?" He looks at me. His eyes are pleading. "I was wrong, I admit it. But I didn't think you'd notice. You opened the account six months ago and it has been inactive ever since. I figured you were one of those guys who just wanted to put his money in the cooler for a little while. That's the way it is with lots of these accounts I handle, especially those that come through Arzghanian. So I thought I could use the money for a few weeks, then return it, and no one would be the wiser."

"Use it for what?"

"Real estate investment. Guy I know is building some condos out near Tucker's Town. A place called Governor's Pointe. Ultra high-end. Very exclusive. I bought six of them at preconstruction prices, thinking I could flip them."

"And you haven't been able to."

Trimmingham shrugs.

"The market has gone soft. It's taking longer than I predicted."

"So why are you sweating it? It's my goddamn money sitting out there."

Trimmingham looks down at the table.

"It's more complicated than that," he says.

"I've got all the time in the world."

I settle back in the booth with my Tennants. Trimmingham jiggles the ice in his glass, finishes off the little bit of gin that's left.

"I've had to borrow money from other people to get me over the hump," he says. "Payment on the property is running almost seventy thousand a month."

"How much have you had to borrow?"

"A lot," he says. "And the interest on it is piling up."

"Am I right in guessing that the people you had to borrow this money from are not the kind of people who are amused when you miss a payment?"

"Bloody understatement, that," says Trimmingham. "Listen, I really need to use the men's room. Why don't you order us another round."

He slides out of the booth and disappears down the hall. I watch as the hall floods with daylight, then goes dark again as the back door slams shut.

Men's room, my ass.

I'm not the only one who sees Trimmingham cut and run. The bartender spots him, too. He pulls out a cell phone and punches numbers.

I throw down money on the table and head for the back door.

13

By the time I step outside, Trimmingham is a third of the way down the long alley that runs behind Benny's Lounge, heading for Queen Street. He's fairly fast on his feet for a fat guy. And, cocky bastard, he doesn't even look back to see if I'm following.

I could catch him, even with my gimp foot. But where's the sport in that? More interesting to see where he goes. Who knows? I might even learn something. And the more I learn about Trimmingham, the closer I get to my money.

I hang back, waiting to see if he goes left or right when he hits Queen Street. But he never makes it there. As Trimmingham nears the end of the alley, a white Toyota screeches in from Queen Street and cuts him off.

Two guys get out, leaving the driver in the car. One is short, the other tall, and both of them wear sweatsuits like they've just come from the gym.

The short one carries a flat, wooden paddle—a cricket bat, it looks like—the handle wrapped in tape. He slaps it against an open palm as he stands beside the car.

Trimmingham stops. He turns back my way, but the tall guy is already on him, hooking an arm around Trimmingham's throat, shutting off his air as the short guy moves in with the bat.

I start running down the alley. Or, running as best I can anyway.

"Hey!" I yell.

The two guys don't even glance my way. The short one rears back with the bat.

Trimmingham throws up both arms, trying to ward off the blow. I hear the sharp, sick crack as bat meets bone.

The short guy flips the bat around and jabs the handle hard into Trimmingham's chest. Trimmingham groans. The short guy jabs him again.

The tall guy releases his grip and Trimmingham folds onto the ground. The short guys rears back with the bat.

"Stop!" I yell, closing in.

The short guy delivers another whack, this one to Trimmingham's head. Then another. And another. Then the two of them hop in the car and it squeals away.

By the time I reach Trimmingham, he is trying to prop himself up on an elbow. But he doesn't have it in him. He collapses on the pavement, head lolling to one side.

He doesn't look like the same guy I was just sitting across from in the bar. His eyes are battered shut, and blood oozes from wicked gashes along both cheekbones. His nose is split down the middle and flattened against the pulverized mess that is his face.

Trimmingham tries again to sit up, but falls back, cradling an arm against his chest, moaning in agony.

"Just lie still," I tell him.

Trimmingham sucks in air, gets a mouthful of blood. He coughs and blood splatters my face and shirt.

I try to apply pressure to the gashes on his cheekbones, but he jerks away.

"Try not to move," I tell him. "Deep breaths."

He breathes, coughs, splatters me with blood again.

The bartender from Benny's steps out the back door, spotting us as he lights a cigarette.

"Call an ambulance," I tell him.

He doesn't move.

"Do it!" I yell. "Now!"

The bartender hurries back inside.

People gather at the mouth of the alley. A woman kneels

beside me. She pulls a handkerchief from a purse and I try to keep Trimmingham still while she dabs at the wounds on his face, trying to stop the bleeding.

There's shouting from the street, then a siren.

Trimmingham's breaths turn fast and shallow. He's slipping into shock.

As the ambulance arrives he tries again to sit up.

"Help me," he says.

"It's going to be fine. They're taking you to the hospital."

He reaches out, finds my arm, seizes it.

"No, you have to help me. With them," he says. "Please . . ."

He collapses on the pavement as the ambulance crew swarms in.

14

'm way late returning to the spot where J.J. is supposed to pick me up outside Richfield Bank, but he is parked and waiting for me. I slide into the front seat of his van.

"Sorry I took so long. Ran into a few problems."

"More than just a few, by the looks of it." J.J. eyes my blood-spattered shirt. "You going to the Mid Ocean Club like that?"

"I was hoping to buy something, but all the stores are closed."

"What size jacket you wear?"

"A forty-eight long."

"I probably got something that'll fit. My house is on the way. Might rustle up a shirt, too."

"Well, thanks. I appreciate it."

"Oh, don't be thanking me for anything yet."

He raises an eyebrow, shoots a look at a rear seat. Only then do I notice the other passenger in the van—a woman, thirtyish, her long black hair pulled back tightly against her head then tied in a ponytail that just barely manages to control it. She wears a tight black T-shirt and jeans, a pair of funky red glasses.

"My niece," J.J. says.

"Janeen Hill," the woman says. "From the *Royal Gazette.*"

"You were there yesterday when we found the body."

"Yes," she says. "That's what I was hoping to talk to you about."

I look at J.J. He puts up a hand in protest.

"Wasn't my idea," he says. "I told her she shouldn't be ambushing you like this."

"Why, listen to you," Janeen says. "You're the one called me and told me you'd driven Mr. Chasteen downtown this afternoon. So don't be playing Mr. High and Mighty with me."

J.J. mutters something, pulls the van onto the street.

"How can I help you, Ms. Hill?" I say.

She scoots forward in the seat, pushes the glasses up on her nose. She is wound tight, ready to pounce.

"Need you to confirm something for me," she says. "Tell me about the condition of the body when it was pulled from the water."

"I'm guessing you want to know about the eyes, right?"

"Yes, that."

"They were gone," I say. "But isn't that common knowledge by now? Your uncle knew about it. Plenty of other people apparently did, too. Why do you need me to confirm it?"

"Because I refuse to rely on secondhand information," Janeen says. "The rumor was floating around the newsroom last night, but there was nothing about it in the preliminary report, and the police wouldn't comment on it, on or off the record. I refuse to allow conjecture to be a part of anything I write."

"Makes you a rare breed of journalist," I say.

"Not really. But that's neither here nor there," she says. "I've got a stake in this story."

"How's that?"

She looks out the window. We're bogged down in traffic, just creeping along.

"Seven years ago, when I was just starting at the paper, I covered a story that was a lot like this one," she says. "Two bodies were found then, both bound in similar fashion, both with their eyes missing."

"Yeah, your uncle mentioned something about that," I say. "He said the case was never solved."

"Never fully pursued is more like it. At least, not by the authorities." There's bitterness in her voice. "Everything died down and the police just sort of put it on a shelf and conveniently forgot about it."

J.J. clears his throat. He glances at Janeen in the rearview mirror.

"Just because I'm letting you ride in my van doesn't mean I need to be hearing your conspiracy theories," he says. "Talk about conjecture. I've heard you conject all kinds of things about what got those two men killed, Janeen."

"Yes, you have. But I've never written about it."

"Good thing, too," says J.J. "Because no one in their right mind would believe it."

"Well, now maybe they might."

"Believe what?" I say.

Janeen shakes her head, turns away.

"Go ahead. Tell the man," J.J. says. "I'd like to hear what he thinks of it."

Janeen doesn't say anything.

"What's the matter? Afraid he might not believe your nonsense either?" J.J. looks at me. "My niece, she's usually got a pretty good head about her. Except when it comes to this so-called story of hers. And then she gets crazy."

Janeen ignores him, reaches into her purse, pulls out a pack of cigarettes, and starts to light one.

"Unh-uh," says J.J. "Not in my van you don't."

Janeen takes the cigarette out of her mouth. She folds her arms across her chest, looks out the window.

The traffic eases up. We whip through a roundabout and are soon riding along Point Finger Road toward the south coast.

J.J. splits off onto a narrow lane lined with eucalyptus trees. He stops the van outside a house half-hidden by jacaranda bushes.

"Might take a few minutes," he says, getting out of the

van. "I have to heat up the iron and put it to the shirt, get the wrinkles out of it."

"You don't have to go to all that trouble," I tell him. "I don't mind wrinkled."

"Maybe not," he says. "But Mrs. Ambister? She does."

15

As soon as J.J. is gone, Janeen steps out of the van and lights her cigarette. She stands with her back to me, facing the street.

I open my door and perch on the side of the seat.

"Funny," I say. "You don't look that crazy."

Janeen cuts me a look over her shoulder. She blows smoke out the side of her mouth, allows herself a smile.

"Oh, believe me, I have my moments," she says.

"We all do. Matter of fact, I'm teetering on the brink of insanity right now myself."

She turns around, sizes me up.

"You seem to be holding it together fairly well. For a guy wearing a shirt that looks like it mopped up a butcher's shop. What's up with that?"

"Oh, let's just say I've got a couple million reasons for not getting into it. Besides, I'd rather hear about those two other murders you were talking about. Your uncle told me earlier that they were scuba divers."

Janeen takes a drag on her cigarette, flicks the ash.

"Not just your ordinary scuba divers," she says. "One of them, Martin Boyd, was a treasure salvor. A pretty famous one. He'd worked with that guy in Florida, Mel Something-or-Other, I forget . . ."

"Mel Fisher. Discovered the *Atocha* down in the Keys."

"That's it. Anyway, Boyd had some successes of his own

after that, mostly at sites in the Mediterranean. Which is where he met and eventually teamed up with Richard Peach."

"That the other dead guy?"

She nods.

"Ever heard of him?"

"No, can't say that I have."

"Neither had I, at least not until after I started working on the story. Since then, I've become something of an authority on Richard Peach. For all the good that's done me."

"Was he another treasure salvor?"

"No, Peach was an academician. Had dual doctorates in archaeology and biblical studies from Oxford. Used to be a professor there. Wrote a book called *The Legend of the Lost Cross*."

"The Lost Cross?"

"Yeah, also known as the True Cross. The one they used to crucify Jesus Christ."

She takes a drag on her cigarette, gauges my response. I don't really have one, not unless puzzlement counts.

"How good is your biblical history, Mr. Chasteen?"

"Pretty spotty. I was raised Episcopalian. Not exactly Bible thumpers."

"Know anything about the True Cross?"

"Next to nothing," I say. "Except that it's one of those holy relics that people are always trying to find, like the Holy Grail or the Ark of the Covenant. Then again, some folks might lump it in with searching for the Lost City of Atlantis. Or signs of aliens in the pyramids."

"You sound like a skeptic," she says.

"About most things."

"That include religion?"

"On most days," I say.

Janeen smiles.

"Let's leave religion out of it then."

"Always a good idea," I say.

"From a purely historical perspective, the whole Son of God thing aside, would you agree that someone named Jesus

Christ really did exist and that he really was crucified on a wooden cross in Jerusalem, roughly in the year AD 33?"

"Yeah, I can go with that. I mean, it's been fairly well proven as historical fact."

"Ever wonder what happened to that cross?"

"No, not really. I mean, that was two thousand years ago. I'd guess it had long since disintegrated, turned to dust."

"Yeah, you'd think. Still, there are cathedrals all over Europe that claim to have pieces of the True Cross, tiny slivers of wood enshrined in jeweled cases for the faithful to worship. They had to come from somewhere, right?"

"The faithful tend to worship some pretty wild things," I say. "The image of the Virgin Mary in the windows of a bank. The face of Jesus on a piece of burnt toast. There's lots of bogus stuff out there."

Janeen laughs.

"No doubt about that," she says. "And there's reason to believe that many of those so-called pieces of the True Cross are bogus, too. Back during the Crusades era, plenty of pilgrims returned from the Holy Land with bagfuls of fake relics that they sold to unsuspecting believers. Chips off the rock that sealed the tomb of Jesus. Thorns from the crown of thorns. The early Christians, especially the rich ones, used to pay big money for that sort of thing."

"Buying their way into the kingdom of heaven, a noble tradition. Make your faith pledge now, brothers and sisters. Our operators are standing by."

A long look from Janeen.

"I take back what I said before," she says. "You're really more of a cynic than a skeptic, aren't you?"

"As far as I'm concerned, there's not a lot of difference between organized religion and organized crime. At least the Mafia is honest enough to admit that it's only in it for the money."

"I'd have to agree with you," she says. "And Richard Peach probably would have, too. He was a scholar, not a cleric. Yet, he was utterly convinced that the True Cross really did exist.

And he believed that a sizable chunk of it had survived the ages."

"Exactly how sizable a chunk are we talking about?"

"Well, according to various sources that I've read, it was ten centimeters by sixteen centimeters and five centimeters thick."

"You mind doing that conversion for my nonmetric brain?"

Janeen smiles.

"Roughly four inches by six." She shapes it with her hands. "About the size of a paperback book, although not at all uniform. It was just a fragment, a piece that had broken off the original cross."

"What kind of wood?"

She shrugs.

"That's up for speculation. Some accounts say it was olive. Others cedar. And still others say it was gopherwood, probably a form of cypress, like Noah used to build the ark."

"You mean to tell me that a piece of wood like that survived two thousand years?"

"Hey, it's a piece of the True Cross. It has supernatural powers. It can survive anything." She smiles. "You know what a reliquary is?"

"I've heard of them. They're used to store holy relics, right? The hair of John the Baptist, the bones of St. Paul, stuff like that."

"Uh-huh. Something very elaborate, made out of silver and gold with all kinds of jewels adorning it. I've seen drawings of what it was purported to look like—shaped like a cross and maybe twice the size of the wood that was displayed inside it. It was the reliquary of all reliquaries—the Reliquarium de Fratres Crucis. The reliquary of the Brothers of the Cross."

"Brothers of the Cross?"

"One of those secret orders of Christians, like the Knights Templar, that started up around the time of the Crusades. From Portugal originally. They're said to have come into possession of the remains of the True Cross and commissioned the reliquary to hold it."

"So how did it wind up in Bermuda?"

"Long story," Janeen says. "Longer than you've got time to hear tonight."

She looks past me to the house. J.J. hurries out the front door, a blue blazer over an arm, a freshly pressed white shirt on a hanger.

"But Peach and Boyd . . . they thought the reliquary was somewhere out there? On a wreck or something?"

Janeen nods.

"They thought they'd located it and were closing in on it."

"And that's what got them killed?"

"Apparently," Janeen says, flicking her cigarette to the ground, crunching it out with the toe of a shoe. "But then, what do I know? I'm crazy."

Janeen offers me her hand.

"A pleasure chatting with you, Mr. Chasteen. I need to get back to the *Gazette* office. I've got a story to file." She reaches into her purse, produces a business card. "If anything else comes up that you think would be helpful, then I'd appreciate it if you gave me a call."

16

It's just past sunset when J.J. delivers me to the Mid Ocean Club.

Aunt Trula scrutinizes me as I arrive at the table. She is swathed in something shiny and blue, mere backdrop for a white gold pendant with a whopper of a diamond brooch that rests just above her décolletage. A bit more décolletage than I would prefer to see, thank you very much, but hey, it's her show.

I'm expecting something catty from the old girl, especially since I'm so late. But she surprises me.

"You look quite nice," she says.

"Thanks. The jacket's a loaner. From J.J."

"The driver?"

"Yep. Shops were closed and he let me borrow something from his closet."

Aunt Trula forces a smile.

"Well, it shows off your shoulders nicely."

She's trying, I guess.

"And that's some necklace you're wearing," I say.

"Why, thank you." She puts a hand to a cheek, demure, as if she's ready to blush. "It was a gift."

I swoop in and give Barbara a peck on the cheek. She's wearing a simple black dress and the black pearl necklace I gave her for Christmas. I have yet to check out all the other women in the room, but I know she's the best looking one in it. She always is.

Boggy sits next to her. I'm pleased that Aunt Trula has seen fit to invite him, but more than a little startled by his outfit—a starched white shirt under a blue blazer with brass buttons and a gold crest on the jacket's pocket. It's no loaner. And no way it was wrapped up in his blanket-cum-suitcase.

Barbara reads my mind.

"We found something of Uncle Taylor's," she says. "It was a perfect fit."

Boggy gives no sign whether he's enjoying himself or just enduring his circumstances, like a cat being given a bath. He studies me, eyes furrowed.

He says, "Your afternoon, Zachary, did it go well?"

"Yeah, just dandy."

He can tell I'm lying. Barbara can, too. But no need to get into it here.

There's a fifth chair at our table, next to Aunt Trula, with a drink sitting in front of it. And now its occupant returns from visiting a group of people near the bar. He's an older gentleman—short, barrel-chested, with close-cropped white hair, a ruddy weatherworn face, and eyes of the palest blue.

He sticks out a hand. His grip is firm, his grin congenial.

"Teddy," he says. "Teddy Schwartz."

"Sir Teddy is an old, old friend," says Aunt Trula. "You've heard of him, no doubt."

The moment she adds the title, it clicks with me who he is.

"Of course," I say. "What a pleasure."

"Sit," says Teddy. "What are you drinking?"

"Gosling's, neat," I tell the waiter at my elbow.

"Same here," Teddy says. Then to me: "So you favor our local rum, do you?"

"I favor all rum," I say.

"Ah, that's a lad," says Teddy, giving me a slap on the back.

Strictly speaking, Gosling's isn't from Bermuda. It's a blend of rums imported from several different Caribbean islands, with a few secret ingredients added to give it a flavor all its own. It goes down good, so why mince details over its pedigree with the likes of Teddy Schwartz?

I'm in a state of minor awe just sitting next to him.

In my former life, after I stopped playing football and before I got railroaded into jail then got out and started raising palm trees full-time, I used to have a modest charter boat operation. Fishing was always the biggest part of it, but I would run the occasional scuba trip if there were paying clients.

So I am on fairly solid ground when it comes to diving, enough to know that if you were to make a list of the top ten pioneers of underwater exploration, then Teddy Schwartz's name would surely be on it, right up there with Jacques Cousteau, Zale Parry, and that crew. In the late 1940s, with scuba diving in its infancy and Teddy barely in his teens, he had been one of the first to strap on a tank and go nosing around in the waters of Bermuda.

Over the years, he had discovered and subsequently salvaged dozens of shipwrecks. And although he had no formal training in the field, he was considered one of the fathers of marine archaeology, an innovator in technique and technology.

He was also considered something of a rogue and a scoundrel, at least in the eyes of the Bermudian government. Beginning in the 1960s, it had enacted a series of increasingly strict laws that sought to license treasure salvors and lay claim to anything they found. Teddy had long railed against such laws, and although he had donated many of the artifacts he'd found, not only to the government but to different historical societies and maritime research institutes, there was little doubt that he had probably sold off an even greater portion to various international collectors.

The most notorious instance was the ongoing mystery of Schwartz's scepter. Discovered by Teddy in the early 1960s on the wreckage of a seventeenth-century British ship, the scepter was thought to have been a gift from Queen Elizabeth I to the ship's captain, both as a good-luck talisman and the seal of royal approval. With its long gold staff and emerald-encrusted head, the scepter was the single most dazzling bit of treasure ever plucked from Bermuda's waters. The tale of its discovery had even warranted a cover story in *National Geographic,* and led to Teddy Schwartz's eventual knighthood.

After nearly twenty years of wrangling with Bermudian authorities over who was its rightful owner, during which time Teddy kept the scepter on public display at a small museum he once operated in downtown Hamilton, a truce was finally reached. Teddy would sell the scepter to the British Museum for a token amount, just a few thousand dollars, and split the proceeds with the Bermudian government.

But when curators arrived from London to prepare the scepter for transport, they discovered that the piece on display was just a replica, albeit a very good one. The official explanation: Thieves had broken into the museum at some unknown point and switched out the pieces. The unspoken subtext: Teddy had sold the scepter on the international market and substituted the fake. In any event, the original had never been recovered.

As much as I would like to spend the evening chatting with Teddy Schwartz, it doesn't happen. Between Aunt Trula monopolizing the conversation and a steady stream of people stopping by the table to pay their regards to Sir Teddy, dinner is soon over. The only real moment we have is when the plates are being cleared and Barbara and Aunt Trula step to the ladies' room.

"So tell me," Teddy says in a low voice. "What I'm hearing about the body on Cutfoot Beach, is it true?"

"Depends on what you're hearing," I say, knowing full well what he's talking about and wondering if there's such a thing as a secret in Bermuda.

"The eyes."

"Yeah, I'm afraid that's true."

Teddy doesn't say anything, but it's clear that he's unsettled by my confirmation of the rumor.

"I heard something similar happened several years ago," I say.

Teddy nods, but offers nothing by way of further explanation. He seems consumed with his own thoughts. We sit in silence until Aunt Trula and Barbara return.

"Time for us to go, Teddy," announces Aunt Trula.

Boggy springs to his feet. He's more than ready to call it a night, too. Teddy gets up and offers Aunt Trula his arm.

I stand, but Aunt Trula waves me back down.

"No, you and Barbara stay, enjoy yourselves," she says. "The night is young, the band will start playing soon, and the two of you need some time together. I'll make sure that J.J. is here to take you home."

I catch a look from Barbara: Your call.

"That'd be nice," I say. "We'll stick around a bit longer."

I need some one-on-one time with Barbara.

And, considering the day it's been, I wouldn't mind another rum.

17

The band isn't awful, a three-man combo with a vocalist who has opted for a look somewhere between Mary Travers and Peggy Lee—a little too blond, a little too chunky, but not all that hard on the eyes. They play old white people's music, mellow sounds of the '60s with flabby takes on newer stuff. Still, it sets a nice enough mood, wallpaper for the evening.

Barbara and I order more drinks. I tell her about the scene at the bank and my run-in with Brewster Trimmingham. Which calls for even more drinks.

"So what next?" asks Barbara.

"I'm still trying to figure that out."

"Did you call Freddie Arzghanian?"

"Why would I do that?"

"To ask him why he set you up with this thief Trimmingham, of course."

I shake my head.

"I'll tell Freddie when the time is right," I say. "The fewer dealings I have with him, the better."

"I was just thinking that he might be able to apply some pressure on Trimmingham and get your money back, that's all."

"I'm a big boy."

"And big boys take care of themselves?"

I nod.

"Besides," I say, "Brewster Trimmingham has all the pressure he can handle right now."

"Is he going to be OK?"

"Yeah, I think so. The ambulance crew got him stabilized. A few days in the hospital maybe, but he should be all right."

I sip some Gosling's. Maybe if I sip enough of it I'll figure out the secret ingredients. That way I'd accomplish something useful on this trip.

I sip some more. I'm thinking bitters and a touch of vanilla . . .

"The men who beat him up, who do you think they are?"

"No earthly idea."

"Did you get the license plate number?"

I shake my head.

"Stuff like that, I think it only happens in the movies. I was too busy taking everything in. I didn't even think of it until they were long gone."

We order more drinks. It's a good thing they don't let tourists drive in Bermuda because this one can't.

"Zack, may I ask you a question?"

"You may."

"It's a bit touchy."

"There's no one I'd rather get touchy with than you."

Barbara smiles.

"OK, then," she says. "Do you ever stop to think where your money came from?"

"Yes, believe me, I think about that all the time. It came from bad guys. Very bad guys."

"And you don't have a basic moral issue with that?"

"No. Because I worked for that money. I worked hard. I obtained it honorably. And at great sacrifice."

"And is that money any less bad because it came into your possession?"

"Yes, I think it is less bad because of that. I redeemed it, purified it."

Barbara laughs.

"Oh, you did, did you?"

"Yes, I did."

"You don't think it's just a massive rationalization on your part?"

"Oh, of course, it's a rationalization, but I don't think it's a massive one. I think it's tiny and, all things considered, pretty benign. And I really do think that money was made good again by its association with me."

"I do, too," she says. "I believe everything is made good by its association with you."

"I believe maybe you're getting a little carried away there," I say. "Plus, we're both more than a little drunk."

The band starts playing "Have I Told You Lately That I Love You?" The blond woman is no Van Morrison, or Rod Stewart, but she isn't that bad.

"Let's dance," Barbara says.

We're the only ones on the floor, but even when it's crowded that's the way it always feels with Barbara. She rests her chin on my shoulder. We move without even thinking. It feels right.

Barbara says, "Whisper sweet nothings in my ear."

I nuzzle her hair, pull her even closer.

"Think Aunt Trula can recommend a good attorney?"

Barbara stops dancing. She looks up at me.

"You call that a sweet nothing?"

"Sorry," I say. "I'm preoccupied."

She puts her head back on my shoulder. We sway with the music.

"I'm sure Aunt Trula can recommend an attorney, Zack. But why? You aren't in some kind of trouble, are you?"

"No, not yet," I say. "But I'm getting ready to stir the pot."

18

don't sleep worth a damn. Too much to drink, too much on my mind. It's still dark when I slip out of the bed in Barbara's room—to hell with Aunt Trula and her bunking arrangements—throw on clothes, and tiptoe down the hall toward the kitchen.

I'm just passing Aunt Trula's bedroom when I hear her door creak open behind me. Aw, hell. Having a hangover is punishment enough. I don't need Aunt Trula on my case.

When I turn around, it's not Aunt Trula who is stepping into the hall. It's Teddy Schwartz. Well, well, well . . .

Teddy flashes a conspiratorial grin.

"Appears I've been caught," he says.

"Appears we both have."

He gives me the once-over. If the outside of me looks half as bad as the inside feels, I'm a horrifying sight.

"I know where they keep the coffee," he says.

"You're a righteous man," I say.

"And the aspirin."

"A living saint."

"I've found that some cheese toast also helps."

"If there's none of that," I say, "I'll settle for a morphine drip."

Teddy leads the way. He's a spry old guy, certainly spryer than me at this particular moment. I resolve to limit all further inquiries into the nature of Gosling's to three drinks or less. Surely no more than four.

A peculiar odor—imagine sweat socks boiling in turpentine—assaults us as we make our way downstairs. My stomach does a somersault. Followed by a triple axel.

"Boggy's up."

"How can you tell?" asks Teddy.

"By the smell."

We arrive in the kitchen to find Boggy sitting at the table, huddled over a mug of something hot and steamy. He nods at the stove where the pot responsible for the vile aroma sits bubbling on a burner.

"Please, drink," he says. "I made enough for all of us."

"How very thoughtful," I say.

Teddy, his curiosity mixed with revulsion, lifts the lid on the pot, unleashing a fresh wave of noxiousness. He quickly puts the lid back on.

"Exactly what kind of wretched concoction is that?" he asks.

"Just some tea," says Boggy.

"Don't believe him. Whatever he's got cooking in there it's not just some tea," I say. "Where's the coffee?"

Teddy points to a cabinet. I find a canister of ground beans and a French press. I get water going in a kettle on the stove.

I find the aspirin, too. The dosage is two. I need three. I take four.

Teddy lifts the lid on the pot and takes another cautious whiff.

"Do I detect ginger?" he says.

Boggy nods.

"Also, bark of cedar, pulverized husk of mango seed, and . . ." A leather pouch sits on the table. Boggy reaches into it and pulls out a small bottle of black liquid. "Elixir of pig's bile."

"Kindly shut the hell up," I say. "Unless you want to experience projectile vomiting on a personal level."

Still, the so-called tea piques Teddy's interest.

"This some sort of secret recipe?" he asks Boggy.

"Not secret," says Boggy. "I just told you. Bark of cedar, pulverized husk of . . ."

"I'm warning you," I say. "When I hurl, I'm hurling your way."

"If you like, Zachary, I can also make a tea for rum poisoning."

I ignore him. I drink a glass of water. Then another. The pipes are really burning this morning.

"This tea, it is an old recipe," Boggy tells Teddy. "Handed down through the ages."

"What's it do?"

"All those things, they are natural antihistamines," says Boggy. "They reduce the amount of fluid in the ears. This tea, it is good to drink before one goes out on the water. Or under it."

"You have plans for today that I don't know about?" I ask him.

Boggy looks at Teddy.

Teddy says, "Well actually, Zack, I did mention something to Boggy last night about the three of us heading out on my boat this morning."

"Sorry, I've got some business matters I need to take care of."

"Ah, come on. I'll have you back long before noon. A good dive will cure all your ills," Teddy says. "Plus, I thought you might be ready for a bit of diversion from Trula."

I start to say something, then stop myself. Teddy laughs.

"I know, I know," he says. "She can be a handful. But we've become quite fond of each other in recent months. She's been trying to figure out a way to tell Barbara about us, but I guess my lurking about at five A.M. has taken care of that, eh? I suppose both Trula and I were feeling a bit randy last night."

Entirely too much information.

The kettle whistles. I pour water into the French press and stir the grounds.

I find mugs in a cabinet. I hand one to Teddy.

"I think I might sample that tea first," he says.

Boggy gets up, pulls a strainer from the sink, pours the tea through it, and hands the mug to Teddy. He blows on it, takes a sip.

"Tastes better than it smells," he says.

"To damn by faint praise," I say.

I plunge the press and pour a cup of coffee. It's way too hot to drink and I'm impatient.

I go to the refrigerator and pull two cubes of ice from the freezer. I plop them in the mug and as soon as they have melted I take a long pull of coffee. The world remains grim but hope is ascendant.

Teddy drains his tea and smacks his lips.

"So," he says. "Who's ready to go diving?"

19

We arrive at Teddy Schwartz's house in Somerset, near Bermuda's westernmost tip, just as first light dapples the water of Mangrove Bay.

Given the opulence of Cutfoot Estate, I'm expecting something equally grand, especially for a Knight Commander of the British Empire. But Teddy's house is modest by any comparison—one-story, solid in the way of most Bermudian dwellings, embraced by a wild tangle of bougainvillea and ligustrum.

Teddy nods us to the dock. I can just barely make out the profile of a boat, a pretty good size one.

"Just give me a minute to change clothes," he says. "I'll meet you down there."

As Boggy and I reach the dock, the morning's coffee and the previous night's overindulgence collide to create the perfect storm in my stomach. I need to do some serious purging before we venture out on the water.

A long, low concrete-block building—the boathouse, I presume—sits nearby. I try the door. It opens. I reach for a light switch, find a rack of key chains instead, manage to knock some of them on the floor, onto a pile of dirty towels and boat rags. I fumble around some more, find a switch, and flip on a light.

The room is giant, the size of a four-car garage, and it's a study in clutter. There's stuff piled everywhere. I spot the bathroom on the far side, hurry to it, and do my business.

When I come out, Boggy is nosing around the room. I nose around, too. There's a lot to take in.

One corner is a repository of underwater equipment. It's like a tactile timeline of diving, everything from old brass hard hats that predate the Aqua-Lung to antiquated regulators and an assortment of masks and fins. Elsewhere there are old tools and the relics of a lifetime spent in and on the water—anchors and chains, deck cleats and oars.

Stacks of lumber consume one entire wall, everything from teak and mahogany to more exotic woods that I can't identify. There's a table saw and a lathe and various woodworking tools.

I join Boggy beside a massive workbench that occupies the middle of the room. A blue tarpaulin covers most of it. A carpenter's box holds a variety of small tools—pliers, tweezers, screwdrivers—made for precision work. They are arranged neatly alongside glass jars filled with gold and silver bric-a-brac, bits of wire, shiny odds and ends.

Stacked at one end of the workbench are several glossy, coffee table–type books along with some that would fall into the reference category. I notice a couple of titles: *Ornamentation in the Elizabethan Era* and *Fundamentals of Metalsmithing*. There's also what appears to be an assortment of catalogs from museums and auction houses all over the world.

I'm trying to figure out what it might mean when Teddy steps inside the boathouse. He does not look pleased.

"How did you get in here?"

"The door was open," I say.

Teddy examines the doorknob, turning it back and forth. He casts a worried look around the room.

"Is something wrong?" I ask.

He ignores me. He steps across the room to the other side of the workbench. He lifts the tarp, looks under it. Then he looks at Boggy and me.

"If you don't mind . . ."

He gestures us to step outside.

Heading for the door, I stoop to pick up the key chains that I knocked off the rack.

"Never mind about those!" Teddy barks. "I'll get them."

Jeez, what a bear. Maybe Boggy's tea did a number on him or something. We wait for him on the dock.

When Teddy finally emerges from the boathouse he carries a big, black neoprene dive bag over one shoulder. It has something inside, something fairly bulky.

"Look," I say. "I'm sorry if you didn't want us going in there. But nature called."

Teddy shrugs it off, smiles. He slaps my back.

"Forget it," he says. "Old men living alone tend to get a little too set in their ways. Let something upset the normal course of things and we react like fussy hens."

We board Teddy's boat. It's an old Rehmbauer 32 with twin diesels, worn by the years but well maintained, a sturdy rig that could easily accommodate a dozen divers and all their gear. *Miss Peg,* it's called.

Teddy carefully stashes his dive bag, then steps to the wheel, opens a compartment in the console. He pulls out a worn and weathered log-book that contains page after page of coordinates for various dive sites. He finds the one he's looking for, punches its numbers into a GPS mounted on the console.

He cranks the engines, lets them run a couple minutes while he tends to matters that always need doing on a boat: spraying WD-40 on the corroded pedestal of the captain's chair, wiping mildew off a seat cushion, stowing gear that has mysteriously escaped its lodging.

"You boys grab the lines," he says.

We make free from the dock. And we're off.

20

Forty-five minutes later and about eight miles offshore, Teddy backs off the engines. He consults the GPS, makes a couple of adjustments in course, slows down to idle speed.

There's nothing to distinguish our position from the miles and miles of open water that surround us, except for a slight darkening of the water about fifty yards off our bow and the occasional whitecap that crests over it. Teddy keeps an eye on the spot as he maneuvers the boat.

Boggy is already at the bow, ready to drop anchor. Another glance at the GPS and Teddy gives him the signal. The line feeds out, the anchor hits bottom. Teddy pops it into reverse, the anchor holds. He shuts off the engines.

As Teddy busies himself around the boat, I ask him how *Miss Peg* got her name.

"After my late wife, bless her. Died long before her time," Teddy says. "It's more boat than I need these days, but I can't bring myself to part with her. We've been through it, the two of us. It was on *Miss Peg* that I found the *San Miguel de Verona* and, just a few months later, the *Beatrice*."

"*Beatrice* . . . that's the wreck the scepter came from, right? Schwartz's Scepter."

Teddy nods.

"And after that, *Miss Peg* was so well known that every time I went out on her to look for something new, there would be boats following us, hoping to pick up the scraps. Got so bad I had to buy another boat and send *Peg* out in one direction as a decoy while I went in the other," says Teddy. "Rough and wooly days, I'm telling you. Used to be you could come upon a boat out here and risk getting yourself shot at."

He lifts a hatch seat and in the compartment below I see a leather rifle case, a box of ammunition.

"Old habit to keep it aboard," Teddy says. "I fire off a few rounds every now and then, just to make sure it still works. You can never tell."

Teddy opens a locker, pulls out a wet suit, and starts putting it on. I stand around, waiting for instructions. It's Teddy's boat and I don't want to start yanking gear out of lockers until he gives me the go-ahead. Particularly after his little scene back at the boathouse.

He hasn't laid out our dive plan yet. Trips like this, though, you go to all the trouble of packing up and heading out, they're usually two-tank dives. Depending on how deep you go, the first dive might last forty-five minutes or so, followed by a surface interval to get rid of the nitrogen that builds up in the blood when you're breathing compressed air at depth. The second dive is typically a bit shallower.

Boggy doesn't do scuba. He's strictly a free diver. So we've already decided that he'll keep an eye on things topside while Teddy and I blow bubbles down below.

While Teddy suits up, Boggy sits atop the boat's transom in full lotus position, eyes closed. He inhales deeply, exhales slowly.

After a couple of minutes of this foolishness, he stands and says: "I go now, take a look below."

"You've got about a hundred feet of water down there, right off the boat," says Teddy.

"Good," says Boggy.

And then he springs overboard, hardly making a splash as he slices into the water.

I'm antsy, ready to get into the water myself. But Teddy still hasn't pointed me to my gear.

"So what's this site called?" I ask him.

"Sock 'Em Dog," he says. "There's a seamount juts up about fifty yards astern, looks like the head of a Labrador, at least in the eyes of some. It's poked holes in many a boat, the most famous being the *Victory,* a stern-wheeler used by the South as a blockade runner during your Civil War. When she broke up, part of her went down one side, part of her the other. There's not all that much left to look at, but I like to come out here because the commercial dive boats seldom venture this far and I can have it all to myself."

Teddy stands up and adjusts his wet suit. He attaches his buoyancy compensator vest to one of the dozen or so steel tanks lined up in their slots behind a bench that runs along one side of the deck. He grabs a regulator, hooks it up to the tank and vest, then checks the gauges.

He looks overboard, to where Boggy entered the water.

"It's been a couple of minutes," he says. "Is he all right?"

"He's fine. Just showing off."

Teddy sifts through a plastic crate, pulls out a weight belt, checks the lead on it, then fastens it around his waist. He slips on a mask and lets it dangle under his chin.

He looks overboard again, this time with real concern.

"Don't worry," I say. "He's good for at least six or seven minutes."

"You're joking."

"Afraid not. I've timed him."

"Has it got something to do with that tea he made?"

"It might, along with that breathing thing he was doing. He calls it 'putting on his fish brain.' Boggy, he sets his mind on doing something, and then he does it."

"Quite a remarkable fellow."

"He has his moments," I say.

The ice chest sits under one of the benches. Teddy opens it. Inside, there's a block of ice and some jugs of water.

Teddy pulls an ice pick from a drawer by the console and chops off two chunks of ice.

"A little trick of my own," he says, taking a chunk of ice in each hand. He wedges them behind his ears and presses them against his skull. "Causes the inner ear to contract, makes it a little easier going down."

He keeps up the ice treatment for another minute or so, until the chunks have melted away. He reaches into the drawer again. This time he pulls out a Ping-Pong paddle. He holds it in one hand, the ice pick in the other.

"A treasure hunter's two best friends," he says.

"A Ping-Pong paddle?"

Teddy nods.

"Nothing works better for fanning away sand and silt. And an ice pick is still the tool of choice when it comes to prying something loose without totally destroying it."

"We looking for something down there?"

"Not really. Believe me, if anything's down there, then I've already found it," he says. "But it never hurts to be prepared."

His bulky dive bag hangs from the console. He zips it open, puts paddle and pick inside, along with whatever else he's got in there. He hooks the dive bag onto his BCV. He sits down on the bench, slips his arms through the BCV, and cinches it around his waist and chest. He grabs a pair of fins from below the bench and puts them on.

I'm beginning to wonder if I'll be joining Teddy on this dive. He's ready to go, and I'm still just standing around.

As Teddy stands and begins backing his way toward the transom, Boggy pops out of the water. A couple of strokes and he's at the boat. He climbs aboard, barely winded.

"Is nice down there," Boggy says.

"How deep do you figure you went?" asks Teddy.

"To the bottom."

Teddy seems skeptical.

"Oh, really now?" he says.

"Yes, there is a big coral ridge and it is shaped like . . ." Boggy traces it in the air.

"Sock 'Em Dog, all right," says Teddy. "That's one impressive display of free diving, I must say."

Boggy shrugs off the compliment. He turns to me and says: "You will like, Zachary, there are many fish and the water it is very clear."

"Can't wait," I say. "But I'll need to get geared up first."

Only then does Teddy seem to realize that I'm lagging way behind him.

"Oh, I'm sorry," he says. "I was operating purely on instinct, just thinking about myself. Help yourself to whatever gear you want. If you don't mind, I'll be waiting for you down below."

He steps backward off the stern, surfaces briefly to let all the air out of his BCV, and then he's gone.

It's another ten minutes before I find gear that will fit me. Boggy sips at a bottle of water, watching me while I put everything on.

"What troubles you, Zachary?"

"Just not accustomed to diving like this, that's all. I'm used to everyone going down together. You know, never lose sight of your buddy and all that."

"Teddy, he started diving long ago, before there were so many rules."

"Yeah, he's an old mossback. I guess it's just his way," I say. "It'll be all right."

I step to the transom, slip the mask over my face, stick the regulator in my mouth. Then I take a giant stride and hit the water.

21

In diving parlance, I am what is called a "slow descent." Some people zip right to the bottom. But for me, the first 45 feet are hellish.

Maybe I should have tried Teddy's ice treatment, but I was in too big of a hurry to catch up with him. I swallow and gulp, pinch my nose and blow, trying to equalize the pressure against my eardrums. It's painful, but after I get over the hump, everything's good.

It takes me a couple of minutes to level off at about sixty feet. I check my air—just under 3,000 psi. Meaning, I didn't consume that much on the way down.

The visibility is good, 150 feet or so. Schools of reef fish swim all about—blue tangs and parrot fish, wrasses and snapper.

But there's no sign of Teddy Schwartz.

While I can't make out anything even vaguely resembling a Labrador's head, I spot the seamount and start swimming for it. It would be impossible to miss, actually, thrusting upward from the murky depths to within twenty feet or so of the surface, like some crazy underwater skyscraper. Pity any ship that collided with it.

I fin along, getting into the scuba groove. Breathe in, breathe out. Relax, relax. It's like yoga and flying all at once, the closest I'll ever come to being an astronaut at zero gravity.

The relaxing part is important. The more relaxed you are,

the less air you use, the longer you can stay down. And I'd like to stretch out this dive as long as I possibly can. Partly because it's plenty beautiful down here and I want to see everything there is to see. But partly, too, because I want to look good in front of Teddy Schwartz.

Scuba diving isn't supposed to be a competitive sport. Still, there are all sorts of ways that divers take measure of each other.

For some, it's the gear—who has the most technologically advanced dive computer, the newest state-of-the-art fins. For others it's a dicks-on-the-table, depth thing. You did 140 feet at that blue hole off Andros? Well, at Cozumel, we shot the tubes at Maracaibo Reef down to 152.

Just a lot of swagger and macho bullshit. Because the real yardstick is air consumption. The slower you are to drain your tank, then the greater your cred as a diver. It means you move through the water with efficiency, are at ease with your surroundings. The coolest divers don't suck much air.

The equation is stacked against big guys like me who just naturally need more air to keep us going. Then again, I've been diving with hundred-pounders who were in constant motion, flapping their arms and legs and getting all excited. Their tanks were empty before they knew it.

Experience levels the playing field. The more you dive, the more comfortable you feel pretending to be a fish. Bottom line—when your tank hits 500 psi and you have to go sit on the boat while everyone else enjoys another ten minutes of bottom time, then that definitely places you on a lower rung of the scuba hierarchy.

Breathe in, breathe out. Relax, relax . . .

As I near the seamount, I pick out scatterings of ship's timber on the sandy bottom, most of it encrusted with coral and anemones. Part of the *Victory,* I assume. I hang in the water and turn slowly, looking in all directions. Still no sign of Teddy Schwartz.

I can no longer see the hull of *Miss Peg,* but I've got a pretty good idea of her general vicinity perpendicular to the seamount.

I check my air—2,500 psi. I've barely dented the tank. Yep, Zack, you're one cool diver guy.

I start swimming to my left, the shortest route for getting to the other side of the seamount. I figure that's where Teddy must be. I keep close to the coral wall, stopping occasionally to peek under a crevice or to watch tiny fish—redlip blennies, I think they are—poke their heads out of hidey-holes.

As I move around the far side of the seamount, the bottom begins to drop off and I can make out another scattering of timber on the seafloor, maybe 120 feet below.

I'm not familiar with the story of the *Victory,* don't know how many aboard her perished. I can only imagine the sheer and utter horror of chugging along on a ship in the night— the night, it's always the night—and then comes the sudden tumult, the awful noise, the impossibility of escape.

I pause a moment, pay tribute to those souls now resting in the deep.

Just ahead of me there's an overhang in the seamount. I move past it, peer underneath at the lip of a shallow cavern. And there, flat against the sand, lies what's left of *Victory*'s paddle wheel—a half-circle skeleton, spokes radiating from a rusted iron hub.

The water is murkier here, as if there has been a recent commotion. I see movement near the remains of the paddle wheel—a figure swimming toward me. It's Teddy.

When he's just a few feet away, I give him the OK sign, meaning: Everything's fine with me. How about you? He returns the OK.

I swim past him, heading toward the paddle wheel. The rubble around it looks ripe for exploration.

But there's a tug on my fin. Teddy stops me. He signals for me to follow him around the seamount.

We angle upward, past purple gorgonians and bucket sponges. Nothing quite nearly as interesting as the wreck of the *Victory,* but Teddy's the tour guide. I'm just tagging along.

Suddenly, Teddy stops. He rolls over, looking up at the

surface. I look up, too, glimpsing the silvery trail of a boat, a big one, as it churns past the far side of the seamount.

Teddy turns to me. He makes a hatchet-chop signal: Back to *Miss Peg*.

Then he's off, finning like a madman. It's everything I can do to keep up with him.

We make a slow ascent on our way back until we come to *Miss Peg*'s anchor line. At about 30 feet, I grab hold of the line to make my safety stop. I only need a few minutes to decompress since I didn't have much bottom time.

I check my air gauge—2,000 psi. Hell, I was just barely getting started. Wonder what made Teddy want to head back?

That's when I realize that he hasn't stopped. He's heading straight for the surface. These crusty, old divers. They just don't play by the rules. The bends be damned . . .

I look up the length of the anchor line. I see the hull of *Miss Peg* with its blue antifouling paint.

I see something else, too.

The other boat, its red hull sitting right alongside *Miss Peg*.

22

By the time I surface, Teddy has already stripped off his gear and is talking to a tall, bearded man who stands on the other boat.

The other boat's engine is running. I can't hear over it, but I can tell that "talking" does not fully describe what Teddy is doing. He's in the other guy's face. At least, as much as he can be in the other guy's face considering the two of them are on separate boats with the gunwales between them. Which is probably a good thing. Because it looks as if Teddy is ready to leap out and grab the tall, bearded man by the throat.

The other vessel is what we in Florida call a "go-fast" boat—sleek, powered to the hilt, and the favored craft of drug smugglers. The U.S. Coast Guard uses the same kind of boat to chase the bad guys, only the coast guard calls it a DPB, a deployable pursuit boat.

Whatever the name, it flat-out hauls ass. This one looks like a forty-eight-footer. There's a second man on it, sitting at the wheel. He's young, in his twenties, olive skinned with black wraparound sunglasses.

It's not until I climb aboard *Miss Peg* that I notice the official seal of Bermuda emblazoned on the side of the other boat, white and green with a red lion in the middle.

And I hear Teddy shouting: "This is harassment, you son of a bitch, and I'm tired of it!"

Boggy takes hold of my tank and helps me slip out of my vest.

"What's going on?" I ask him.

"Government man," says Boggy. "He wants to search Teddy's boat."

The other boat rides high in the water so it gives the tall, bearded man the advantage of looking down on Teddy. He stands with his arms folded across his chest, wire-rimmed glasses low on his nose. He looks like a professor, patient and unruffled as Teddy hurls invective after invective at him.

When Teddy finally stops, the bearded man puts up a hand, trying to calm him down.

"Sir Teddy, please," he says, "I apologize for any trouble that this might cause you. It is not my intent to harass, merely to carry out the law. And the law gives me full authority to board any vessel that I suspect may be in violation of the Salvage Act."

"I told you, goddammit, I'm not in violation of anything!"

"Then you shouldn't have a problem with me carrying out this inspection."

"It's an insult. I intend to file a formal complaint with the minister's office."

"That is your right," says the bearded man. "Still, I will ask one more time for permission to come aboard. And if you do not comply, then I will impound this vessel."

Teddy fumes, but he stops arguing. He steps away from the gunwale.

The bearded man grabs a line from his boat and ties it off on *Miss Peg*'s stern cleat. The young guy behind the wheel shuts down the engine and fastens a line from the bow. Both of them wear navy blue shorts, light blue shirts, and navy blue caps that bear the seal of Bermuda.

The bearded man hops aboard *Miss Peg*.

"Again, Sir Teddy, I'm sorry for the inconvenience."

"Just hurry up with it," says Teddy.

It only takes a few minutes for the bearded man to search all the compartments, deckside first, then in the cabin. When he's done, he walks up to me.

"You were diving as well?" he asks.

"I was."

"Then I need to take a look at your vest."

"And I need to know who you are."

The bearded man looks briefly startled, but he recovers with a smile.

"Oh, my apologies," he says, sticking out a hand. "Dr. Michael Frazer, with the Ministry of Environment. I'm curator of wrecks."

"Curse of the wrecks is more like it," says Teddy. "A goddamn plague on us all."

Frazer ignores him, shaking his head as if to say he's grown accustomed to being cussed and it doesn't really bother him.

"Curator of wrecks?" I say. "Interesting title."

Frazer shrugs.

"And an interesting job to go with it," he says. "But you know that old Scottish curse."

"May you live in interesting times?"

"That's it." Frazer smiles. "And well applied to what I do."

He points to my BCV.

"May I?"

"Knock yourself out."

He goes through all the pockets.

"Thank you," he says when he's done.

He steps toward the bench where Teddy's vest sits.

"May I, Sir Teddy?"

"What is this, some bloody child's game? Mother, may I?" Teddy says it with a sneer. "Just finish up with it, will you?"

Frazer goes through Teddy's vest, finds nothing. Sitting next to it on the bench is Teddy's dive bag.

"That your dive bag?" asks Frazer.

"You saw me climb out of the water with it, didn't you? And you saw me put it down. Yes, it's my dive bag."

"Then I'd like to have a look in it, too."

"You've arse-ended everything else on my boat," says Teddy. "Might as well stick your hands in there, too."

Frazer picks up the dive bag. He unzips it, removes the ice pick and the Ping-Pong paddle. He casts a suspicious look at Teddy.

"What?" says Teddy. "There a law saying I can't carry the tools of my trade?"

"You know the law, Sir Teddy. No disturbance of an archaeological site without proper permit."

"Only disturbance here is you."

Frazer lets it roll. He turns the dive bag inside out. There's nothing else in it. He puts it back on the bench.

"Satisfied?" says Teddy.

"Yes, thank you," says Frazer. "We'll be on our way."

"Damn right you will," says Teddy.

Frazer hops aboard his boat and casts off the lines. The young man takes the wheel and fires the engine.

The boat moves slowly away. When it's at a distance where its wake won't rock us, the boat throttles up with a loud *va-room* and hits its planing speed.

Teddy watches the boat until it becomes just a speck on the water.

"Let's haul anchor," he says. "We're heading in."

23

By the time we return to shore and load into his car for the drive back to Cutfoot Estate, Teddy Schwartz seems to have shaken his sour mood.

I ride shotgun. Boggy takes the backseat. And as we bump along, the conversation soon turns to Michael Frazer's surprise inspection of *Miss Peg*.

"Ah, the bastard's just doing his job, I suppose," says Teddy. "Still, I don't see why the government has to interfere with tradition."

"The salvaging tradition, you mean?"

"That exactly," says Teddy. "Generations of Bermudians have been going out in these waters to find what they can find. There's hardly an old-time family here on the Rock doesn't have a little trinket of some sort that was plucked from the sea."

"It's like having your own personal treasure chest out there, huh?"

"Ha!" snorts Teddy. "That's what the world would like to believe, anyway. That we treasure salvors just went out for a nice swim and came back rich men."

"Didn't work like that, huh?"

"No, the way it worked, you invested lots of time, lots of money, risked your life, and often for naught," says Teddy.

"You've done pretty well by it though."

"Ah, technology lent me a hand. I was lucky enough to be

a young man with his eye on salvaging when scuba first came along. Doesn't mean I was any brighter than the rest."

"Come on," I say. "Something tells me that even if scuba hadn't come along you would have still found a way to do what you were obviously meant to do."

Teddy smiles.

"Yeah, you're right about that," he says. "Five years old, I was going out in a rowboat with a bucket, the bottom cut out and a piece of glass stuck in it so I could see what lay down there. By the time I was twelve I'd rigged up this little gasoline motor to pump air down a garden hose. Didn't occur to me that I needed to figure a way to filter out the carbon monoxide when I did it. Almost killed myself the first time I tried it, had to work out the kinks. I was seventeen when I first strapped on a scuba tank. Seldom been far from one since."

"And the rest, as they say, is history."

"Yeah, I had a good run at it. But that was in the so-called good ol' days, before the new salvage law took effect."

"Changed things, did it?"

"In a big and everlasting way. The Historic Wrecks Act, they called it. Said all shipwrecks within three hundred miles of shore are historical sites that belong to the nation of Bermuda. Created a fancy-ass position, curator of the wrecks—that would be our man Frazer—and said anyone who discovers a site of potential salvage must register for a permit with his office. Some joke that is."

"How's that?"

"Care to guess how many people have registered for permits since the new laws went into effect?"

"Don't have clue."

Teddy holds up a hand, touches index finger to thumb.

"Exactly zero," he says. "Nary a one."

"The permits cost a lot of money?"

"No, man, they're free. Don't cost a damn thing."

"So, I don't get it. People have just stopped salvaging?"

Teddy cuts me a look.

"What kind of fool ya be? Of course they haven't stopped.

Salvaging goes on like it always did. Only these days when folks go out there to look for something they just don't find it. You know what I mean?"

"They salvage on the sly."

Teddy nods.

"Who's to blame them? The law says the government retains ownership to anything they find."

"And doesn't have to pay them for it?"

"Oh, the law provides for just compensation," says Teddy. "But it's the government that gets to decide the compensation. And believe me, it's nowhere near just. That's why, people who salvage nowadays, when they find something of value, they sell it on the black market to some rich collector who secrets it away for his enjoyment and his alone. The public doesn't hear about it. And worse, the public doesn't get to share in the history of what was found. All the Historic Wrecks Act did was make sure people would never get a chance to see historic marine finds again."

"It was different when you found Schwartz's Scepter, right?"

"Oh yeah, it was altogether different. It was years before the Wrecks Act when I found Betty's bat." He looks at me, winks. "That's what I called the scepter. I never much liked the idea of naming it after me. Better to give a nod to Queen Elizabeth I. A beauty it was."

"Something to behold, huh?"

"Oh yeah, man, like you've never seen. Three dozen emeralds, the biggest, fattest ones you can imagine, and better than a hundred diamonds. All set in the finest gold. Weighed nearly a hundred pounds it did. I was the proudest man on the face of this earth when I came ashore in *Miss Peg* holding Betty's bat." He takes a moment to relish the memory. "And after I found her what did I do? I put her on display for all to see, that's what. More than half a million people walked through that little museum of mine over the years. They got to see history close up. At a dollar a head."

"Not a bad turn of coin."

Teddy laughs.

"No, not at all. Made even more selling T-shirts and replicas and whatnot. And I was due it, too. A return on my investment," he says. "But that's what got in the government's craw, seeing me make a little money and them not. Got to where it was costing me more in lawyers than I was taking in, so I just gave in to them, agreed to sell the scepter to the British Museum."

"And then it got stolen," I say.

"Yeah," he says. "Then that."

We ride for a while, neither of us speaking.

Teddy looks at me.

"I know what you're wondering," he says.

"What's that?"

"Same thing as everyone else wonders. What really happened to the scepter? Did ol' Teddy pull a switcheroo? That what you're wondering?"

"Well, now that you mention it."

He grins, gives me a wink.

"You just keep wondering about that," he says.

24

It's only midmorning by the time Teddy drops us off at Cutfoot Estate.

Boggy and I check on the hole-digging crew in the backyard. They're making minor progress against the bedrock. The first Bismarck is ready to set. Finally.

I do the math. If we average a little better than a hole a day, then we just might have all the palms planted in time for the big party. I leave Boggy to oversee everything, then head inside.

I find Barbara sitting in the front parlor with Aunt Trula. There's a third woman with them—blond, pretty, outdoorsy looking. Her yellow sundress shows off a nice tan. Nice legs, too. Not that I'd stare.

She's been crying. She wipes her cheeks with the back of a hand.

"You poor, poor dear," Aunt Trula says, getting up and patting the woman on her back. "Rest assured that I shall help you however I can. And for starters, I want you staying here with us."

The woman shakes her head.

"No, no. I couldn't possibly do that. It's a great imposition. And I didn't come here with that in mind," she says, in an accent I'm pretty sure is Australian. "I just wanted to . . . to see, that's all."

"I will not hear it," says Aunt Trula. "You are staying, and that is that. For as long as you need to."

The woman lets out a long sigh.

"Well, thank you," she says. "It is very kind. And I am dead on my feet. Been traveling for the better part of the past two days."

Barbara stands, gives me a hello hug.

"Zack," she says, "this is Fiona McHugh. It's her brother whose body . . ."

She stops. She doesn't say anything else, doesn't need to.

"My condolences," I say.

The woman nods, offers a grim smile.

"Fiona just arrived this morning from Australia," says Aunt Trula, continuing to comfort her. "I'm sorry, dear, but I didn't catch exactly what part of the country you are from."

"Perth," says Fiona. "On the west coast."

"The most isolated big city on earth," I say. "Home to the Kings Park Botanic Gardens."

Fiona brightens a bit.

"Why, yes. Do you know Perth?"

"No, but I've had some contact with the botanic gardens. Provided them with the seeds of some Malaysian palms after a weevil infestation wiped out their collection."

Aunt Trula says, "Zack is one of the leading authorities in the world on palm trees."

"Well, that's not exactly true," I say. "In fact, it's not even anywhere near true."

"Oh, shush. You're brilliant, absolutely brilliant. You should see what Zack is doing to my backyard, Fiona. Transforming it into a regular Nebuchadrezzar's garden," says Aunt Trula. She takes Fiona's hand. "Come, dear, let me show you to your room."

She leads Fiona from the parlor. When they're gone, I sit down on the couch beside Barbara.

"Wow," I say.

"Wow?"

"Double-wow. As in, wow, when did I suddenly become ace-high with Aunt Trula? And wow, the dead guy's sister is here."

"The dead guy's name was Ned," says Barbara. "Ned McHugh."

"No disrespect intended," I say. "I'm just surprised to see her, that's all."

"We were, too. She got here about an hour ago," says Barbara. "Said she wanted to see where her brother's body washed ashore. So I took her down to the beach, then left her there to have some time alone. We'd been sitting here for a few minutes when you arrived."

"Pretty lady."

"Yes, I saw you staring at her legs."

"That wasn't staring. It was a professional appraisal."

"And you approve?"

"Very much so."

"She's a cop," Barbara says.

"No way."

"What? Pretty women with nice legs can't be cops?"

"I didn't say that. But the women cops I know? They don't look like that."

"All I know is that she's not exactly thrilled by the way the Bermuda police are handling this. They aren't telling her much."

"Could be because they don't know much."

"That's what bothers her. She said she intends to do some looking into things herself."

"How old was her brother?"

"Just twenty-six. He was spending a couple of years traveling. Wound up here, working at a dive shop. Full of life, the world was his oyster," Barbara says. "It's just so unfair."

I put an arm around Barbara. She rests her head against my chest. We're quiet for a moment. Then . . .

"Did you happen to ask Aunt Trula about an attorney?"

Barbara looks up at me, eyebrows angled in a way that tells me she's a little irked.

"Excuse me, but weren't we just cuddling?"

"We were," I say. "It was nice."

"So can't you turn it off for just a little while, Zack?"

"Sure, I can. Sorry."

I kiss the top of her head. We settle back into the couch.

I wonder how Brewster Trimmingham is doing. I need to check on him before I do anything else. I need to check on a couple of other things, too.

"Stop it," Barbara says.

"Stop what?"

"Tapping your foot like that. It's driving me crazy." She sits up. She pulls a slip of paper from a pocket, gives it to me. "Here's the attorney's name."

She gets up from the couch.

"Listen, Barbara, I'm sorry. It's just that . . ."

"It's just that your mind is elsewhere. And I understand, darling." She pulls me up from the couch, kisses me on the lips. "Now, go do what you have to do. Because I want you back again."

25

What I have to do first is call J.J. He tells me he's dropping off someone at the Naval Dockyard, but can be at Cutfoot Estate as soon as he's done. Say, thirty minutes.

As much as I like J.J., the whole routine of waiting on a driver to show up and then haul me somewhere is beginning to cramp my style. It's not that I'm in a giant hurry. But it's the American in me—when I'm ready to go, I'm ready to go. And I'd just as soon drive myself there.

"Where you heading this time?" J.J. asks after I hop into his van.

"The hospital."

He shoots me a look, concerned.

"Something wrong?"

"Yeah, I've got a bug up my ass."

He laughs, throws the van into gear, and rolls out of the driveway.

"Plenty of that going around," J.J. says. "Speaking of which, I just got a call from that niece of mine, Janeen."

"And?"

"And she wants you to help her set up an interview with that dead fellow's sister."

"Hell, J.J., the poor woman just flew in this morning. You mean to tell me that Janeen already knows she's staying at Cutfoot Estate?"

"When it comes to knowing things, Janeen seldom comes up short."

"I'm getting that impression," I say. "Tell Janeen I'll do what I can, but I'm not making any promises, OK?"

At the hospital, a receptionist tells me Brewster Trimmingham has been released from intensive care and transferred to the third floor. When I enter the room, a nurse is adjusting Trimmingham's bed and tending to the various tubes attached to him.

Trimmingham's face looks worse than the day before. Both eyes are black and swollen shut. A wire brace encases his head.

"How's he doing?" I ask the nurse.

"Quite well, actually, all things considered," she says. "The doctors were a bit concerned about the swelling in one part of his brain. But it seems to have subsided. He suffered a nasty concussion, but he'll be all right."

"His jaw broken, too?"

The nurse nods.

"Yes, it's wired shut and will be for the next few weeks. Whatever happened to the poor man?"

"Cricket accident," I say.

The nurse looks at me funny.

"Are you a relative?"

"No," I say. "Business associate."

"Well, as you can see, he's not very responsive at this moment. Still heavily sedated. I would ask you not to stay too long."

"I just want to pay my respects," I say.

She steps out of the room. She leaves the door open. I go over and close it.

I step to the table beside Trimmingham's bed. I open a drawer. A plastic storage bag sits inside. It holds Trimmingham's wallet and two sets of keys.

I open the bag, take out the keys, and leave the wallet. I stick the bag back inside the drawer and close it.

I stand by the bed, looking at Trimmingham. One of

those air mask things is stuck over his nose and mouth and he's making sucking sounds.

"Yo, Trimmingham," I say. "Can you hear me?"

Nothing.

"If you're faking being asleep, then I'm wise to you."

But apparently, he really is out for the count.

"You said you wanted me to help you, right?"

More nothing.

"I'll do what I can," I tell him. "But it's going to cost you. It's going to cost you a lot."

26

I tell J.J. to drop me off at Trimmingham's office and come back in a couple of hours.

The first key I try opens the door. I take this as a positive omen, endorsement that I'm doing the right thing, not embarking on yet another ill-conceived scheme in a career that has seen plenty of them.

Trimmingham's office is not the hellhole I'd imagined it might be. The furnishings are fairly luxurious—good leather chairs by a big mahogany desk, a good leather couch along a wall, expensive oriental rugs covering the crummy carpet that came with the office.

No photos of loved ones on the desk. I'm relieved by that. I'd just as soon not know if Trimmingham has a wife and kids and people who depend on him. It makes what I plan to do a little easier.

A computer sits in the middle of the desk, but I don't bother with that. I head for a bank of file cabinets that occupy the rear wall. I roll a desk chair with me. This could take a while.

Thirty minutes later, after going through files in two of the cabinets and moving on to the third, I've learned a lot about Brewster Trimmingham. Forty years old. Born in Hamilton. Divorced. His former wife, Alice, an American, now living in Charlottesville, Virginia, where Trimmingham sends a monthly check to cover a mortgage and expenses.

No mention of children. He rents an apartment in Hamilton. His various credit cards carry a balance, per last month's statements, of just under $20,000. Member of the Somerset Sailing Club. And a founding officer of the Bermuda Chapter of the Morris Minor Owner's Club.

I eventually dig out the real meat: a big accordion folder marked "Governor's Pointe."

I roll the chair to the desk, put my feet up on it, and spend the next ten minutes studying the papers in the folder. There's a thick stack of them, with surveys, settlement sheets, and mortgage payoff schedules.

There are also a couple of slick full-color brochures. Photos of well-groomed elegant couples toasting each other with flutes of champagne, lounging in lush living rooms, swimming in an infinity-edge pool.

"Governor's Pointe: Bermuda's Most Prestigious Address," reads the brochure copy. "Only a fortunate few, drawn from the world's elite, will be lucky enough to call Governor's Pointe home. Don't miss this ground-floor opportunity to be part of the luxury investment of a lifetime."

Each of the six residences that Trimmingham bought at Governor's Pointe has its own deed, the mortgage held by the National Bank of Bermuda. I look the deeds over and when I'm done, I use Trimmingham's phone to call the office of Daniel Denton, the attorney recommended by Aunt Trula. After the necessary happy talk I explain what I have in mind.

Denton is not overly enthusiastic about helping out.

"This seems the sort of proposition that might have serious repercussions," he says.

"Yes, it might."

"I don't know that it is the sort of thing in which our firm should be involved."

"Gee, that's too bad," I say. "I'm sure Aunt Trula will be disappointed to learn that."

Denton coughs.

"Is Mrs. Ambister your aunt, Mr. Chasteen?"

"No, she's the aunt of my significant other," I say. "But she's even dearer than family to me."

Straight to hell, that's where I'm going.

Denton hems and haws.

"What does your firm typically charge for something like this?" I ask him.

"My firm does not typically do something of this nature."

"Well, let's pretend you're expanding your services. What would be a reasonable fee?"

He tells me.

"Double that," I say.

Denton doesn't require much time to consider it.

"Very well, Mr. Chasteen," he says. "I will be at my office for another hour or so. You may drop off the papers and I will review them."

You gotta love lawyers.

27

By the time I finish in Trimmingham's office and take the stairs down to the parking garage, it's the end of the day and the place has emptied out.

A blue Morris Minor convertible sits in one of the spaces. It's a cartoon of a car, but it's not without a sort of friendly appeal.

I take the other set of keys from my pocket. One of them unlocks the door of the car. I slide behind the wheel.

Whatever sort of mess Brewster Trimmingham has made of his life, those screw-ups have not extended to his care for this car. It doesn't look perfectly new—they stopped making Morris Minors back in the 1960s—but it has aged well.

The leather seats are soft and supple. The dashboard is shiny and aligned in that peculiarly British way that might make sense to them but is counterintuitive to the American brain. It would be cool to put the top down, but one look at all the latches and cranks involved with the procedure and I know it will take a while to figure out exactly how to do it.

I start the car, put it in gear, and drive out onto the street. I pull alongside J.J.'s van. He rolls down his window.

"Has Mrs. Ambister paid you in advance for driving me around?"

"Yes, sir. Paid me for the whole two weeks. Except for any incidentals."

I take some money from my wallet and give it to him.

"I appreciate all your help," I say.

"You plan to drive yourself now?"

"I do."

"Police will raise hell if they catch you at it."

"That's why they're the police."

J.J. looks over the Morris Minor.

"That car, it ought to be in some museum."

"Now, J.J., show a little respect. This is a vintage automobile, a classic. I think it fits me to a T."

J.J. smiles.

"I don't want to know how you came by it, do I?"

"No, J.J., you don't."

28

Dinner that night at Cutfoot Estate proves to be a relatively sedate affair. Fiona McHugh, still sleeping off her journey, doesn't make it down to join us. The evening's fare is sirloin broiled beyond recognition and something that may or may not be potatoes. The conversation is all about Aunt Trula's birthday party.

"I've hired a string quartet to open the festivities," Aunt Trula says. "Then, after dinner, I thought you youngsters would appreciate a boogie-woogie band."

She pronounces it "boojie-woojie."

"Plus," Aunt Trula says, "I thought the stage would be useful for those who want to stand up and pay a few words of tribute, that sort of thing."

"Better get one of those take-a-number machines like they use at the Publix deli," I say. "There's sure to be a line."

"What's that?" Aunt Trula says.

"Oh, Zack's just trying to be clever," Barbara says, shooting me daggers. "How many people have you invited anyway, Titi?"

"The guest list is right at five hundred," Aunt Trula says. "And there have been very few regrets thus far, I'll have you know. I am quite renowned for my parties."

After we're done eating, Barbara heads back to her room to get some work done. Boggy begs off, too.

I'm not quite ready to call it a night. So I enlist a tumbler of Gosling's to keep me company on the terrace. It does a fine job. I've invited a second tumbler to sit down and join me when Aunt Trula steps out from the house.

"You look content," she says.

"Like a baby with bourbon in his belly."

"I've never heard that one before," Aunt Trula says. "But I rather like it."

"My grandfather used to say it. I think it referred to the old Southern tradition of giving crying babies a little toddy to help them relax for the night."

"Your grandfather raised you, isn't that right, Zachary?"

"Yes, he and my grandmother."

"And did they give you toddies before bedtime?"

"Only until I was two," I say. "After that, I poured my own."

Aunt Trula laughs.

"What a delightful sense of humor you have," she says. "I can see why Barbara thinks so highly of you."

"It's a mutual admiration society."

She takes the chair beside me.

"I must say, I had my doubts about you at first, Zachary. You and Barbara just seem so . . . so . . ."

"So what?"

"So unsuited for each other," she says. "I hope that doesn't offend you."

"Not at all. I've heard it from other people. Barbara has, too. Neither one of us would argue the point."

"It's just that Barbara is so . . . so . . ."

"Refined," I say.

Aunt Trula nods.

"And you are so . . ."

"Not."

Aunt Trula laughs.

"You have your own sort of refinement," she says.

"I'll take that as a compliment."

"As it was intended," Aunt Trula says. "Still, I must ask: What are your intentions with my niece?"

I somehow avoid spewing out rum.

"You mean, what are my intentions as far as . . ."

"You know very well what I mean, Zachary Chasteen. Do you intend to marry my Barbara?"

"I love her."

"That does not answer my question. Do you intend to marry her?"

I drain the rum. I don't say anything.

"Do not think me just a prying old woman who must control everything and everyone around her."

"I don't think that."

"Oh yes, you do. Because everyone thinks that about me. And rightly so, because that is exactly the way I am. I cannot help it. I like having things my way," says Aunt Trula. "Be certain of one thing: Barbara is quite dear to me. And it would grieve me to see her hurt."

"I would never hurt her. My intentions are totally honorable."

Aunt Trula considers me for a long moment.

"That still is not an answer, but it is good enough for the time being," she says. "I just want you to know, Zachary, that whatever your intentions with Barbara, you have my blessing."

"Thank you."

Aunt Trula smiles.

"And now I must ask you a favor," she says. "I would very much like it if you could help that poor dear Fiona settle this business with her brother."

I don't say anything.

"She needs to bring some closure to this ordeal. She is all alone here and I'm quite sure she's at her wit's end."

I don't say anything.

"Of course, I would step in to help her myself, but as you know I have my hands quite full with the party."

I don't say anything.

"You're not saying anything," Aunt Trula says.

"That's because I really don't know what I can do to help."

"Oh, I'm sure a resourceful chap like you will rise to the

occasion, Zachary." She gets up from her chair, bends down and, wonder of wonders, plants a kiss on my cheek. "Nighty-night."

After she's gone, I sit on the terrace, stewing things over. I really could use some company to help me stew. Good thing there's more Gosling's.

29

'm up early to see Barbara off. She has planned one of her typical pack-it-to-the-hilt days. A half-dozen meetings with hoteliers, hoping to snag some new ad contracts for *Tropics*. A dinner down in St. George's with the new minister of tourism. She doesn't expect to return until late tonight.

I hang out with Boggy and the hole-digging crew, pretending they require my help and expertise as they set the third Bismarck in place. Only five to go. And six days until Aunt Trula's party. Piece of cake. They seem to have it under control.

It's still too early to check in with the attorney, Daniel Denton, to see if he's done what I asked him to do. Therefore, it's still too early to drop by the hospital to visit Brewster Trimmingham and do what needs doing there.

I'm just a knight-errant at loose ends. So it's appropriate that I chance upon Fiona McHugh, who is punching away on her laptop in a corner of the study.

Full of chivalrous intent, I offer my services.

Fiona McHugh scrutinizes me with her blue eyes. She has freckles on her nose. They're fetching in an altogether wholesome kind of way.

"Exactly what sort of help do you think you can provide me, Mr. Chasteen?"

I open my mouth to say something, but discover I don't really have anything to say. Fiona picks up the slack.

"Do you have any experience in police work?"

"I've created lots of it from time to time."

Fiona allows herself the hint of a smile.

"Is that the sort of help you are offering? Comic relief?"

"Well, I'm good at heavy lifting, too."

She closes the laptop, rests her chin in a hand, and considers me.

"Do you have any insight regarding my brother's death?"

I flash briefly on my conversation two nights earlier with Janeen Hill. This doesn't seem the appropriate time for trotting out the reporter's wild speculations about some misbegotten quest for a chunk of biblical lore. And despite the grisly similarities between Ned McHugh's death and the murders of Martin Boyd and Richard Peach, I'm not on firm ground when it comes to discussing them. So . . .

"No," I say.

"Are you well acquainted with Bermuda, know your way around, have any particular connections that might prove valuable?"

"No, no, and no. I only arrived here four days ago."

"Then I have to ask again: What possible help can you provide me?"

"I've got a cool car. A Morris Minor convertible. It's blue."

"So you're offering to be my chauffeur? Is that it?"

"Sure, why not? The comic relief I'll toss in for free. Mainly because the radio in the car doesn't work."

"That's very kind of you, really. But I intend to rent a car for myself."

"I don't think so," I say.

I tell her about Bermuda's law prohibiting tourists from driving cars. And when I'm done, she asks: "How is it then that you are driving a car?"

So I give her the abridged version of how I came to liberate Trimmingham's Morris Minor from the parking garage the night before.

"Still," she says, "you don't have a license to drive it."

"A mere technicality. Besides, you're a cop. I'm thinking

if we get pulled over you can flash your badge," I say. "You do have a badge, don't you?"

"Of course."

"Can I see it?"

She gives me a look.

"What, you don't believe I'm with the police?"

"Sure, I believe it. I just want to see what a police badge from Down Under looks like, that's all."

Fiona reaches into her purse, pulls out a billfold, and flips it open.

"It's really not terribly exciting," she says.

She's right. It's shiny and it looks like any other police badge. The emblem reads: Western Australian Water Police.

"Water police?"

Fiona nods and puts the billfold away.

"Rather like your coast guard, only we're civil service not military," she says.

"You get a lot of experience with murders in the water police?"

"Mr. Chasteen, if you are challenging my credentials, then . . ."

"Not challenging, just asking."

She gives me a glare, a surprisingly harsh one for such a pretty face.

"For the record, I graduated from the Western Australian Police Academy with a specialty in investigative procedure and administration. I worked four years in Perth proper, first fraud, then felony, then homicide. Australians don't murder each other with nearly the frequency as you Americans, Mr. Chasteen. Our homicide rate is barely a tenth of yours, about one murder per day spread out over the entire country. Still, we do get the odd stiff in Perth and, yes, I've had a hand in several such investigations.

"As for the water police part of the equation, I saw my career evolving into a series of desk jobs. Promotions, yes, and better pay. But not for me. I asked for my transfer to the water police and have been there about a year. We've got fast boats and thirteen thousand clicks of coastline to watch over, from Scorpion Bight north to Doubtful Bay. Every day's a corker now, all grouse for me."

"That means you like what you do, right?"

"Yeah, I like it. I like it a lot." She smiles. "Any other questions?"

"Uh-huh," I say. "Do I get the job or not?"

"What job?"

"The job of helping you do whatever it is you need to do."

"You don't give up, do you?"

"You know the old saying: 'Obstinancy is the better part of valor.' "

"I thought discretion was."

"Obstinancy gets you what you want," I say. "You can be discreet about it later."

Fiona takes a moment to consider that, then rightly decides that it's really not worth considering.

"Why do you want to help me, anyway?"

"Aunt Trula asked me to."

"So you're just offering to be nice?"

"That's the way it started, but after you spurned me, it became a personal cause."

"Men," she says. "The whole conquest thing. They can be really screwed up like that."

"Yeah," I say. "They can. Meanwhile, my offer is still on the table."

Fiona cocks her head, looks me up and down. I don't feel the least bit objectified.

"So let me get this straight," she says. "You don't have a background in police work. You don't know your way around. And yet, despite that, you are offering to drive me. In a car that you stole. In a country where you do not hold a driver's license."

"That pretty much sums it up."

Fiona smiles. Her teeth are very white, her lips plump and pink.

"Works for me," she says. "So where's this cool car of yours, anyway?"

30

I futz around with the Morris Minor, trying to get the top down. But it's no go. And just as well, since a rain shower descends upon us the moment we pull onto Middle Road, heading south to Hamilton. Fiona has an appointment at the coroner's office to review the official findings.

"Barbara told me you met with the police after you arrived yesterday. Said you weren't too pleased with the way things are going."

"To put it mildly," Fiona says. "Granted, it was a very brief meeting and I was jet lagged out of my skull. Still, the detective in charge of things . . . Worley, I think his name was . . ."

"Same guy who showed up here the day your brother's body was found. Seemed decent enough."

"Yeah, maybe. But not exactly forthcoming, not even after I played the just-between-us-cops card. What little information I got, I felt like I had to pry it out of him. Plus, he kept asking all these rather irksome questions about Ned. I got the feeling that my brother was under more suspicion than his murderer."

"What kind of questions was he asking?"

"Mostly regarding Ned's reasons for coming to Bermuda. Worley seemed to think he had a motive or something. It wasn't like that."

"So why did your brother come here?"

"It was just a lark, that's all. Ned had been going to university for six solid years. Got his master's degree. Decided to do some traveling before he settled down. Financed it by working at dive shops along the way. A few months in Thailand, then in the Maldives and Seychelles. Arrived here in Bermuda last fall. Next stop was supposed to be home. He was finally hankering to get on with his life, I think."

"What did he study in college?"

"Marine archaeology," she says.

I let that rattle around in my head. She keeps talking.

"A couple of months ago, Ned got word that he had won a position with the Australian National Maritime Museum. He was going to be charting some seventeenth-century shipwrecks along the north coast. Living on a research vessel, diving every day, putting together pieces of the past—it was his dream job. He was on top of the world.

"We were ecstatic that he'd finally be coming home, even if he'd be way up in the north territory. My mom and dad had even started planning a party to welcome him back. And then—poof!—he pulled the plug on everything."

"What do you mean he pulled the plug?"

"I mean, two weeks before he was set to fly home, he called to tell us he had turned down the job and was staying here."

"What reason did he give?"

Fiona shrugs.

"In typical Ned fashion, he was vague. Just said it was important that he remain in Bermuda because he could make a name for himself."

"Make a name for himself?"

"That's what he said."

"Nothing more than that?"

"No, not really. Why?"

Best not to let laundry lie around in the hamper. Time to air it out . . .

"Listen, Fiona. When you spoke with Inspector Worley yesterday, did he mention anything about two other murders? They happened several years ago. Both scuba divers.

Both apparently killed in a fashion much like that which happened to your brother."

The look on Fiona's face tells me it's news to her.

I spend the next few minutes telling her what little I know about the deaths of Martin Boyd and Richard Peach, courtesy of my conversation with Janeen Hill. Skimpy stuff, but it's all I've got.

When I'm done, Fiona doesn't say anything for a while. Then . . .

"Bastard," she says.

"Who?"

"Worley, that's who. I went to see him. I talked to him cop-to-cop. He should have told me."

"Maybe he was just waiting until he got all the details from the coroner's report."

Fiona shakes her head.

"Bullshit. He should have told me. The bastard should have told me." She looks at me. "Do you know how to get in touch with that newspaper reporter?"

I fish around in my wallet, find Janeen Hill's business card, and give it to Fiona. She punches numbers on a cell phone. I listen as she works her way through several layers at the *Royal Gazette* office, asking for Hill.

"Oh, really? As of when?" I hear her say. "Well thanks, then. I appreciate it."

She turns off the phone.

"That was Janeen Hill's editor."

"Is he going to put her in touch with you?"

"I don't think so."

I look at her.

"Janeen Hill no longer works at the *Royal Gazette*," Fiona says. "She turned in her resignation yesterday."

31

The coroner's office is a small, stuffy room at the rear of the main police complex on Parliament Street. The chief coroner—a stout, dark-haired woman named Dr. Patterson—points us to chairs beside her desk.

"First, my condolences," Dr. Patterson says. "My heart is with you."

"Thank you," Fiona says.

Dr. Patterson pats a stack of papers on her desk.

"You will be pleased to know that I have been authorized to release your brother's remains. But there is some necessary paperwork that I must trouble you with," she says. "To begin with, do you intend to ship the body back to Australia, Miss McHugh?"

"No," Fiona says. "I discussed it with my family. We've decided to have a simple memorial service for him in Perth. As for here, I'm hoping to arrange a burial at sea. I know that's what Ned would have wanted. Will that be a problem?"

"Not at all," says Dr. Patterson. "Sea burials are quite common here in Bermuda. I'll be glad to recommend someone who can assist you with the arrangements."

The next few minutes are taken up with paperwork. When the formalities are over, Dr. Patterson pulls a manila folder from a desk drawer.

"This is the official autopsy report. I performed it myself," she says. "If you like, I can summarize."

"Please," says Fiona.

Dr. Patterson opens the folder, scans its contents. Then she puts it back down on the desk. She steels herself for what she is about to say.

"In brief, your brother's death was caused by a disruption of the inner ear ossicles and the petrous ridge, which severed the internal carotid artery and, ultimately, punctured the brain stem."

"A disruption?"

"Via the forcible insertion of a sharp instrument," says Dr. Patterson. "Judging by the relatively confined size of the puncture, roughly three-point-five millimeters, it would rule out anything much larger, say, than a long needlelike object of some kind. We are still assessing the exact nature of the weapon involved."

Fiona closes her eyes, shudders.

"My brother bled to death?"

"No," says Dr. Patterson. "Although the artery was severed, his death was a result of contusions to the medulla oblongata. He died almost instantly."

"So, he didn't suffer?"

Dr. Patterson considers the question. Her look is grim.

"I wish I could tell you, no, he didn't suffer, but . . ." She stops. "Are you quite certain that you wish to know all the details?"

Fiona nods.

"Tell me. Everything."

"Very well, then." Dr. Patterson studies the folder for a moment. "Your brother sustained a significant, although not lethal, loss of blood approximately two hours before his death. This would be consistent with trauma observed in both of the ocular cavities."

It takes a moment for the stilted terminology to sink in.

"His eyes?" Fiona says. "You mean to tell me that whoever did this yanked out my brother's eyes and then waited two hours to kill him?"

Dr. Patterson nods.

"He also received numerous contusions to the upper

torso, along with three broken ribs, mostly likely the result of being kicked."

Fiona bites her lip, hangs her head.

"My God," she says.

Dr. Patterson gets up from her chair and steps around the desk to comfort Fiona.

"Can I get you anything? Do you want some time to yourself?"

Fiona shakes her head.

"No, I'll be all right."

She reaches for the folder on the desk.

"There are photographs in there, Ms. McHugh," Dr. Patterson says. "You might not want to . . ."

"I can handle it," Fiona says.

She flips though the folder. She flinches a couple of times at what she sees, but remains composed. She puts the folder back on the desk.

Dr. Patterson reaches out and grips Fiona's shoulder, offering solace.

"I realize how difficult this must be," she says. "If there's anything I can do . . ."

"There is, actually," Fiona says. "You can tell me about the two other murders."

It catches Dr. Patterson by surprise. She pulls back her hand, looks away.

"I'm not prepared to talk about that," she says.

"Did you perform the autopsies on them?"

Dr. Patterson answers with a reluctant nod.

"Can I see the files?"

Dr. Patterson shakes her head, no.

"Why not?"

"Because the files are no longer in my possession, Ms. McHugh."

"Detective Worley?"

"That's right," says Dr. Patterson.

"If you don't mind me asking, exactly when did you give them to him?"

"It would have been three days ago. Shortly after your brother's body was discovered."

Fiona settles back in her chair, studies the coroner.

"But I'm guessing you reviewed everything that was in those files before you turned them over to Worley. Didn't you? Just to refresh your memory."

Dr. Patterson meets Fiona's stare, holds it.

"I did, yes."

"So maybe you don't need those files to answer my question, do you, Dr. Patterson?"

Dr. Patterson doesn't say anything.

"It's a very simple question: My brother's murder and the murders of those other two men—are they connected?"

Dr. Patterson weighs her response, grappling with how best to proceed.

"I cannot speak as to how the murders might be connected. I can only offer an objective analysis of the forensic evidence in each case and any similarities that might exist between them."

"OK, then," says Fiona. "Are the murders similar?"

"You understand that this is unofficial and off the record?"

"Yes," Fiona says. "I understand."

"You understand that I am only telling you this because I believe that you, as a family member, have the right to know."

"I appreciate that."

Dr. Patterson steps back behind her desk, sits down in her chair.

"In answer to your question, Ms. McHugh, the murders are more than just similar. They are practically identical," Dr. Patterson says. "So much so, that I have little doubt they were all committed by the same person."

Fiona looks at me, then back at Dr. Patterson.

"And did you tell that to Detective Worley?"

Dr. Patterson shakes her head.

"I didn't have to tell him. Those other murders? That was his case, too. I'm sure he knew they were connected the moment he saw your brother's body."

32

et me guess," I say as we leave Dr. Patterson's office. "Next stop is to see Detective Worley, where you will proceed to cut him a brand-new asshole."

"That's if I'm feeling merciful," says Fiona. "Which, right now, I'm not."

We find Worley's office, but he isn't in. No one knows where he is or when he'll return. Fiona leaves Worley a card with her cell number, the number at Cutfoot Estate, and a message: "Call me ASAP."

"So where to now?" I ask her when we step outside.

Fiona pulls out a sheet of paper on which Dr. Patterson has written down the name of a funeral home that can help arrange the burial at sea.

"Guess I might as well get this taken care of," she says.

We head for the visitor's parking lot. The Morris Minor is right where I left it, in the shade of a mahogany tree.

Perched on its hood, smoking a cigarette—Janeen Hill.

She wears a tight blue dress and a pair of blue glasses that match it. Her abundant hair is pulled together on top of her head, spilling out from a beaded scrunchie. With the plume of cigarette smoke wafting skyward, it looks for all the world like a small volcano is erupting from her skull.

Janeen slides off the car, straightens her dress as we approach.

"Heard you got yourself some wheels," she says. "Saw this thing parked here and thought I'd take a chance."

"And I heard you no longer work for the *Gazette*," I say. "What happened?"

Janeen shrugs.

"Just decided the time was right to move on," she says.

"So what now?"

"Oh, I've got a few ideas," she says. "One thing for sure—I intend to keep following this story."

She looks at Fiona.

"Are you . . . ?"

"Sorry, I'm forgetting my manners," I say. "Janeen Hill, this is Fiona McHugh. And vice versa."

The two women shake hands. Janeen cuts straight to the chase.

"We need to talk," she says.

Fiona nods.

"I'd be happy to, but I have another matter I really should take care of first."

"Now is better than later," Janeen says. "There are some things you need to know. And there are some things that I could learn from you, as well."

"You mean, about my brother?"

"Yes, mostly, but other things, too. Do you mind?"

"No, I don't mind. It's just that . . ." Fiona looks at me. "What about it, Zack?"

"It's your call," I say.

Janeen already has Fiona by the arm, leading her away.

"My apartment is only a few blocks," she says. "We can walk."

33

We cut down to Front Street, past the cruise ship terminal. The berths are empty, but an incoming arrival is visible on the horizon, a giant wedding cake chugging in from the east.

We tell Janeen about the autopsy reports. She asks Fiona a few questions about Ned McHugh, learning about his background and his studies in marine archaeology.

For Janeen, it all amounts to further proof that the murders are somehow linked by what brought Richard Peach and Martin Boyd to Bermuda—the search for the Reliquarium de Fratres Crucis. She conducts a miniseminar on the topic as we walk along the busy thoroughfare.

"You have to understand, there's no iron-clad evidence that the cross used in Christ's Crucifixion was ever found in Jerusalem," she says. "Everything is based on the accounts of Helena Augusta."

"Sorry," I say. "The name's not ringing any bells."

"The mother of Constantine the Great, who was the first Christian emperor of the Roman Empire. She eventually became Saint Helena. When she was in her seventies and a recent convert to Christianity, this would have been sometime in the early part of the fourth century, Helena left Rome and began a pilgrimage to Jerusalem. Once there, she commanded workers to begin an excavation that eventually is said to have unearthed the True Cross."

Fiona and I share a skeptical look.

"Yeah, right," Fiona says. "Out of all the places to dig and all the crosses the Romans executed people on over the years, an old woman shows up and just happens to find the exact same cross they used to crucify Christ."

"I'm not saying I buy into it," Janeen says. "I'm just throwing it out there, OK? Because, in the end, it doesn't matter if Helena really did find the cross. What matters is that, through the ages, millions upon millions of people have believed that she found it, have believed in the existence of the True Cross. That belief has led them to die for it. Kill for it, too. And even if it's just a myth, it's a powerful one. Powerful enough to make guys like Richard Peach devote their lives to sorting it all out."

We stop at a corner to let a truck wedge into the traffic on Front Street. Janeen takes the opportunity to light another cigarette. Then we're walking again.

"When did you say Helena was supposed to have dug up the cross?" I ask.

"Somewhere around AD 326."

"OK, here's what I don't get," I say. "If the cross was so important, how come the followers of Jesus left it buried for nearly three hundred years after the Crucifixion?"

"Because those early Christians had other things to worry about. Like their own survival. Besides, it took a few hundred years for Christianity to catch on and for its followers to begin seeing the cross in the same way they see it now. Up until then the cross had been an instrument of death, something they would just as soon leave buried.

"Then along came Helena. She was a newbie Christian and, perhaps even more important, she was a shrewd politician. Her son had just taken over the throne of the Roman Empire and was trying his damndest to expand his power, while stamping out the last vestiges of paganism. So dear ol' Mom provides him with the perfect symbol to solidify his power, something that would not only rally the troops but add to the divine nature of Constantine's cause. Quite brilliant, really."

Janeen steers us off Front Street and onto a narrow, pedestrian-only walkway that runs between a phalanx of office buildings. We can no longer walk three abreast, so I let the two of them take the lead.

"Let's pretend Helena really did find the True Cross," Fiona says. "What happened to it after she dug it up?"

"That's where things start to get a little fuzzy," Janeen says. "What was left of the cross, after all those pieces were hacked off as holy relics, probably remained in Jerusalem for much of that time. Then, around 1100, the Crusader kings began carrying it into battle. They saw the cross as a talisman, a good luck charm that helped ward off their Muslim enemies. That's how the cross really began its ascendancy as a symbol. It became the Holy of Holies, almost supernatural in its powers, something that had to be defended at all costs. And that's why its capture became the primary objective of Sultan Saladin."

"Someone else I've never heard of," I say.

"He was a Kurd, from the city of Tikrit, in what is now Iraq. Went on to be king of Egypt. His troops slaughtered the Crusaders at the Battle of the Horns of Hattin, sometime around AD 1180. Saladin's army supposedly seized the cross, and after that it was never officially seen again."

"What do you mean, officially?"

"Well, there were stories that subsequent Muslim leaders often dragged the cross through the dirt before battle to fire up their armies. That only fueled the passions of true Christian believers who launched forays to get it back. One of Saladin's successors was even said to have turned down a ransom payment for the cross—forty bags of gold or something like that," Janeen says. "And over the years, as it endured further degradation, the cross was reduced to just a small piece of wood, no bigger than a book."

"So how did the Fratres Crucis get hold of it?" I ask.

"Hard to say exactly. They were a pretty secretive bunch. Didn't keep written records. And if any member of the brotherhood talked about their activities to those on the outside—even to a wife or a close friend—they were summarily put to death," says Janeen. "Best guess is that they just bided their time, waited for the fervor of the Crusades era to die down, waited all the way until the mid-1400s when the Ottomans seized Constantinople and Sultan Mehmed took over the empire. By then, as far as rousing the Muslim troops went, that tiny little piece of the cross had lost its sizzle. The Fratres Crucis didn't have nearly the manpower to lay siege to Constantinople and take it. But they had money. Lots of money. And most likely they just bribed the sultan or one of his emissaries and got what they wanted."

"Either that or the sultan knew a bunch of rubes when he saw them and sold them a worthless chunk of wood," I say.

Janeen laughs.

"Yeah, there's always that. Still, belief is a powerful thing, you know? The brotherhood believed they had the last remaining piece of the True Cross. And, in the end, that's what mattered above all else. They returned with it to Portugal and hired a goldsmith to create a reliquary to properly enshrine their treasure. And, not long after that, they built a ship."

"A ship?" Fiona says. "What for?"

"Constantinople fell to the Ottomans in 1453. Things moved a heck of a lot slower back then. The Fratres Crucis didn't just rush off to see the sultan and zip back home. It could have taken them thirty or forty years to pull everything off. By then it was the 1490s. And we all know what was going on around that time."

"In fourteen-hundred-and-ninety-two, Columbus sailed the ocean blue," I say.

"And so did the Fratres Crucis," says Janeen. "Well, not exactly. It was a few years later before they set out aboard the *Santa Helena.*"

"That was the name of their ship?"

Janeen nods.

"After Helena Augusta, discoverer of the True Cross. They launched it in November of 1497."

"You sound pretty exact about that date, considering what you said about the brotherhood not keeping any records," Fiona says.

"As secretive as the Fratres Crucis were, building and launching a ship is pretty hard to hide. There are port logs in the archives of the Museu de Marinha in Lisbon that mention the *Santa Helena*. They don't go into any detail about its mission, but that's not hard to figure out."

"I'm guessing they weren't on the typical let's-find-India-and-bring-back-some-gold cruise, right?"

"Not by a long shot," Janeen says. "The Fratres Crucis were out to establish their own Christian kingdom in the New World, one far from the Muslim hordes, and one that would enjoy the power that came from possessing the most holy relic of their religion."

"And they planned to do this in Bermuda?" Fiona asks.

"No, they didn't even know that Bermuda existed. No one did. It wasn't even on any maps until 1520 or so. The *Santa Helena* was probably on a course that would have taken it somewhere near what is now Virginia. Only Bermuda just sort of popped out and surprised them. In any event, the ship was never seen again. And the reliquary was lost with it."

We stop at a door near the rear entrance of an office supply store.

"My place is upstairs, on the second floor," Janeen says, riffling through her purse to find a key.

"You really think this reliquary of theirs could have survived more than five hundred years on the sea bottom?" I ask. "Seems highly doubtful to me."

"Well, even though it was made out of precious metal and jewels, it was still a pretty substantial piece of work. It was built to endure."

"How do you know that?" Fiona asks.

"Because the goldsmith who created the reliquary made drawings of his work, several of them, and showed them around, probably just trying to drum up more business. One of them is in the Museu de Marinha."

"The brotherhood couldn't have been too happy about that," I say.

"Oh, they were outraged. They killed him." Janeen unlocks the door and swings it open. "After they plucked out his eyes."

34

Janeen's apartment is a tiny place—one bedroom with a glimpse of the harbor from a window in the living room/kitchen. Overstuffed sofa draped with blankets. Rattan chairs around a wooden dinner table upon which sits an oldish desktop computer. Piles of books everywhere. And a well-fed black cat lounging on a windowsill.

"The thing with the eyes," Fiona says. "Was that like their trademark when they killed people or something?"

"It came to be," Janeen says. "Originally, before they gained possession of the cross, members of the brotherhood first cut out the tongues of those who talked out of school about them. And then they killed them. Later, they switched to removing the eyes of the offenders, perhaps to signify that while the victim had seen the Reliquarium de Fratres Crucis, they were no longer worthy of such an honor."

Fiona broods, plainly unsettled by the information.

"How does this relate to my brother?" she asks. "Do you mean to tell me that there are still members of this insane brotherhood out there, plucking out people's eyes?"

Janeen holds her gaze for a long moment, then says: "Look, why don't I make us all some tea? How's that sound? Then we can sit down and talk."

I nose around the apartment while Janeen puts water on to boil.

A worn copy of *The Legend of the Lost Cross*, by Richard

Peach, sits on the table. I pick up the book. Janeen notices me flipping through it.

"Came out about a dozen years ago," she says. "Got mediocre reviews. Even the best of them said it was little more than a rehashing of other works on the subject and did little in the way of breaking new ground. It stung Peach, stung him bad. He became obsessed with setting the record straight about the Lost Cross once and for all, and he spent the next six years, right up until the time of his death . . ."

"Wait, wait, wait," I interrupt. "How do you know all this stuff? About the Fratres Crucis? About Richard Peach? How do you know he was obsessed? You'd never even heard of him until after he and Boyd were killed, right?"

My words come out more strident than I intended. They cause Janeen a moment's pause.

"Yes, you're right. And sorry, I can get carried away on this subject. But after covering the story of their murders for the *Gazette,* I became rather obsessed myself," she says. "I interviewed Peach's wife when she came here to claim his remains. She's the one who told me what Boyd and her husband were doing in Bermuda and how they came to believe that the *Santa Helena* wrecked here."

Janeen plops tea bags into mugs, fills them with hot water, hands one to Fiona and then me. We sit down around the table.

"Margaret Peach and I kept in touch after she returned home to England, and I did my best to keep her updated on the progress of the investigation, such as it was. We grew to be friends. Margaret was a dear, dear lady. She could never quite bear to return here to Bermuda, but I visited her in England on three or four occasions.

"Shortly before her death, this was just last year, she asked me to come and help catalog her husband's papers. It had gotten to be too much for her, and she wanted the papers to be in some sort of order before she donated them to the University of Leeds, where Peach began his teaching career. Let's just say it turned out to be a more extensive project than I had envisioned. I wound up taking a three-month

leave of absence from the *Gazette* so I could see it through
to the finish."

The black cat leaps onto the table. It sniffs Fiona's mug,
then jerks its head away.

"Come here, you." Janeen picks up the cat and cradles it,
stroking it as she looks at Fiona. "I must ask you to promise
me something."

"What's that?" Fiona says.

"That you will give me the exclusive rights to your
brother's story."

"My brother's story?"

Fiona and I look at each other. Neither one of us says
anything.

"I don't want to come off as paranoid or anything," says
Janeen, "but I have to look out for my own best interests
here." She lets go of the cat and it leaps off her lap. "You
should know that I resigned from the *Gazette* because I want
to give my full attention to this. I want to get to the bottom
of it. I'm planning on writing a book."

"A book?" Fiona says.

"Yes, Margaret Peach was adamant that her husband's
work not just get stuffed away in some dusty old library. She
wanted his death to count for something. And she gave me
the publication rights to her husband's research. It was one
of the last things she did before she died."

Janeen grips her mug with both hands, takes a sip of tea.

"The only strings Margaret attached were that, should a
book get published, I share credit with her husband, list him
as the coauthor. I had no problem with that. He had already
done so much of the research. It's solid stuff. And the story
of how the reliquary may have wound up in Bermuda is fas-
cinating. Had Peach and Boyd actually succeeded in finding
it, there's no doubt the book would have been an international best-seller, maybe even a movie. Even as it is, based
just on Peach's research and some other information I've
cobbled together, well, let's just say I've got high hopes for
the book I intend to write. But I want to keep all that under
wraps, OK? I don't want someone coming along, stealing

this story away from me, and coming out with a book of their own."

Fiona sips tea, considers Janeen across the top of her mug.

"So how far along are you on this book of yours, anyway?" she asks. There's a distinct edge to her voice. But Janeen doesn't seem to notice as she lights another cigarette.

"Well, having the rights to Peach's work helped me get an agent. A good one in New York. Still, nothing has really happened as far as landing a publisher. I mean, it has been a long time since Peach and Boyd were killed. Plus, as my agent keeps telling me, the story is unresolved. The murderer has never been caught. The cross has never been found." She takes a drag on her cigarette, blows smoke out the side of her mouth. "But when I called him the other day and told him about your brother's murder, he got really excited and . . ."

She stops.

"I'm sorry, Fiona. I don't want to make it sound as if I'm exploiting Ned's death to my own advantage."

Fiona bristles.

"But that's exactly what you're doing, isn't it?"

Janeen looks away, doesn't say anything. Fiona sets down her mug, sloshing tea onto the table.

"I am so glad your agent was excited by my brother's murder. Hope it lands you a giant book deal. Good luck with the goddamn movie rights, too."

"Fiona, please, I didn't mean for it to come out like that." Janeen turns to her, pleading. "Just hear me out on this. There's more, so much more."

Fiona ignores her. She gets up from the table, looks at me.

"I'm done here," she says.

She marches across the living room and out the door. To her credit, she does not slam it.

Janeen slumps into a chair at the table. She takes a final drag on her cigarette, then snubs it out in a seashell ashtray.

"Guess I really blew that, huh?"

"Not what I'd call a diplomatic coup."

"I didn't mean for it to come out sounding like that, really I didn't."

I get up from the table, look down at her.

"Cut to the chase, Janeen. Do you know who committed these murders?"

She doesn't say anything.

"You better tell me what you know and you better tell it to me now."

"There are still some pieces missing," Janeen says. "I still can't say for sure."

"But you've shared what you know with the police?"

She looks away.

"No," she says. "I haven't."

"Why not?"

She doesn't say anything.

"Let me guess why not, Janeen. You're saving it all for this book of yours, aren't you?"

She doesn't say anything.

"Because it's in your best interest if the police don't catch the killer. It gives you a little more juice. You can reap the glory, watch your book climb the best-seller list. Pretty goddamn selfish, if you ask me."

Janeen looks up at me. Her eyes are hard.

"I've worked my ass off for this," she says. "I deserve something out of it."

"The three dead guys deserve something, too. It's called justice. Go to the police, Janeen."

I head for the door.

"Zack, please," she calls out. "There's so much you don't know."

"Story of my life," I say.

35

Fiona is waiting for me in the alley behind Janeen's apartment.

"Sorry for storming out like that," she says as we walk back to the car.

"Don't blame you," I say. "Don't blame you at all."

"But the idea that she would try to capitalize off Ned's death . . . I just lost it. Was I wrong?"

"No, you weren't wrong."

She looks at me.

"You think I should have just bit my tongue?"

"No."

"No, but . . . ?"

"But, yeah, I do think Janeen knows some things. Maybe more than the cops know, even. Or certainly more than what they've been willing to share with you so far. I don't think it could hurt matters to hear her out."

Fiona stops.

"OK, then. Let's go back up there. I've cooled off. Let's listen to what she has to say."

"Not just yet. She deserves to wallow in a little guilt for handling that the way she did. Besides, we might wind up learning more from her if we give her time to stew."

We get back to the car and drive to the funeral home recommended by Dr. Patterson. The funeral director says he can arrange Ned McHugh's burial at sea for the day after to-morrow.

We'll need a boat. So I make a call to Aunt Trula, who calls Teddy Schwartz, and, just like that, we've got *Miss Peg*.

"I'm done in," says Fiona as we leave the funeral home.

"Still working off the jet lag?"

"Yes, that, plus I never could have imagined that I'd be arranging Neddie's funeral. And this whole thing with crosses and reliquaries and secret societies, it's just so . . . so . . ."

She stops. She looks exhausted.

"I need to call my folks and let them know where every-thing stands," she says. "Do you mind if we head back now?"

"Fine by me."

"And one other thing, Zack."

"What's that?"

She takes my arm, gives it a quick squeeze.

"Thanks," she says.

"For what?"

"For insisting that you help me out."

"Aw shucks, ma'am. It weren't nothing. Besides, I was just looking for an excuse to tool around in my cool blue car."

I drive us to Cutfoot Estate, and when we get there I make a call of my own—to Daniel Denton, the attorney.

"I was rather hoping you might have changed your mind about going through with this," he says.

"Nope. Did you do everything I asked you to?"

"Yes, but I can't say that I like it any more than when we first spoke."

"You don't have to like it, Denton. When can we do this?"

He sighs.

"I'm available after three P.M."

I tell him where to meet me.

36

As soon as I hang up the phone with Denton, I round up Boggy. Together, we figure out how to lower the top on the Morris Minor and set out down the coast.

The morning's rainstorm is long gone. It's a lovely afternoon. The air is warm but not too warm, the sky a flawless blue.

As we drive along, I bring Boggy up to speed on everything, from Fiona's meeting with the coroner to our encounter with Janeen Hill.

"This book the man Peach wrote, and the one woman Janeen is writing," says Boggy. "They are books I would like very much to read."

"Oh, really. And why is that?"

"Is like some Taino stories. This search for the cross, it reminds me of how we Taino always hope to find Yaya's gourd."

"Yaya's gourd?"

Boggy nods.

"Yes, for Taino, it is our creation story. Yaya, the father of the world, had a son, Yayael. And Yayael, jealous of his father's power, plotted to kill him. But Yaya caught him at this and he killed his son instead."

"Jeez," I say. "Why is it that so many religions get started by families from Dysfunction Junction? The whole Cain and Abel thing. God cuckolding Joseph and then sending Jesus on a suicide mission. This guy Yayael trying to kill his old man."

"You want to hear how the story ends, Zachary?"

"Is it a happy ending?" I say. "I could really use a happy ending for a change."

Boggy ignores me.

"So after Yaya killed his son, he put the bones into a gourd and hung the gourd in his house."

"Sick bastard," I say.

Boggy cuts his eyes my way, keeps talking.

"Then one day, wanting to see his son again, Yaya asked his wife to fetch the gourd and pour out the bones. She did this. Only, it was not bones that came out, but water and fish. Enough water and fish to cover the world."

I look at Boggy.

"That the end of the story?"

Boggy nods.

"It is a happy ending, Zachary, no?"

"What's so happy about it?"

"Yaya and his wife, they get to eat the fish."

"Gee, nothing at all whacked-out about that, seeing as how those fish were once their son's bones."

"Yes, but death creates life, Zachary. That is the story of all religion. And just as there are people who would want to find this Lost Cross, so, among the Taino, we have always dreamed of finding Yaya's gourd. Is out there. Is real. He who finds the gourd finds everlasting life." He looks at me. "Why is it that you are smiling, Zachary?"

"Oh, nothing."

"No, Zachary. It is something. What is it?"

"I was just thinking that maybe the Taino religion is the most honest of them all. It admits that it's based on someone being out of their gourd."

Boggy looks at me.

"I do not understand this," he says. "Please explain."

"Never mind. You believe what you believe. And I believe what I believe."

"Very well then, Zachary. And what do you believe?"

"I believe we are getting close to the place I want to see."

We're outside of Tucker's Town, near a bluff overlooking the ocean. There's a small sign just ahead. Back in Florida, where billboards grow wild, it would be a giant sign with Day-Glo lettering and a stop-traffic headline. But this one is fairly tasteful as such things go.

FUTURE SITE OF GOVERNOR'S POINTE, it reads. EXCLUSIVE RESIDENCES. PRECONSTRUCTIONS PRICES.

I pull onto the side of the road.

Below us sits a tiny cove. The green-blue water is so clear that you can make out the outline of sea fans waving atop coral heads twenty feet below the surface. Pelicans dive-bomb schools of fish. The beach is a glistening strand of pinkish sand.

"Only one thing could improve a view like this."

"What is that, Zachary?"

"A bunch of condos stuck on the side of the hill."

Boggy smiles.

"And maybe a golf course, too," he says.

"With a clubhouse and a spa."

"It's the way of man," Boggy says.

"What? To improve something that doesn't need improving?"

"Yes, that. And to think that he can own the land. Man cannot own the land, Zachary."

I look at him.

"OK," I say. "I'm waiting for the next part."

"Next part?"

"Yeah, you know, something like: Man cannot own the land because the land will wind up owning him."

"Yes, that is true."

"Also, man cannot own the land because, long after man is gone, the land endures."

"Wise words, Zachary," says Boggy. "It is the way of the Taino."

"Well, don't go thinking you've got a convert. Because I'm looking at that land right there in front of us and I'm thinking that someone has taken a big chunk of my money so that he can own a tiny part of it. And I don't get any comfort out of knowing it will endure long after I'm gone. I'd like my money now."

"You are very attached to your money, Zachary."

"Yes, I am."

Boggy doesn't say anything. I start the car.

"It's not that I'm greedy," I say.

"You only wish to have that which is yours. Eh, Guamikeni?"

"Right," I say. "And maybe just a little something extra to go along with it."

37

Brewster Trimmingham is sitting up in bed, doing much better than the day before.

"Umph-emmph," he says.

With his jaw wired shut, it's hard to make out exactly what he's saying, but I'm pretty sure he's cussing me.

"Easy there, Brew," I say. "I'm doing you a big favor."

"Oddy-astad," Trimmingham says.

"I am not a sorry bastard. I'm the guy who rescued you after you got your head cracked. And I'm the guy who is going to relieve you of your financial responsibilities to whomever did the cracking. Plus, I intend to make sure it doesn't happen again. You should be thanking me."

I turn to Daniel Denton. He's sixtyish, a tall man with a patrician's bearing. He wears a good suit and an expression that says he would rather be anywhere else but here.

"You're up," I tell him.

Denton edges to Trimmingham's bed and presents him with a thick stack of papers.

"Now, please listen very carefully, Mr. Trimmingham, as I explain in more detail the proposition that Mr. Chasteen has just laid out," says Denton.

Denton launches into a protracted lawyerly lecture that boils down to this: For the token amount of one dollar per unit, I will become the proud owner of six condominium residences at Governor's Pointe. I will assume the mortgages with the National Bank of Bermuda. And I will further assume, as Denton has so craftily phrased it, "any prior debts to parties mentioned or unmentioned herein that are directly or indirectly related to the purchase of said units."

There's also a lot of legal rigmarole that I interpret to mean that neither Daniel Denton nor his firm can be held liable in the event that this whole deal blows up in our faces. It's all so guardedly worded that I'm surprised Denton isn't wearing gloves out of fear his fingerprints might be traced back to these documents.

Denton hands Trimmingham a pen.

"Now, sir, if you would just sign your name at those places which I have highlighted."

Trimmingham slings the pen across the room. It almost hits Boggy, who is standing by a window.

I tap Denton on the shoulder.

"If you don't mind," I say, "I'd like a few moments alone with Mr. Trimmingham."

Denton steps away from the bed. On his way to the door, he leans close to me and speaks low.

"I will not be a party to coercion," he says.

"Coercion sounds so harsh, don't you think? I prefer to think of it as playtime."

The moment Denton leaves the room, Trimmingham launches into a tirade. I can't make out a word he says.

When he's done, I pick up the pen from the floor and grab a notepad from the bedside table. I hand them to Trimmingham.

"Might help if you wrote down what it is you're trying to tell me," I say.

Trimmingham scribbles something on the pad and shoves it at me.

I LOSE $200,000!!!, it says.

"Sorry, but I'm afraid that's the cost of doing business, Brew. Consider that two hundred thousand dollars your payment for my services. The way I look at it, you're getting off pretty cheap."

Trimmingham rips the sheet off the notepad. He wads it up and throws it at me. He writes something else.

NOT FAIR!!!!

"Not fair? Come on, Brew. You took two million dollars of mine and it's sitting out there. You want not fair? That's not fair. So I am assuming my role as majority partner in this little enterprise you've gotten us into. And I'm calling in the chits."

Trimmingham starts in on another rant. I grab a pillow from the bed and shove it down on his face. Trimmingham shuts up. I remove the pillow.

Trimmingham glares at me. But at least he has the good sense to be quiet.

"Look at it this way," I say. "Sign these papers and you're home free. No overhead to worry about. No bad guys on your tail. Everything is on my shoulders. All you have to do is take it easy and get well."

"Goosh-gotumpph," Trimmingham says. "Izznot-tokus . . ."

I move in with the pillow. Trimmingham shuts up.

"Of course," I continue, "if you refuse to sign then that means your ass is in a sling. You still owe all that money. To the bad guys. And to me. And I'm a whole lot badder than they are. You might as well take up permanent residence in this hospital. That's if you're lucky."

Trimmingham seethes. He starts to say something, thinks better of it. He scribbles on the notepad and holds it up so I can see.

I WANT ALL MY MONEY!!!!

"Sure, no problem." I take out my wallet, pull six dollar bills from it. I put them on the bed. "There you go. Now sign the papers."

I pick up the pen and hold it out to Trimmingham.

"Gafuk yusef," he says.

I fluff the pillow, move in with it again.

He reaches for the pen.

38

Despite my success in getting Brewster Trimmingham to sign the papers, I have no luck on another front: Getting him to tell me who beat him up.

He stonewalls. And keeps stonewalling. And when his blood pressure spikes so much that a buzzer goes off, a nurse comes in and asks Boggy and me to leave.

"These people, the ones Trimmingham owes money to, don't you think they will soon reveal themselves?" asks Boggy as we leave the hospital.

"Yeah, I do. But I prefer they reveal themselves on my terms. And I prefer they do it sooner rather than later."

I drive to downtown Hamilton and park in the alley behind Benny's Lounge. We step inside. Not much of a crowd. A few people occupying booths. No one sitting at the bar.

The same bartender from a couple of days earlier is wiping down the bar, talking on his cell phone. Boggy and I take stools near him. If he recognizes me, he doesn't show it. He flips shut his phone.

"What can I get you?" he asks.

"A name."

Blank stare from the bartender. He's a big, pig-faced guy, clearly not hired for his looks.

"What name is that?"

"Whoever it was you called the other afternoon when Brewster Trimmingham got his butt kicked in the alley."

"Don't know what you're talking about," says the bartender.

He gives me his bad-ass look. It's a good one, as looks like that go. I'd rate it about number 713 out of the 10,000 or so I've been given in my life. I hope he doesn't see me quivering in my sandals.

"Gee," I say. "I must have made a mistake."

"Yeah," says the bartender. "You must have."

I smile.

"In that case," I say, "my friend and I will each take a pint of Guinness and review our options."

The bartender isn't sure he likes the sound of that, but he draws our pints anyway. He sets them down in front of us.

I pick up my mug and study it. There's at least three inches of brown foam sitting on top of the black stout.

"You know, you really rushed this one," I say.

"Oh, yeah?" says the bartender. "How's that?"

"Well, the right way to draw a Guinness, it takes time. You pour a little, let it sit. Then pour a little more, and let it sit. Maybe scrape off the head with a knife. I don't like it when my Guinness is rushed," I say. "I can't possibly drink this."

I toss the Guinness in the bartender's face.

As he sputters, I grab Boggy's mug.

"You mind?" I ask Boggy.

"I hate Guinness," he says. "Gives me gas."

"Then 'tis a far, far better thing I do."

I give the bartender another faceful of stout.

He reaches across the bar to grab me and I slam the mug against the side of his head. He drops like a bag of bricks.

The people in the booths eye me with no small degree of alarm. Can't say that I blame them.

"Big guy like him," I say, "you'd think he could hold his liquor."

I vault over the bar. The bartender lies groaning on a plastic mat. I roll him onto his back. I sit down on his chest.

There's a red welt near his temple. He'll be all right.

I give his right cheek a slap.

"A name," I say.

"No way, I can't."

"Oh, but you can."

A backhand slap to his left cheek. Then another to his right.

"I'm just getting into my rhythm," I say. "Maybe you'd like to hum along."

Left, right, left . . .

"OK, OK," the bartender says.

I stop slapping.

"They're Papi's guys. That's all I know. Swear to God."

"Who's Papi?"

"I don't know. I've never met him. Just heard about him. Everyone's heard about Papi Ferreira. He's, like, the local Godfather or something."

"What's he got to do with Brewster Trimmingham?"

The bartender shakes his head.

"All I know, these guys they come in the other day and they tell me that I'm supposed to call them whenever Trimmingham gets here and whenever he leaves."

"You ask them why?"

The bartender snorts.

"Not the kind of guys you ask why," he says.

"So all you've got is a phone number?"

"Yeah, and that's all I know. Swear to God."

"What's the number?"

"I don't have it in my head. I've got to look it up."

I slide off his chest. We both stand.

"You can't tell them where you got it," the bartender says. "You've got to promise, OK?"

"Sure, cross my heart, hope to die. What's the number?"

The bartender pulls out his cell phone, punches some buttons.

"OK, here it is. Six-oh-three . . ."

He stops.

"You want to write this down?"

"No, don't think so."

I grab the cell phone. The number is displayed on the screen. I hit the green button, hear it dialing.

"No, man, you can't . . ."

The bartender moves toward me. I push him back.

"Quiet," I say. "Can't you see I'm on the phone?"

"But they'll know you got the number from me. They'll see the caller ID."

"Technology," I say. "Ain't it a beautiful thing?"

39

"What makes you think they will come, Zachary?"

"They'll come," I say. "They want to see who they are up against."

"You and me."

"Yeah," I say. "You and me."

"And we will strike fear into their hearts."

I look at Boggy.

"Did you smile when you said that?"

He shakes his head, no.

"Well, you should have," I say.

We're sitting in Brewster Trimmingham's office. We've been sitting there for almost three hours.

I am in the swivel chair, my feet up on the desk. Boggy leans in a corner, near the door. We've traded positions a couple of times, just to break the monotony.

The ceiling fan spins round and round. Its long metal chain rattles against the fan's frame.

Irritating.

I get up, turn off the fan, sit back down with my feet on the desk.

Now it's hot.

I get up, turn the fan on again.

The guy who answered the phone when I called from Benny's Lounge, I told him we would be here until 7:00 P.M. It's almost that time.

"You didn't happen to bring that big-ass knife of yours, did you, the one that can slice through a watermelon in midair?"

"No," Boggy says. "I did not think it would get past airport security."

"You could have at least tried."

Boggy shrugs.

"That would have been foolish," he says.

"Unlike calling the bad guys on the phone, inviting them to come see us, then actually hanging around for three hours to see if they show up. And not taking into consideration that there might be a whole bunch of them and they might just decide to wipe the floor with us."

"I think it will not be that easy for them."

"Not if you had that big-ass knife."

As it turns out there's three of them. They actually knock at the door. How very polite.

I nod Boggy to stay put in the corner. I leave my feet on the desk. All the better for impressing them with my laid-back demeanor and convincing myself that I'm not even a teeny bit scared.

"*Entrez-vous*," I say.

Maybe I can impress them with my international flair, too.

The door swings open. They step inside.

It's the same two guys who worked over Trimmingham—one big, one small. The third guy, I'm thinking, must have been the driver. He's the biggest of them all.

They notice Boggy behind them and back away, fanning out so that they can keep their eyes on both of us. Ah, already we have them running scared.

"So glad you could join us," I say. "I wish I could offer refreshments, but . . ."

"Cut the shit," the small one says. "What is it you want?"

"All business, huh? OK, if you want to play that way," I say. "I'm putting you on notice that you are not to lay another hand on Brewster Trimmingham."

The small guy looks at the other two. All three of them snicker.

"Oh really," says the small guy. "Why is that?"

"Because he no longer owes you any money."

"He doesn't?"

"No. I have assumed all of Mr. Trimmingham's debts." I point to the stack of papers on the desk. "The details are in there if you care to read them."

"You can wipe your ass with those papers," the small guy says.

"I prefer Charmin. Citrus scented, double ply."

"Listen, Jay Leno, just give us the money."

"No, no, no," I say. "It doesn't work like that. First, I need to know who 'us' is. You guys work for Papi Ferreira, right?"

The three of them exchange looks.

"It is none of your business who we work for," the small guy says. "You need to pay us the money and get out of Bermuda."

"And what if I were to tell you to go straight to hell?"

The small guy shrugs.

"Then you would get the same thing that Trimmingham got. Only worse."

"Go straight to hell," I say.

The two big ones move first, toward me. And as they do, Boggy leaps from the corner, clipping the small guy with a shoulder, taking him down.

I lean back in the chair, put my feet on the side of the desk, and push. The desk catches the two big guys at their knees, stopping them. I scramble out of the chair, set a shoulder against the desk—just like football practice, working against the blocking sled—driving the desk back until the two guys are pinned against the wall.

One of them, the driver, starts to squirm loose. I hit him a couple of times, then slam his face against the table. He stops squirming.

The small guy breaks free of Boggy. He reaches behind to his back, pulls a pistol, aims at me.

In an instant, Boggy grabs the chain on the ceiling fan, breaks it loose. He loops it over the small guy's head, around his neck, squeezes.

The small guy jerks back, fires wildly, the shot striking the ceiling. Paint and plaster shower the room.

Boggy squeezes harder. The small guy drops the pistol. Boggy grabs it.

And that's pretty much that.

We take their wallets and make them sit on the floor. I pat them down while Boggy keeps the pistol on them. There're no other weapons.

I sit on the side of the desk and check out their IDs. The short guy is Paul Andrade. The driver is Luiz Barros. The third one—Hector Moraes.

I find a notepad in a desk drawer, write down their names on it.

"Let's see, I've already got your phone number, so that should do it. It's been fun. Let's stay in touch, OK?"

"You have fucked up big-time," says the short one, Andrade.

"I'd say the jury's still out on that. But right now? You're leading in the fuck-up department." I toss them their wallets. "Now get out of here. And tell Papi we need to talk."

They get up. They go out the door.

Not even a good-bye.

40

Trimmingham's office is trashed. So, nice guys that we are, Boggy and I spend the next several minutes straightening it up.

Who knows? Things have gone so well that maybe I'll redecorate the place and conduct more business here. Get some nautical charts for the walls. Install a wet bar. Febreze the hell out of the carpet.

We've just about got everything put back together again when there's a knock at the door.

A voice from the hall says, "Police."

I open the door. There's two of them, hands resting on their holsters.

"We got a call," says the cop who's standing closest to the door. "Someone reported hearing a gunshot."

Across the hall, the guy from the other office has his door cracked open and is peering out. The Neighborhood Watch Committee.

"Yeah," I say. "I thought I heard something, too. You figured out where it might have come from?"

The cops look at each other.

The one who's doing the talking says, "We detained three men who were leaving the building when we arrived. They claim they were here to visit you."

"They claim correctly."

"And you are?"

I give him my name. He writes it down on a notepad.

"Those three guys," the cop says. "They work for Papi Ferreira."

"Cute name, Papi. Don't you think? Perky."

"What was their business here?"

"Training seminar." I nod at Boggy. "My associate and I were teaching them some new sales techniques, helping them sharpen their people skills."

The cop cocks his head.

"I need to look around," he says.

I step back from the door and let him in. His partner stays in the hall.

The cop walks around the office, his eyes eventually finding the hole in the ceiling.

"What happened there?"

"Termites," I say. "I've complained to the landlord, but . . ."

"The truth," he says.

"Well, actually, we're in the middle of a remodeling project and that's where we'll be hanging the new chandelier. We're thinking brass, but I'm not averse to something a little more sparkly. Crystal, maybe. Any thoughts?"

The cop gives me a long, hard look. I manage not to wither.

"Those three guys," the cop says. "They looked like they'd been roughed up."

"My associate and I are serious about our work," I say. "We take a very hands-on approach."

The cop looks around the office some more, but it's only for show. He writes some more stuff down in his notepad. But that's mostly for show, too.

He rejoins his colleague in the hall. They spend a few minutes interviewing the guy in the other office.

I hang out in the doorway just in case they need me to offer any further illumination to the situation. But, no, I get the snub treatment.

When they're gone, I turn to Boggy.

"That gun you grabbed from the short guy. Where is it?"

Boggy pats a pocket in his pants.

"You want it, Zachary?"

"Not yet," I say. "Just hold on to it."

We lock the office, take the steps to the garage, and get in the Morris Minor. On the drive out of Hamilton, I take a detour down a dirt road to Baxter Bay.

Boggy gives me the gun and I get out of the car.

I've got a pretty good arm. I imagine the gun lofting in a tight spiral as it sails out above the water, the sound of its splash lost against the wind.

41

It's double-overtime against the Patriots. In Boston. In the snow. Tony Eason drops back to pass for the Pats and launches a long one. Irving Fryar fakes to the outside, but I don't fall for it. I'm in the perfect position between him and the ball. I plant my right leg. I pivot. And even above the roar of the crowd I can hear . . .

The creak of a door.

I cock an eye to see Barbara slipping into my bedroom. The clock says 1:17 A.M.

There's the rustle of clothes as they drop to the floor, and then she is crawling into bed beside me.

"Sorry to wake you," Barbara says.

"No you're not."

"You're right, I'm not." She draws herself close, arches her back as I rub my hand down her spine. "And I intend to make sure that you aren't sorry either."

"I never am. Besides, I was about to blow out my knee and help us lose the AFC championship."

Barbara looks at me.

"Say again?"

"Never mind," I say. "But aren't you a little scared?"

"About what?"

"About getting caught in the boy's dormitory after curfew. Aunt Trula might place you on double-secret probation."

"Adds to the thrill," she says.

And then we don't talk for a while. We kiss, we clutch, we moan, we laugh. It is sweet and warm and dear.

It is also more rambunctious than usual.

Afterward, I say: "Are you a little drunk?"

"A little. Why?"

"I don't know. It's just that you showed some moves a few minutes ago that were, shall we say, rather innovative."

"I've got moves, darling," she says. "Moves you've never imagined."

We talk. I tell Barbara about my day. She tells me about hers.

"I hit it off well with the new minister of tourism. He's quite charming," she says. "I think he has a crush on me."

"Sounds like I need to eliminate the competition."

"Not until he has signed the ad contract I'll be presenting him. It will be quite the big deal should I pull it off."

"Oh, you'll pull it off," I say. "You always do."

"Just as you'll pull off whatever it is that you're up to."

"Glad you're confident about that."

"Oh, I'm confident. But I'm also a little troubled."

"By what?"

She rolls over to face me, rubs a hand along my cheek.

"By the fact that you and I aren't getting to spend nearly enough time with each other on this trip."

"Well, Aunt Trula seems to be your top priority. When you're not off charming tourism ministers."

"Just as you seem to be preoccupied by your money woes. When you're not off gallivanting around with pretty Australian cops."

"She is rather pretty, isn't she?"

"For the record, John Traylor is no burden to gaze upon either."

"Who's John Traylor?"

"The tourism minister."

"So go for it," I say.

"Perhaps I will. If only I can get beyond his goiter."

"He has a goiter?"

"I'm not sure. Perhaps my eyes were playing tricks on me. It might have been all the wine he plied me with."

"And are you pliable?"

"Oh, very."

She kisses me. We lie quietly for a while.

And then she says: "I would like to propose . . ."

She stops. I sit up.

"Propose?"

She looks at me, smiles.

"Yes, I would like to propose that we have a playdate to-morrow."

"Oh. Right. A playdate. Like kindergartners you mean?"

"No, like grown-ups. A grown-up playdate. We will put everything aside no matter what and we will devote our-selves only to one another."

"And where will this playdate take place?"

"I have a spot in mind," she says. "Think you can make time for me?"

"Oh, I think so. When?"

"How about noon? Food and drink will be involved."

"Well, in that case, I know so. But if I'm running a little late . . ."

"Why would you be running late, Zack?"

"Because I promised Fiona that I would help her out with a few things in the morning. I don't know how long it will take."

She raises up on her elbows, considers me.

"My, my. You are quite the helper these days, aren't you? Helping Fiona. Helping that Trimmingham fellow."

"Yep, just call me Zack the Kindhearted. I'm thinking about nominating myself for sainthood."

She pulls me down to her, rubs a hand along my leg.

"Right now, I could use a little help."

"Oh, really? Help doing what?"

She rubs a little lower.

"Practicing my moves."

42

By nine o'clock the next morning, Fiona and I are in downtown Hamilton, sitting across the desk from Chief Inspector Worley.

"I assure you, Ms. McHugh, we are not trying to shut you out of this investigation," Worley says. "We intend to keep you in the loop every step of the way."

"Then why didn't you tell me about the other two murders?"

Worley falters for a moment.

"I apologize for that. I was waiting for the appropriate moment."

"That would have been the moment I first sat down with you two days ago. As it was, I knew nothing about the other murders until Zack told me."

Worley looks at me.

"I heard about it from a taxi driver," I say. "Then his niece told me more. Janeen Hill. She works for the *Gazette*. Used to anyway."

"Yes, I know Janeen Hill." Worley says it with more than a little weariness. "I've dealt with her many times over the years. Spoke with her again yesterday."

Fiona and I share a look.

Fiona says, "She called you?"

"That's right."

"When?"

"Late. I was getting ready to call it a day."

"What did you speak with her about?"

"Spoke some about your brother. She said she had met with you and Mr. Chasteen earlier in the day and learned that your brother was a marine archaeologist. She said she thought he might have been looking for the same thing that brought the previous victims to Bermuda."

"The wreck of the *Santa Helena*?"

"Yeah," says Worley. "That nonsense."

"Nonsense?"

"Let's just say that I don't put much stock in the stories I've heard about that ship."

"And you're an authority in such matters, Inspector?"

If Fiona's words touch a nerve in Worley, then he doesn't let it show. He observes her coolly for a moment, then says, "No, Ms. McHugh, I'm not an authority. But I've consulted on a frequent basis with someone who is—Dr. Michael Frazer."

"The curator of wrecks," I say.

"That's right," says Worley. "You know him?"

"We've met. Briefly."

"Frazer's a smart man, one of the smartest around. If there's anyone who knows shipwrecks then it's him," says Worley. "He says there's no proof that this *Santa Helena* ever existed. Calls it an archaeological urban myth, something that has been floating around for years and years, leading people on wild-goose chases all over the world."

Fiona says, "What about the Fratres Crucis?"

A dismissive laugh from Worley.

"You mean the secret brotherhood that built the ship that doesn't exist?"

Fiona plods ahead anyway.

"I'm told they pulled out the eyes of their victims before they killed them."

"And who told you that?"

"Janeen Hill."

Worley studies Fiona for a moment, shakes his head.

"Ms. McHugh, in training to become a police officer in

Australia, did they teach you anything at all about verifying the credibility of an individual who comes forth with possible information in a case?"

"Of course. Why? Are you saying that Janeen Hill isn't credible?"

Worley shrugs.

"Oh, Janeen's OK. Flaky as hell, but harmless. Typical journalist. More interested in making headlines than anything else. On a ten-point credibility scale, I'd give her about a two."

Fiona mulls it over, says: "Credible or not, Janeen Hill is the only person who has offered me a possible explanation for what might have gotten my brother killed."

"And there's nothing to it, I'm telling you!" Worley's words are sharp, sharper than they need to be. He recognizes it. "Sorry, but I chased that horse for months after Richard Peach and Martin Boyd were killed. The ship. The secret brotherhood. The piece of the cross. All that. Know where it got me? Nowhere."

Worley drums his fingers on the desk, looks at his watch.

"What about Martin Boyd?" I ask.

Worley shoots me a look.

"What about him?"

"Janeen Hill talked a lot about Richard Peach, but not much about Boyd. All I know about him is that he was Peach's partner and a treasure salvor of some reputation."

Worley rubs his chin, serves up a sly grin.

"Had a reputation for a few other things, too," he says.

"Do tell."

"Let's just say that for the short time he was in Bermuda, Martin Boyd cut a pretty wide swath among the women here. Including at least one woman that he should have stayed clear of."

"She was married, I take it?"

"Oh yeah, real married. Married to someone who wasn't exactly open-minded about such things."

"Care to mention any names?"

Worley shakes his head.

"No, not really. Besides, the husband is dead now and his wife has left the Rock. But for a while there—early on, right after Peach and Boyd were killed—it looked like we might have something."

"Thought maybe the husband had killed them?"

Worley nods.

"He looked good for it, considering who he was and everything. Turned out he was off island, down in Miami, when it happened. And as much as it would have made a nice, tidy little package, I'm convinced he didn't do it." Worley lets out a sigh. "Murder typically doesn't get real complicated. Either a man-woman thing. Or a money-greed thing. In any case, it generally all comes down to somebody wanting something that somebody else has got. Simple as that."

"So," Fiona says. "What have you got?"

Worley looks at her.

"Nice segue," he says.

"I take my openings where I find them."

"As it turns out," Worley says, "we're working a lead. A very strong lead."

Fiona and I wait for him to add something more, but no, he's enjoying letting us dangle.

Fiona scoots closer to Worley's desk, puts an elbow on it, says: "Well, since I'm in the loop every step of the way, perhaps you could tell me what that lead might be."

Worley rubs his tongue along the back of his teeth, smiles.

"You superstitious, Ms. McHugh?"

"Sure, about some things. Why?"

"Well, I'm superstitious about some things, too. And more than anything else I'm superstitious when it comes to talking too much about a case when I can feel that I'm about ready to tie all its pieces together."

"Are you telling me that you're close to finding who killed my brother?"

Worley shrugs.

"I would hate to jinx it," he says.

Fiona looks at me. There's hope in her eyes.

Worley pushes his chair back from the desk, stands.

"Now, Miss McHugh, if you don't mind." He looks at me, then back at her. "I need a few moments with Mr. Chasteen. Alone."

Fiona starts to say something, but Worley nods her to the door.

"It won't take long," Worley says. "I promise."

43

No sooner has Fiona closed the door behind her, than Worley grabs a manila file from a drawer, then steps around to the front of his desk. He leans against it, looking down at me. He holds up the file, shakes it at me.

"What the hell were you up to last night, Chasteen?"

"It has nothing to do with the murders, Inspector. It's a private matter."

Worley opens the file, studies it for a moment.

"Says here that the complainant reported gunfire."

I don't say anything.

Worley studies the file some more.

"It says that three men were questioned as they left the building where the gunfire was reported. These three men just happen to be known associates of Papi Ferreira."

I don't say anything.

"It says that these three men looked as if they had been in a scuffle of some sort and had come out on the short end of things. You know anything about that?"

"Wasn't much of a scuffle," I say. "Over almost as soon as it began."

Worley studies me.

"What's your business with Papi Ferreira?"

"Tell you the truth, Inspector, I'm still trying to nail that down. I've yet to meet the man."

"But you don't deny that you are here in Bermuda to conduct business with Ferreira?"

"It's not what brought me here, if that's what you mean. It's more like I inherited a situation after I arrived."

"Care to share the details of this situation?"

"No, I wouldn't."

Worley holds up the file again.

"There's something else in here," he says. "Want to guess what that is?"

"I have a pretty good idea. You've got computers. Ten minutes and you can find out just about everything you need to know about me."

"Didn't take that long," says Worley. "Baypoint Federal Prison Camp. You served almost two years for counterfeiting, that right?"

I look at him for a long while.

I say, "You read the whole report?"

"I did."

"Then you saw the amended writ of adjudication. Cleared on all counts. With special citations for meritorious service from the federal prosecutor and the governor of Florida."

"Yeah, I saw all that," says Worley. "Still . . ."

"Still what?"

"Still, you seem to have a knack for associating with individuals of ill repute."

"Present company excluded?"

Worley doesn't laugh.

"Why is that, Mr. Chasteen?"

"Why is what?"

"Why is it that you regularly find yourself in the company of criminals?"

"Just my gregarious nature, I suppose. A friend to one and all."

Worley tosses the file onto his desk. He folds his arms across his chest and looks at me.

"Bermuda attracts all kinds of people, Mr. Chasteen. People with money. More money than you or I will ever know. And I have no doubt that a goodly number of those people either got their money in a questionable fashion or are trying to hide it in a way that might not be strictly legal. But you know what?"

"What?"

"That doesn't bother me. I mean, I don't like it. But I don't waste my time worrying about people like that. They're aren't good people, but they aren't real bad people either. You know what I mean?"

I nod. Worley looks at me.

"Papi Ferreira is real bad people, Chasteen. Your gregarious fucking nature notwithstanding, you do not want to be friends with him. And if you're up to anything with Ferreira and I find out about it, then I'm coming after you. We clear on that?"

"We're clear."

Worley nods to the door.

"Get out of here," he says.

44

"So you feeling better about things now?" I ask Fiona when we're back in the car.

"Yeah, a bit."

"But not so much better that you want to go back to Cutfoot Estate, lollygag around the pool, and let things take care of themselves. Am I right?"

"Right as rain," she says. "I'd like to visit the place where Ned worked."

"The dive shop?"

She nods.

"Deep Water Discoveries. I've got the address somewhere." She pulls out a notepad, flips through it. "Somerset. Know where that is?"

"Yeah, I've been to Somerset. Teddy Schwartz lives near there."

"Really now? How convenient. Maybe we could drop by, let me introduce myself and thank him in advance for letting me use his boat for Ned's service tomorrow."

"Maybe. I'll have to see what the time looks like after we get finished at the dive shop. I'm supposed to be meeting Barbara at noon."

"So what do the two of you have planned?"

"Don't know. It's her idea. She's calling it a playdate."

"My, my. Sounds like fun. Could mean any number of things, now, couldn't it?"

"Yes, it could. Although I'm hoping that pin-the-tail-on-the-donkey and ring-around-the-rosy aren't involved."

Fiona laughs.

"So what's in store for the two of you?"

"I just told you, I'm meeting Barbara at noon and . . ."

"No, no. Not that." She waves me quiet. "I'm talking long term. You plan on fastening your muzzles, sharing the old feed bag?"

"Excuse me?"

"You going to marry her, Zack?"

She grins an impish grin.

"You know, you're the second person who's asked me that recently."

"The other being?"

"Aunt Trula."

"Oh, now that's serious. And what did you tell her?"

I concentrate on the road, don't say anything.

"Ha," laughs Fiona. "Dodged the question, did you?"

I look at her.

"What's with you women, anyway?"

"Why, Zack," she says, all innocence. "Whatever do you mean?"

"I mean, I've got friends, men friends, who I've known all my life and they would never even once think of asking me if I planned to marry Barbara. Wouldn't cross their minds. Here I've known you, what, two days, and Aunt Trula only a day or two longer, and both of you apparently think you're already on a need-to-know basis regarding me and Barbara."

Fiona laughs.

"It's because women are more honest than men."

"Oh, really?"

"Yes, really. Put four women who've never seen each other together in a room, give them an hour, and they'll walk out of there knowing the nitty-gritty about one another. The names of all their children. Their hopes, their dreams, their fears. How much money they've got in the bank. And how many times their blokes knock boots with them in a week."

She catches the look on my face. "Really, Zack. Women do talk freely about such things."

"And men?"

"Ha, men. You put four men in a room and the sum of all their knowledge would likely be reduced. Unless, of course, it applied to brands of beer or the scores of ball games or what highway to take to get somewhere."

I laugh.

"You're probably right about that," I say.

"I know I'm right. Women get straight to the heart of the matter. Men just nip around the edges. You're very superficial creatures, really. But somehow we manage to love you anyway." She smiles. "You and Barbara are quite lovely together."

"Thank you."

"And I can't even begin to imagine how beautiful your children would be."

I don't say anything.

She laughs again.

"You men . . ."

45

Half an hour later, we're pulling into the parking lot of Deep Water Discoveries. It occupies part of a small marina on a cove just off Great Sound, a squat concrete-block building painted a wake-up shade of aquamarine with an office, gear room, lockers, a retail shop, and a small classroom for conducting scuba certification classes.

A young man perches on a stool behind the shop counter. He's shirtless with a shaved head and no visible space left on his torso for another tattoo.

I tell him who we are and why we're there. After that, I figure I'll let Fiona handle the talking.

"You should really be speaking with Bill," the young man says.

"Bill?"

"Bill Belleville, the owner. He's usually around, but short-handed like we are right now, he's running one of the boats. Should be back any time now from this morning's trip," the young man says in a brogue that hints strongly of Ireland. "Sucks, what happened to Ned. A solid one, he was, don't know how anyone coulda done that to him."

"Did you know Ned well?" asks Fiona.

The young man shrugs.

"Not all that well. Just around the shop here, really. Ned, he'd sometimes join us for a pint down at the Onion, but not so much lately, he didn't. Lately, he seemed to have his own thing going. Even Polly was riding him about it, complaining that the two of them never went out."

"Polly?" asks Fiona.

"Yeah, Polly . . . uh, don't know her last name, sorry. Just Polly. American, tiny little thing, pretty as a bug," he says. "She and Ned were a pair. The two of them shared a place just down the road."

Fiona covers it well, but I can tell that her brother's living arrangements have come as a surprise.

"Can you tell me how to get there?" she says.

"Sure, no problem. Keep going another mile or so and you'll come to Bedon's Alley. Hang a left, go all the way to the end, and you'll see a row of small cottages on your right. Their's is the last one, painted yellow, I believe."

"Have you spoken with Polly since all this happened?"

"Just briefly. She called in after word came down about Ned. Said she wouldn't be in for a few days. She's not scheduled until next week."

"She works here at the dive shop, too?"

The young man nods.

"She's the one supposed to be running the shop, not me. I'm usually out on the boats," he says. "Polly, she was freaked bad by what happened. She was supposed to have gone out on the boat with Ned that day, but she got called in to pull a shift at the Onion. She waitresses there sometime. Cost of living here on the Rock and what a dive shop pays? We've all got to bust a hump working somewhere else. Me, I wash dishes down at the . . ."

"Wait, wait," Fiona says. "You say she was supposed to have gone out on the boat with Ned that day?"

"Yeah, that's right."

"What boat?"

"Right out there," the young man says, pointing to a boat tied off in a slip. It's a Delta, a twenty-eight-footer, a workhorse of the scuba trade. "Police hauled it in yesterday afternoon."

"The police brought it in?"

"Yup, that's right. There was a whole crowd of them out

here earlier. From what I gather, they figure Ned was trying to get away from whoever it was that was after him. Think he might have jumped overboard and let the boat run. They found it jammed up in the mangroves just this side of Daniel's Head."

Fiona looks at me.

"So much for that bastard Worley keeping me in the loop," she says.

She is out the door and on her way to the boat before the young man can get off his stool.

"She can't go on that boat," he says, sliding out from behind the counter.

I step to the door and block his way out. He stops.

"The police said no one can go on it until they give the OK," the young man says.

The phone rings. He looks at it.

"You need to answer that," I tell him.

He watches Fiona as she reaches the dock. The phone rings again.

"The phone," I say. "Now."

The young man steps back behind the counter and answers the phone. He's on it for a few minutes, telling the caller about the availability and pricing of dive trips.

After he hangs up he looks outside to the boat. Fiona stands near the wheel, inspecting the console, going through storage compartments.

He shakes his head.

"It's her ass, not mine," he says.

"That's the attitude," I say. "Now, you just sit tight and keep an eye on the shop, OK?"

As I step outside to join Fiona, a boat pulls in from the sound and makes its way to the dock. It's a bigger Delta, a forty-footer, with the Deep Water Discoveries logo emblazoned on its hull. A couple dozen people are on board, divers and crew.

A husky, bearded guy leaps off before it docks. He hurries to the slip where Fiona is still searching through compartments on the boat that was hauled in by the police.

By the time I walk up behind him, the guy is yelling at Fiona.

"I don't care who the hell you are, I want you off my boat!"

"Almost done," Fiona says, ducking into the cabin, out of view.

"No way, lady . . ."

As he starts to climb aboard, I grab his arm. He whips around, ready to square off against me. He's a pretty tough-looking guy—thick shoulders, broad chest, a sun-worn face. His appearance is made even grizzlier by a crusted-over gash on one of his cheekbones that looks as if it should have had stitches. Above it—the yellowed remainder of a black eye.

I've got a couple of inches and several pounds on him. Plus, I am who I am. He thinks better of the match-up and backs off.

"You Belleville?"

"Yeah. Who are you?"

"I'm the lady's helper."

Belleville grinds his jaw. He looks at the boat. Fiona is still down below.

He looks back at me.

"Well, you're going to be helping both your asses straight to jail," he says. "I'm calling the police."

"Do what you have to do," I tell him.

As he moves past me, Fiona emerges from the cabin.

"That won't be necessary," she says.

She hops off the boat and stands beside me on the dock.

"My brother was aboard that boat before he died. I needed to see it for myself," she tells Belleville. "I'll take full responsibility with the police."

Belleville is still fuming.

"You going to take full responsibility for your brother's gas bill, too? Ned had been going out a lot on the boat. He was running a tab. He owed a couple of hundred."

I step in, tap Belleville on the chest.

"Listen, asshole," I say. "Her brother just died. How about you play bookkeeper some other time."

As Belleville swats away my hand, Fiona moves between us.

"It's all right, Zack. Mr. Belleville is entitled to look after his best interests, just as I am entitled to look after mine." She looks at Belleville. "I intend to honor all my brother's debts. You may present me with a bill whenever it suits you."

She turns and leaves the dock. I give Belleville a friendly pat on the shoulder.

"A real pleasure," I say.

He grunts something in response.

I can't make out exactly what it is. Probably just as well.

46

W hat a dick," Fiona says once when we're both inside
the car.

"He was almost a dick with a broken nose."

"That wouldn't have gotten us anywhere."

"Except that I would now be basking in the afterglow of
manly accomplishment."

"Spare me," says Fiona. "Besides, looks like someone
else already got a crack at Belleville. You see that gash on
his face?"

"Pretty hard to miss."

I crank the car, check the time on the dashboard clock.
Already after noon.

"Look," I say, "I know you probably want to go by your
brother's house and . . ."

"And meet the girlfriend? Bloody well right I do. I mean,
the girls were always thick around Ned. He could never settle on just one. Now to hear he had a live-in? Bit of a surprise that." She looks at me. "But we can swing by later,
Zack. We need to get you back to Barbara."

"You sure?"

"Drive," she says.

We're a mile away from Deep Water Discoveries before
Fiona opens her backpack.

"Gee, look what I found," she says, pulling out a black

plastic something-or-other the size of a cell phone. It has a small, green LCD screen and a keypad.

I take it from her, look it over.

"A GPS?"

She nods.

"It was Velcroed underneath the console. I missed it the first time through. Battery has run down. Otherwise, it looks to be fine," she says. "You familiar with this particular model?"

"No, the one I've got is a few years old, nearly twice the size."

"Same with the ones they issue the water police. Shit for memory. But these newer ones, you can program them to spit out a log of every site you've marked for weeks. With any luck, it might just tell us where the boat stopped on the day Ned was killed."

"If he used the GPS."

"Yeah, if. But Ned was a gadget guy. Never met a gizmo he didn't like. I'm betting he used it."

"Hypothetical question here, Fiona."

"Ask."

"You think maybe you ought to turn it over to the police?"

"Oh, yes, by all means," she says. "You're absolutely right, Zack."

She returns the GPS to her backpack. She looks at me, smiles.

"Then again," she says. "I am the police, aren't I?"

47

Barbara's playdate involves us using Aunt Trula's mopeds. I threaten a boycott, but she lures me with the prospect of a picnic lunch she's packed. She won't tell me where we're going, but that's OK. I'd follow her anywhere, even on an infernal moped.

After zipping along the south coast, past Horseshoe Bay and Elbow Beach and, finally and appropriately, Hungry Bay, we arrive at the Bermuda Botanical Gardens.

We cut across a broad lawn and head for a small, circular stand of cedar trees with ancient arthritic trunks and branches low to the ground.

It takes some scrambling to cut through to the center of the stand, but once inside there's a big payoff. It's as if we've entered a room wholly apart from the rest of the world.

Barbara is beaming. She sets down the picnic basket. She lies faceup on the ground and stretches out her arms.

I lie down beside her. I stare up at the cedar-branch ceiling. Light streams in, all soft and golden, the way it does in paintings. The air is cool and comforting, as if set by the ideal thermostat.

"So what do you think?" Barbara says.

"I'm thinking I haven't really done anything like this since I was a little kid."

"I know," she says. "It's great, isn't it?"

Barbara closes her eyes. She takes a deep breath, lets it ease itself out.

"My mother used to have this giant cedar chest at the foot of her bed. It's where she kept all her prettiest things. And when I was a little girl, she would let me sit in it while she sorted through her clothes, picking out something to wear. That cedar chest, its smell, I think it's the first real smell I ever remember.

"Later, whenever we went to church and the priest would talk about heaven, I couldn't really picture it, you know? But I could smell it," says Barbara. "It smelled just like that cedar chest. It smelled just like this."

I roll onto my side. That way I can see her better.

"How did you find this place?"

"It was right after my father died. Mother and I spent that summer with Aunt Trula. She used to be big in the Royal Botanical Gardens and whenever she came here for meetings she'd let me have the run of the place."

"You were how old?"

"Not quite ten."

"Hard age to lose your dad."

"Weren't you about the same age?"

"Nine," I say.

"And to lose both your parents at once like you did."

I don't say anything.

Barbara looks at me, says: "You think that's what draws us together?"

"You mean, other than the knockdown, drag-out killer sex?"

"Yes, other than that."

"I've thought about it," I say.

"And your conclusion?"

"I don't know. It could be that each of us has the same hole in our heart and somehow, without even knowing, without even trying, we manage to fill it for the other one."

Barbara takes my hand, gives it a squeeze.

"Back then," she says, "this was where I came to fill that hole in my heart."

We lay there for several minutes, not talking, not needing to, enjoying the quiet.

Then Barbara sits up. She crawls to a tiny opening in the trees. She motions me to join her. We peer through the opening onto a wide bed of flowers, their creamy yellow petals in full audacious bloom.

"They're freesias," Barbara says. "Double Fantasy freesias. They import the bulbs from Holland."

"Pretty darn gorgeous."

Barbara nods.

"That's where I saw him," she says.

"Saw who?"

"John Lennon."

I look at her.

"The Beatle?"

"Uh-huh, he was kneeling on the ground, right there, in the middle of all the freesias."

"Was this like an apparition or something?"

She shakes her head.

"No. The real thing. He used to visit Bermuda all the time, he and Yoko. This was after he'd split up with the others. He spent lots of time walking around in the gardens."

"And you saw him standing right there?"

"I did."

"And you recognized him?"

"What do you think? I am from England. He was a Beatle. Of course, I recognized him," she says. "I was lying in here, off in my dream world, and I heard someone humming. I crawled over here, just like we are now, and there he was, kneeling in the freesias."

"By himself?"

"No, he had his son with him. Sean. He was four or five, a few years younger than me," says Barbara. "They glanced up, saw me staring out at them. And John Lennon said: 'Ah, will you look, Sean. It's a wee troll of the woods.' "

"And then you crawled out and joined them and the three of you became fast friends."

Barbara laughs.

"Not hardly. I scooted back behind the trees and hid there. I was very, very shy back then," she says. "He died later that same year, right after his last album came out. You remember what it was called?"

I rack my brain, but don't come up with it. Truth is, I've always been more of a Stones fan.

"Double Fantasy," says Barbara. "Like the flowers."

"And you were here to witness the moment of inspiration."

"My solitary claim to fame."

"Aside from knowing me."

"Yes," she says, "aside from that."

She puts her arms around my neck. We hug. The moment is broken by the sound of my stomach in full feed-me mode.

Barbara pulls away and opens the picnic basket.

"I've got rare roast-beef sandwiches with horseradish sauce," she says.

"And?"

"And some havarti."

"And?"

"And a pinot noir from Oregon."

"Not a bad spread," I say. "For a wee troll of the woods."

48

After lunch, we stroll across the botanical garden to an adjoining park called Graydon Reserve. Atop a grassy bluff, with a commanding view of the south shore, sits a tiny chapel.

It's as plain and unadorned a place of worship as I've ever seen. No steeple, no arches, no architectural frills of any sort—just four whitewashed mortar walls and a cedar shingle roof. Behind it sits a small cemetery, with headstones old and new.

We stop so I can read the historical marker that stands alongside the path.

> Graydon Chapel, built 1764, in memory of Capt. William Graydon, lost at sea. Erected by his loving wife, Ingrid, who mourned him until her own passing on January 27, 1811.

"Forty-seven years," I say. "That's a long time to mourn someone."

"I think about her every time I come here. I've got this picture of her in my head."

"Standing on the bluff all alone, looking out to sea, wiping back a tear from her eye, forsaken and forlorn?"

Barbara shakes her head.

"No, not like that at all actually. I see her sitting here, her skirt spread out on the grass, surrounded by children, her grandchildren probably, telling them stories about their grandfather, the sea captain. Smiles and lots of laughter." She looks at me. "Happy mourning, I suppose."

We walk up a stone path to the chapel. Three narrow wood-frame windows line the chapel's side walls. They are open to take full benefit of the ocean breeze.

From inside the chapel comes the sound of singing. Well, not so much singing as chanting. There's not a lot of melody to it, but it sounds pleasant enough.

"We're in luck," Barbara says. "They usually only sing at early morning and evening services."

"Who's they?"

"The sisters who look after the chapel."

"Sisters as in nuns?"

Barbara nods.

"But they aren't your typical nuns. They're part of a small nondenominational order that lives on the property. Both men and women. It's like a commune, a collective. Some of the nuns are even married to some of the men."

"No, not your typical nuns at all."

"I think they take a vow of celibacy."

"I'll pray for them," I say.

The door to the chapel is open. We peer inside. There are only four rows of pews with room for no more than a couple of dozen worshippers.

Two women kneel in a front-row pew. One is quite old, her white hair pulled back in a braided bun. She is large and round and soft looking, wearing a tunic of coarse gray fabric draped over a long skirt made from the same cloth.

The other woman is much younger, in her thirties perhaps, her dark hair cropped short. She wears a yoke-necked dress of light blue, a long-sleeved white blouse beneath it.

The older woman chants a verse of psalm, then the younger woman repeats it with a slightly altered tone. The words are Latin, not that I can make out any of them.

"It's the old Gregorian method of chanting," Barbara whispers. "Quite lovely, isn't it?"

I nod. Because it is quite lovely—ageless, soothing, all that.

The women finish singing and spot us by the door. They smile and nod hello. "Please, join us," says the older woman.

"You don't mind?" Barbara says.

"Oh, my goodness, no. We'd be delighted," the older woman says. "Sister Eunice just arrived yesterday to help us with our work here. We were letting our voices get to know each other."

"I'm afraid my voice is being a bit standoffish," Sister Eunice says. "Sister Kate must indulge me."

"Nonsense," Sister Kate says. "You sing beautifully."

Barbara steps inside and goes to a pew in the back row. She kneels, closes her eyes, and prays.

I kneel beside her. I pray the prayer I always pray on those rare occasions when I frequent a church: "Dear God, let good things happen. And if you can't do that, then let the bad things be less bad. Thanks a lot. As for my part of the deal, I'll try to do better. Amen."

Barbara finishes her prayer and sits back in the pew. I do the same.

Sister Kate holds up a stainless-steel tuning fork and thumps one of its tines with a finger. She matches its note with her voice and begins another chant. Sister Eunice chimes in when it's her turn.

We sit listening to them for twenty minutes or so and, yeah, I start feeling all warm and holy. I mean, it's not a moment of epiphany with the fiery hand of God reaching out to embrace me. And I am not so overwhelmed by the experience that I feel a need to speak in tongues or put aside my venal, corporeal ways to seek eternal salvation. Nothing like that. But it is elevating, and I'm getting a nice little buzz just being here.

The cozy little chapel is comforting in the same way that the stand of cedar trees creates its special sanctuary. It is utterly humble. The altar is a plain pine table. A simple brass crucifix hangs on the wall behind it.

My gaze drifts upward to the ceiling. A rough-hewn

beam runs the length of it. A second beam intersects it, acting as a brace. It's a nifty combination of form and function—both roof support and a large cross, sheltering parishioners from above. The beams are not cut from single pieces of timber, but cobbled together from various types of wood. It took some work to put it together and the effect is like a piece of sculpture. It's beautiful.

When Sister Kate and Sister Eunice finish singing, Barbara and I thank them for sharing their voices with us. An alms box sits by the door and I slip some money through its slot.

On the wall behind the alms box, there's a bronze plaque.

"In thanks to Sir Teddy Schwartz," it reads. "Whose hard work and determination restored this chapel to its original condition following Hurricane Emily in 1987."

"Have you seen this before?" I ask Barbara.

"No, matter of fact, I've never noticed it."

Sister Kate sees us studying the plaque.

"Are you acquainted with Sir Teddy?" she asks us.

I'm tempted to say, "Yep, Barbara's aunt is sleeping with him," but instead, I just tell her: "Yes, we know him."

Sister Kate's face fairly radiates with her smile.

"He's our patron saint, Sir Teddy. When Emily came through, she lifted the roof right off the chapel, broke it all to pieces," Sister Kate says. "We're not a wealthy order, by any means. Sir Teddy more or less adopted us. He put the chapel back together again. Did all the work himself."

"I was admiring the ceiling," I say.

"Oh, isn't it lovely?" Sister Kate says. "It took Sir Teddy months to complete that. The woodwork had to be just so."

At that moment, a bus pulls into the chapel's small grass parking lot. Camera-toting tourists pour out the doors and start heading for the chapel.

"Oh my," says Sister Eunice. "Where did all those people come from?"

"The cruise ships are in town," says Sister Kate. "Get used to it."

49

After only a few near-death experiences on the drive back from the botanical gardens, Barbara and I make it to Cutfoot Estate and park the mopeds in the garage.

"So what's on your agenda for the rest of the afternoon?" I ask her.

She checks her watch.

"Well, it appears as if I am already late for my four o'clock meeting with the tent people."

"Tent people?"

"Yes, you know, the people who rent tents and tables and chairs and things. Titi asked me to come up with an idea for how everything should be laid out for the party. I would guess that they are in the backyard at this very moment, so I better not keep them waiting any longer," she says. "And what are your plans, darling?"

"Think maybe I'll contemplate the origins of the universe, smooth out the wrinkles in a new quantum theory of thermodynamics, that sort of thing."

She looks at me.

"Planning a nap, are you?"

"I find that it sharpens my skills of contemplation."

"Well, I wouldn't get my heart set on it if I were you."

Barbara looks past me to the front door. I turn to see Fiona McHugh hurrying outside. Boggy is with her. She waves and they head our way.

"I believe someone might have plans for you," Barbara says.

She gives me a kiss, then hurries off.

Fiona and Boggy wait for me by the Morris Minor. I walk over to join them.

"Good news," Fiona says. She holds up the GPS that she took from the boat.

"You get new batteries for it?"

"No, Boggy did something to it and it fired right up."

I look at him.

"Since when did you become a GPS technician?"

He shrugs, doesn't say anything.

"I think it might have had a short or something," Fiona says. "This was Ned's personal GPS, not one that belonged to the dive shop. Needed a password."

"And you figured it out?"

"Easy. He always used the same thing—Lebowski."

"As in *The Big Lebowski*?"

She nods.

"He was a giant fan of the movie, was always making me drink White Russians with him." She takes a moment to enjoy the memory. "Anyway, the GPS has at least three months worth of data stored in it. At the beginning there's a variety of coordinates, all over the place. But in the last few weeks, there have been considerably fewer positions, in an increasingly tighter cluster."

"As if he were zeroing in on something."

"Right," she says. "The last half-dozen or so entries, leading up to the day he was killed, are all the same place."

"So what are you thinking?"

"I'm thinking we go to Teddy Schwartz's house and ask him to take us out on his boat."

"This afternoon?"

"Sure, why not? There's still three or four hours of light left," she says.

"And what are we going to do when we find this spot?"

"Why, jump in, of course. Schwartz has scuba gear, doesn't he?"

I don't say anything.

Fiona says, "I need to do this, Zack. I need to know what Ned was doing out there, what he was looking for."

I open the car door.

"OK," I say. "Let's go."

She hops in the front seat. Boggy stays put.

"You coming with us?" I ask him.

"No, Zachary. The palms, I must take the hose to them."

"Take the hose to them? That's cruel and unusual punishment, isn't it? This is Bermuda, Boggy, not Singapore."

He just looks at me. Then he turns and walks away.

Sometimes he's just no fun, no fun at all.

50

Teddy Schwartz's car sits in his driveway, but he doesn't answer when I ring his doorbell. We walk behind the house to the dock, where *Miss Peg* is moored. No sign of him there either.

I step over to the boathouse, stopping at a small window by the door. The drapes are drawn, leaving just a sliver of an opening. I peek through it.

Teddy sits hunched over the workbench that had been covered by a tarp when I was there with Boggy just a couple of days earlier. His back is to me. A high-intensity halogen light sits to one side, beaming down on whatever it is that he's working on.

I rap on the door. Teddy jerks around. He's wearing a headband of some sort. There's something hanging down from it, over one of his eyes. Then I recognize it—a loupe, like jewelers use when they are doing close-up work.

Teddy removes the headband, turns off the lamp, and carefully drapes the tarp over the workbench. Then he steps to the door and opens it, smiles when he sees it's me.

"Well, Zack, to what do I owe this pleasure?"

"We interrupting you from anything?"

"No, no, not at all. I was just piddling around."

He closes the boathouse door behind him and steps outside.

I make the introductions between Teddy and Fiona, and we briefly discuss logistics for Ned's service the next day.

"*Miss Peg* is gassed up and ready to go. I'm glad she can be of service," Teddy says. "Now, can I get the two of you a drink or something? It is getting to be that time of day."

Teddy takes Fiona by the arm, begins ushering her toward his house.

He says, "Have you tried a Dark 'n Stormy, Miss Mc-Hugh? It's our national drink, you know. A shot of Gosling's, a splash of ginger beer, a slice of lime. Just the thing for a warm afternoon."

"Perhaps another time," she says, "because we were wondering if *Miss Peg* might be of service right now."

Teddy stops.

"Now? Whatever for?"

Fiona tells him about visiting Deep Water Discoveries and finding the GPS aboard the boat Ned had used.

"I'd just like to ride out to the site that's marked on the GPS, take a look around," she says. "Here, let me show you."

She pulls out the GPS, switches it on. She punches a few keys. The coordinates flash up: N32° 18.024/W064° 52.622.

Teddy studies the display screen for a long time, doesn't say anything.

"Know the general vicinity of where that might be?" Fiona asks.

Teddy looks at her, his eyes hooded now, his expression grim.

"No," he says.

"Well, that's certainly understandable. There's a lot of water out there," Fiona says. "Still, it would be easy enough to find. I can't imagine that it's . . ."

"I really don't think it's a good idea, Miss McHugh," Teddy cuts her off.

"But there's still plenty of daylight left."

"Miss McHugh, I told you, I'd prefer not to do it. Not today."

The tone of his voice makes it clear there's no further need for discussion. And there's no further mention of drinks.

51

W ell, that was certainly awkward," says Fiona as we pull out of Teddy Schwartz's driveway and wind our way back to Somerset Road. Next stop—Ned's house on Bedon's Alley.

"Yeah, there was something a little off about the whole thing."

"It was like this giant mood shift. One moment he's the gracious gentleman, anxious to pour us cocktails, all friendly and everything. The next he's ready for us to leave."

"Starting from the moment you brought out the GPS."

She looks at me.

"You think he recognized the coordinates?"

"I don't think so. I mean, you've looked at those coordinates a couple of times. Can you tell me what they were?"

Fiona thinks about it.

"Thirty-two something, sixty something. Things like that just don't stick with me."

"They don't stick with most people. That's why they have GPSs. To remember those things for us. An old hand like Teddy Schwartz, all the dive sites he knows, there's no way he recognizes them by their specific coordinates. No, it wasn't that."

"Was it just the sight of the GPS? Knowing that we had it, that it belonged to Ned?"

"That's the only thing I can think of."

"But why?"

We're still muddling that over when I spot the street marker for Bedon's Alley. I whip off Somerset Road and follow Bedon's Alley to a cul-de-sac. A yellow cottage sits under a stand of eucalyptus trees.

I pull the Morris Minor into the driveway, look at Fiona.

"You up for this?"

She nods.

"Yeah, I think so. Has to be done."

We get out of the car and walk up to the front porch of the house. The front door is partly open.

Fiona knocks.

"Hello . . . ?"

No answer.

Fiona gives the door a push, steps inside. I follow her.

For such a small place, it's a big, big wreck—sofa and chairs overturned; drawers pulled from cabinets, the contents scattered everywhere; the refrigerator open and food spilled all over the kitchen floor.

"A dog's breakfast, this is," Fiona says.

"That another colorful Aussie colloquialism?"

Fiona ignores me as she picks her way across the living room, negotiating a path toward the bedroom. She moves past a small mountain of books. The bookshelf that once held them is a heap of splintered wood.

As Fiona nears the bedroom door, she lets out a gasp, freezes. Then she raises her arms, backs away from the door.

A small, dark-haired woman steps from the shadows of the bedroom. She holds a speargun, cocked and ready to fire, a three-foot steel shaft with its double barb leveled at Fiona.

"I'll shoot," the woman says.

She's twitchy, on the point of hysterics.

She wears a faded chambray shirt that falls to her knees, baggy khakis with the cuffs rolled up, red Converse sneakers.

"Just take it easy," I say.

She swivels, points the speargun at me. But the odds aren't in that shot. She aims again at Fiona.

"Who are you?"

"I'm Ned's sister," says Fiona.

The woman shakes her head. "You're lying!"

"No, no, really." Fiona reaches for a pocket.

The woman stiffens, raises the gun. "Don't move!"

Fiona freezes.

"I was just getting my wallet so I can show you some ID." Fiona's voice is calm, soothing. "Is that all right . . . Polly? That's your name, isn't it?"

The woman nods.

"OK, show me," she says.

Fiona pulls out her wallet, flips it open. The woman leans in and looks at it. She's skeptical. She studies Fiona, thinking.

"You're really Ned's sister?"

"Yes, really," Fiona says. "I swear."

"OK, if that's the case," says the woman, "what did Ned give you?"

"What did he give me?"

"Yes, what did Ned give you before he left Australia? If you're really his sister then you'll know that."

For a moment it seems as if Fiona doesn't have an answer. Then it comes to her.

"Jack Black," she says. "His dog. A Clumber spaniel. I had to leave him with my mum and dad."

The woman relaxes, but now she has the speargun trained on me.

"So who is he?"

"A friend," says Fiona. She opens her arms. "We're here to help, Polly. Really."

The woman hesitates, then drops the speargun. She covers her face with her hands.

"Oh, my God," she sobs.

And Fiona rushes to embrace her.

52

A few minutes later, we've restored a small semblance of order to the living room. Fiona shares the couch with Polly. I hold down one of the chairs.

"I got here just a few minutes before you did," Polly says. "The first time I'd been back in three days, ever since Ned . . ."

She stops, chokes up. Fiona pats her back, comforts her.

"I've been staying with a girlfriend not far from here. I couldn't face everything. But then I just figured, you know, get over it, Polly. It's time to get on with your life. Plus, I'd left a lot of my stuff here. Clothes, my yoga mat, a bunch of personal things. I'm really attached to my yoga mat. It centers me, you know? Anyway, I couldn't put off coming by here any longer," Polly says. "But I walked in and saw all this and I just freaked out. And when you drove up and got out and came walking in, well, I just totally lost it. That speargun, it was Ned's. I don't even know how to work it."

"Well, you were faking it pretty well," I say. "You must have gone out on the boat with Ned and seen him using it."

"Are you kidding? I don't even know how to dive."

"And you work at a dive shop?"

"Yeah, go figure, huh? The owner of the dive shop, he's a regular at the Onion. That's the other place I work. Matter of fact, I'm supposed to pull a shift tonight. I really didn't want to, but this friend called up begging me and . . ."

She stops, seeming to have lost her train of thought. Not surprising, since she is all over the place. It's probably one-half nerves and one-half the fact that she's a bit of a space cadet. Cute kid, but ditsy.

"Where was I?" she says.

"You were talking about the dive shop owner," I say. "Belleville's his name, right?"

"Oh yeah, Bill. He was always hitting on me, asking me out. I kept telling him no. Not my type, a little too old for me. He's OK. I mean, he gave me a job. I really needed the money—it's crazy expensive here—so I took it. But it's not like I do any of the real diving stuff. I just run the shop, handle the retail side of it, answer the phone, book trips, that sort of thing."

"So that's how you met my brother," says Fiona. "Working at the dive shop?"

"Yeah, the very first day. And we just clicked, right from the start. I mean, he was gorgeous, that curly blond hair of his, the whole Oz thing going on. He wasn't just a dive bum, you know, like some of the others. He was smart. And passionate. About everything. He was just so . . . so Ned, you know?"

"Yeah," says Fiona. "I know."

Polly wears a rawhide necklace with a piece of red glass in the shape of a bug dangling from it. One of her hands goes to the piece of glass, rubs it.

Fiona says, "I know this might be difficult, Polly, but I have to ask: Do you have any idea who might have killed my brother?"

Polly shakes her head.

"No, just like I told the police—I have no idea at all. That's all I've thought about, believe me. I've racked my brain."

Were I the snide sort, I might say it took precious little racking, but . . .

"Did the police ask you what Ned was doing out there the day he was killed, Polly?"

"Yes."

"And what did you tell them?"

Polly starts to say something, stops. She looks away.

"I guess I didn't exactly tell them everything."

"What do you mean?"

"I mean, I told them that Ned had gone out diving, which was true. But I told them that I didn't know exactly where, which wasn't true. I thought it might get Ned in trouble." She lets out a nervous laugh. "Isn't that crazy? He was already dead. But I wasn't thinking. I was scared. I thought I might get in trouble, too."

"Trouble?" Fiona says. "Trouble for what?"

"For not having the permit," Polly says.

"What permit?"

"I don't know, this government permit Ned kept saying he had to have before he could do anything else."

I say, "Are you talking about a salvage permit, Polly?"

"Yes, that's what he called it," she says.

I share with Fiona what Teddy Schwartz told me a few days earlier about Bermuda salvage laws, how prospective salvors are supposed to apply for a permit with the curator of wrecks before anything can be removed from a site.

"The curator of wrecks. Yeah, that's where we went," Polly says. "I remember the name on the office door. Guy with a beard . . ."

"Dr. Michael Frazer," I say.

"That's him. Nice guy. Kinda cute. Very friendly. Comes into the Onion every now and then. He really helped out Ned a lot. Especially with all the paperwork for the permit. Ned had almost completed everything and was getting ready to turn it in," Polly says. "He'd heard from other people that he really didn't need to get a permit, that no one else ever did, but Ned wanted to do things by the book. He knew what he'd found was important and he planned on dotting his i's and crossing his t's."

Fiona says, "What had Ned found, Polly?"

"Something old, something really old." Her brown eyes widen. "A shipwreck. That's where he found this."

She reaches for her rawhide necklace, holds out the red glass ornament that dangles from it so we can see it better.

"You know what that is?" Polly asks.

"Looks like a bug of some sort," I say. "A beetle or something."

"It's called a soul-saver, a Phoenician soul-saver. Old-time sailors used to wear them on long voyages. They believed that if they died far from home and the beetle ever made its way back to a sailor's family then the sailor's soul would be saved." She rubs the glass beetle, lets it fall back around her kneck. "Anyway, Ned found it on the wreck and gave it to me. Technically, he wasn't supposed to take anything from down there, you know, but this one little thing, he thought it would be all right. At first, it kinda gave me the creeps to wear it. I was thinking, like, whoa, this has got some old-dead sailor guy's soul in it, you know? But then I got over it. After Ned died and everything, it's kinda like it's got his soul in it. Know what I mean?"

Polly gets up from the couch, steps over to the broken bookcase. She rummages through the books on the floor. She pulls one from the pile, flips through the pages, and hands it to Fiona. It's called *Gray's Salvor Compendium: Mediterranean Sea.*

"See, that shows more of them," says Polly, pointing to a page full of photographs of similar glass beetles. "One reason Ned went out that day was in hopes of maybe finding a few more of them. He wanted to show them to investors."

"Investors?" I say.

"Uh-huh. Ned said he would need to raise a lot of money to do the whole thing right. He would have to get a boat of his own, hire people to help him. He was even talking about getting a film crew to document everything from start to finish. He figured the film might make enough money to help pay off the investors," she says. "He expected the project might take several years. But when it was all done he would have . . ."

"Made a name for himself," says Fiona.

"Yeah," says Polly. "That's exactly what he was hoping."

"That's what he told me on the phone," Fiona says, "the last time we spoke."

They're both quiet for a moment.

Fiona finishes studying the photos of the soul-savers. She closes the book. She looks at me, then at Polly.

"The ship Ned found, did it have a name?"

Polly shrugs.

"Not one that I know of. At least, Ned never called it by any name. He just called it 'the wreck.' He was always re-searching, trying to find out what ship it might be. He ordered all these books, looked up stuff on the Internet. When he wasn't working at the dive shop, then he was working on stuff related to the wreck. But he knew it had to be really old."

"Why's that?"

Polly reaches for the soul-saver again.

"Because of these things," she says. "Ned called it a marker, something like that. He said they lost popularity and sailors stopped wearing them in the early 1500s. So if you found them at a wreck site, it meant it probably happened before that. Really old."

Polly kneels beside the pile of books and touches them, as if they bring her comfort. Fiona gets up to join her.

"Would you mind if I took some of his books, Polly?"

"No, I guess not. I mean, I don't really have any use for them, and I'm sure Ned would want you to have them. Let me get something to put them in."

Polly goes into the kitchen and returns with a box of plas-tic garbage bags. She and Fiona start bagging the books. I step over to help them.

"A couple of these didn't actually belong to Ned," Polly says. "They belonged to this other guy he was working with."

"Someone at the dive shop?" I say.

"No, this old guy, some kind of famous diver or some-thing." Polly holds out a well-worn book with a brittle binding—*A Record of Atlantic Explorations: 1200–1600*. "This is one of his."

I take it from her. I open the cover to reveal a label that reads: "From the library of Sir Teddy Schwartz."

I show it to Fiona.

"Ned was working with Teddy Schwartz?" I ask Polly.

"Well, kinda," Polly says. "I don't think they were officially partners or anything like that. But Ned met with him a few times. It was mostly to pick his brain, I think. Ned said Mr. Schwartz knows everything there is to know about shipwrecks."

"Did you ever meet Mr. Schwartz?" I ask her.

"Not until the other day, the day Ned went out in the boat," says Polly. "I was just getting ready to go to work at the Onion when Mr. Schwartz came by. He said he was looking for Ned, and I told him he'd missed him, that he was probably already out on the water."

"Did Mr. Schwartz say why he wanted to talk to Ned?"

"No, I just figured it was something about shipwrecks. That's what they always talked about. He seemed like a nice old guy. But he didn't stick around after I told him Ned wasn't here."

We finish putting the books in the garbage bags. Polly grabs her yoga mat, some clothes, a few other things.

She stands in the living room, looking at the mess that still remains.

"I thought I might move back in here. But now . . ." She stops, looks at us. "You think whoever killed Ned did this?"

"There's a chance of it," Fiona tells her. "Did you notice anything missing?"

"A few things. My iPod, a few pieces of jewelry. Not like I had anything that was worth a whole lot."

"What about a computer, anything like that?"

"No, we didn't have one. The dive shop has a computer that Bill lets us use for e-mail or the Internet."

"Have you called the police about this?"

Polly shakes her head no.

Fiona pulls out her cell phone.

"I'll take care of it," she says.

53

Chief Inspector Worley arrives with a full crew—technicians, investigators, a photographer.

When he's finished interviewing Polly, he pulls Fiona and me aside.

"Got a call from the owner of that dive shop down the road," he says.

He waits for one of us to say something. We don't.

"He seemed pretty mad about you trespassing on that boat, Miss McHugh," Worley says.

She doesn't say anything.

"That boat is his private property. Plus, I left clear instructions that no one was to set foot on it. It is considered part of a criminal investigation and, therefore, it is off-limits to the general public. You, as a police officer, should know and respect that, Miss McHugh."

She doesn't say anything.

"And you, as whatever you are, Mr. Chasteen, should know that, too."

I don't say anything either. It has become a real one-sided conversation.

"Do you mind explaining yourself, Miss McHugh?"

Fiona draws herself up, fire in her eyes.

"Do you mind explaining yourself, Inspector?"

"What are you talking about?"

"I'm talking about why didn't you tell me that you had

found the boat?" Fiona says. "It's so nice being in the loop."

The sarcasm in her voice fairly drips.

"Miss McHugh, please, you must understand . . ."

"I do understand, Inspector. I understand that you can look me straight in the eye and lie when you tell me that I will be informed about every development in this case. Why didn't I know about the boat, Inspector?"

Worley takes a deep breath.

"I thought it better to share that information with you after we had completed a full and thorough inspection of the boat. We are still in the process of gathering evidence and . . ."

"Bullshit," says Fiona. "I should have been told."

Worley rubs his head, blows out air.

"Look, Miss McHugh, I can see now that I made a mistake not sharing that information with you. I apologize. OK? I was wrong. And I promise that from here on out you will indeed be kept informed every step of the way."

Fiona takes it in.

"I wish I could believe you," she says. "Just as I wish I could believe something else you told me."

"What is that?"

"That you are close to tying up this investigation, close to finding who killed my brother."

"We are close. And with luck, this break-in might put us even closer," Worley says. "Now, if you'll excuse me."

We watch him walk back to the house.

Fiona says, "Good thing he didn't ask me if I'd taken anything off that boat."

"Why? What would you have done?"

She looks at me.

"Lied," she says.

54

We give Polly a ride to the Onion. She insists that we stick around for a drink. Seldom have I been known to offer argument on that front.

The Onion is a loud and lively place, and it's packed when we walk in. Polly snags us a table on the deck, overlooking the bay. There's soon a pitcher of Newcastle Brown Ale in front of us, along with bowls of the house specialty—Bermudian fish stew. It's a dilly of a version, finished off with a dollop of Outerbridge's sherry pepper sauce. I wind up eating the better part of Fiona's stew, too.

There's a fresh breeze off the water. It helps lighten the topic at hand, namely, Fiona's plans for the burial at sea.

"We'll be heading out at noon tomorrow," Fiona tells Polly. "I hope you can join us."

"I'll be there. And I'm sure some of Ned's friends from the dive shop would like to come, too. There's a group of them sitting up there at the bar. Why don't I go grab them and have them come over so you can meet them?"

I turn to see Belleville, the dive-shop owner, sitting in a cluster of people. He's been watching us, but glances away when I look in his direction.

I stop Polly as she starts to step away.

"Look, why don't you say something to them about the service after we've left," I say.

"OK, sure." She catches a look between Fiona and me. "Is something wrong?"

"Oh, let's just say we had a bit of a run-in with Belleville when we stopped by the dive shop this morning," Fiona says. She tells Polly the story.

"That's too bad," Polly says. "I mean, Bill started off being so nice, but lately he had really been getting down on Ned."

"What about?" I ask.

"Oh, I don't know, just little things. Criticizing him for dinging the tanks when he took them off the boat or for using too much soap when he washed down the deck. Tiny stuff, really," Polly says. "Ned said it was because Belleville had the hots for me and was taking it out on him."

"Did Belleville know what Ned was working on in his spare time?" I ask.

Polly shakes her head.

"No, that was the other thing," she says. "He thought Ned was using the boat to scope out new dive sites. And he was cool with that because, you know, it could help business. But when it didn't turn out like that and Ned wouldn't let on exactly what he was doing, Bill kinda got his feathers ruffled. He and Ned, they got into it a few times."

"What do you mean, they argued?"

"Yeah, but nothing serious. Not so serious that Bill wouldn't let Ned keep on taking out the boat. But he did start charging him gas money after that. He hadn't done that before."

A couple of people stop by the table to offer their condolences to Polly. She introduces them to Fiona, who tells them about plans for the burial at sea.

While they're chatting, I spot Michael Frazer walking in the door. The tall, bearded curator of wrecks stops to talk with a few people at the bar, eventually making his way to our table. He says hello to Polly and me, then introduces himself to Fiona.

"I was so sorry to hear about Ned," he tells her. "I didn't know him well, just the few times he dropped by my office.

But I was impressed by his intellect, his zeal. He'll be missed."

"Thank you," Fiona says. "You're more than welcome to sit down and join us if you like."

"Well, just for a moment," Frazer says, "I really need to be off. Early morning and all that."

He takes a seat. I pour him a glass of beer.

"Too bad we had to meet the way we did," Frazer tells me. "But if there's one thing I've learned in my years on this job, it's that I have to keep an eye on Sir Teddy."

"The two of you have had some run-ins in the past?" I say.

"To put it mildly," Frazer says. "We're natural adversaries, I suppose. My job is to preserve and protect. Teddy takes a more, shall we say, proprietarial view."

"Meaning . . ."

"Meaning, Sir Teddy has this notion that everything out there in those waters belongs to him and him alone and that he should be able to plunder as he pleases, like he did in the past," Frazer says. "It just doesn't work like that anymore, I'm afraid."

Frazer turns his attention to Fiona, smiles.

"And how long will you be in Bermuda, Miss McHugh?"

"As long as it takes," Fiona says. "Until my brother's murderer is found."

"I understand that you are a police detective back in Australia?"

"Not exactly," Fiona says.

As she tells Frazer about her job with the water police, Polly fetches us another pitcher of beer.

Belleville stops her as she walks past his group at the bar. They speak for a moment, then he gets up and heads to our table.

He stands by my chair, looking down at me. Fiona and Frazer are wrapped up in their conversation, not paying any attention to us.

The cut on Belleville's cheek is festering even worse than before. If things turn ugly, I figure I'll aim for it with the first punch.

"Look," Belleville says. "About what happened earlier on the dock . . . I'm sorry about that. I kinda lost my head."

Not what I was expecting.

"Don't worry about it. Strange situation."

"Man, you can say that again. The whole thing with Ned, the cops, the boat—it stressed me out. I'm sorry, man."

He sticks out a hand. I shake it.

"You mind?" he says, nodding at an empty chair.

"No, have a seat."

Polly arrives with another pitcher of Newcastle and I pour it around. Fiona and Frazer nod our way, then return to whatever it is they're talking about.

Belleville clinks his glass with mine. We take long sips. He grins at me.

"You used to play for the Gators, didn't you?"

"Sure did."

"The Dolphins, too."

I nod.

"Fucked up your knee or something, didn't you?"

"I did."

"The 1986 AFC championship. I remember. I lost a shit-load of money on that game. You guys broke my heart."

I hear it a lot. I never know what to say. So I just shrug and don't say anything.

Belleville says, "You dive?"

"Yeah, when I get a chance."

"How about you come out diving with us while you're here? My treat. I'd consider it an honor hosting you, a former famous football player and all that."

"Well, I kinda have a lot going on right now."

"Sure, man, I understand. But when things free up, you give me a holler. We've got a couple of night dives scheduled out at Bird Reef. That place gets wild after dark. Killer dive. You'd like it."

We talk. About this and that. I finally get around to asking Belleville how he got the gash on his cheekbone. He seems embarrassed by it.

"Oh, it was nothing. Something stupid," he says. "A hazard of the trade."

We talk some more. We finish the beer. Belleville returns to his group at the bar.

Frazer stands up from the table, takes Fiona's hand in both of his.

"A pleasure," he says. "I'll give you a call then."

"I'll look forward to it," she says.

He gives me a nod good-bye.

I watch Fiona watching him walk away.

"Seems like a nice-enough fellow," I say.

"Quite nice," Fiona says. "And fair spunk to boot."

"Translation, please."

Fiona smiles.

"Good looking as all hell."

55

Before they head off to run errands the next morning, Barbara and Aunt Trula join Boggy and me on the back lawn. We've just set the sixth Bismarck in the ground.

Boggy and Cedric are backfilling the hole. The auger crew is moving its equipment to the spot marked for the seventh palm. Two days until the party. We'll be jamming, but we'll make it.

"So what do you think?" I ask Aunt Trula.

Aunt Trula cocks her head and studies the palms. She cocks her head the other way and studies them some more.

"You have planted them too close together," she says.

I glance at Barbara, but she looks away, at the ocean. Boggy and Cedric keep shoveling dirt, pretending like they aren't listening.

"They aren't too close," I say. "You see, the idea is to create a critical mass."

"Hmm," Aunt Trula sniffs.

"Space them any further apart and it takes away from the impact."

"Well, have it your way then. I suppose there's no turning back now." She turns to Barbara. "We really need to get going, dear, if we are to get everything done before we go out on the boat for the memorial service."

As Aunt Trula marches off, Barbara steps beside me. She rubs my back, gives me a nuzzle.

"Don't mind her. I think the palms are magnificent." She gives me a kiss. "See you at Teddy's."

She heads after Aunt Trula. I help Boggy and Cedric finish backfilling around the palm.

When we're done, Boggy scoops up a handful of dirt. He dabs the tip of his tongue to it, tastes it.

"You want, I can bring out some salt and pepper, and you can make a meal of it," I say.

"Magnesium," Boggy says. "The soil is lacking in it."

"And you can taste that?"

Boggy nods.

"Maybe could use some potassium, too," he says. "Otherwise the palms, they will yellow."

Cedric gives us directions to a garden store. Boggy and I take the Morris Minor, find the place, and arrange delivery for enough fertilizer spikes to keep the Bismarcks well fed for the foreseeable future.

When we step out to the parking lot, I see that a gray van has pulled up next to the Morris Minor. Paul Andrade, the short thug whom Boggy had relieved of his gun two nights before, leans against the passenger door, watching us as we approach.

He slides open the van's side door.

"Get in," Andrade says.

I look inside the van. Hector Moraes is at the wheel. Luiz Barros is in the very back seat. Beside Barros sits yet another bruiser. They seem to keep getting bigger and bigger.

I look at Andrade.

"After that ass-kicking we gave you the other day, you only brought along one more of your buddies to help out? I'm deeply offended."

Andrade edges back his jacket just enough to let me see the pistol in a shoulder holster. I let out a low whistle.

"Whoa, went out and got yourself a new one, huh?" Andrade doesn't say anything. "Why didn't you pick out one with a brown grip? It would match your outfit so much better."

"Get in the fucking van," Andrade says.

I slide into the middle seat. Boggy sits down beside me. Andrade slides the door shut, gets in up front, and Moraes puts the van on the road.

56

We ride for twenty minutes and no one talks. We take the detour around Hamilton and keep heading east on Middle Road until we come to Flatts Village.

We wind through narrow streets, past houses built close to the road, slowing every now and then to dodge old women walking with parasols and kids kicking soccer balls.

This is not the rich man's version of Bermuda. It's off the tourist grid, a zone where only locals tread.

Moraes stops the van in the dirt parking lot of a shabby concrete building. A faded sign reads: FERREIRA'S—GROCERY, CAFÉ, PAPER GOODS.

Andrade opens the van door. We get out. The four of them herd Boggy and me toward the store. Along the way we pass a group of men clustered around a picnic table watching a furious game of dominoes.

Our arrival draws only scant attention, but one of the men lets his gaze linger on us as we pass. I recognize him—the young man who was at the wheel of Michael Frazer's boat when they came across us diving with Teddy Schwartz at Sock 'Em Dog.

I give him a nod. He turns back to the dominoes.

We step inside the grocery store. It's neither a clean nor well-lit place, short on shoppers, the shelves not exactly bursting with goods. A bored middle-aged woman, a kerchief around her hair, sits on a stool by the cash register, reading a newspaper.

Boggy and I follow Andrade to the rear of the store. His three beefy associates bring up the rear. I hear music playing—acoustic guitar, the tinkling of a piano.

Andrade opens a door that leads to a back room. The music becomes louder. And now it is accompanied by a woman singing. The words are in a language I don't recognize, but the woman's voice is rich and full and as mournful as anything I've ever heard.

We step into the room. Cardboard boxes are stacked along the walls. A single fluorescent bulb flickers from the ceiling.

Behind a cluttered wooden desk sits an old man, eyes closed, hands folded atop his chest. On a nearby credenza, an LP spins on a turntable, the woman's voice resonating from a pair of speakers.

Andrade motions Boggy and me to step closer to the desk. He and his cohorts maintain their positions behind us.

The old man remains in peaceful repose, a look of contentment on a bourbon-brown face etched deep with lines. His hair is white, and so is his droopy mustache.

As the song reaches its finale, the woman seems to have reached into the depths of her soul—despair, agony, loss.

The music stops. The old man opens his eyes. He looks at Andrade and the others.

"Wait outside," he says.

When they are gone, the old man creaks up from his chair. He is barely five feet tall. Round, but not too round. A bit wobbly on his feet. He keeps a hand on the desk for balance as he steps to the credenza.

He turns off the record player, slips the LP into its jacket, and carries it with him when he returns to the chair.

He pulls a cigar from a desk drawer, clips off the end, takes his time lighting it. He enjoys the first draw. Then another.

He picks up the album and turns it so we can see the

woman's face on the cover. It is an old photograph, from the 1950s maybe, judging by the woman's hairstyle.

"Amália Rodrigues," he says. "The Queen of Fado. Do you know fado?"

I shake my head, no.

But Boggy says: "It is music of Portugal, no? Music of the streets."

The old man smiles.

"Yes, yes," he says. "But it is more than just music, fado. It is the expression of the Portuguese soul. We have a word—*saudade*. It means, well, it is like no word in English. It is about longing, about yearning for something that always seems to be just out of our reach. That is *saudade*."

The old man smiles again, takes a draw on his cigar.

I look at Boggy.

"The music of Portugal? Where did you pull that one from?"

Boggy shrugs.

"I met this woman once, from Lisbon. She used to sing to me."

"She sang to you? How sweet."

"Yes, it was very nice. Her name was Bettina."

The old man coughs. It is one of those coughs that says: OK, enough fooling around. I want you to pay attention.

"I am Manuolo Ferreira," the old man says. "Where is my money?"

He smiles the same smile he has been smiling all along, but there is something now in his eyes, something cruel and cold.

"Look," I say. "Let's start by you telling me exactly how much you think Brewster Trimmingham owes you."

"He owes me one hundred and thirty-three thousand dollars."

"He only borrowed seventy thousand."

"And he was three weeks behind in paying. Thirty percent. Per week. He knew that. It is the way we do business. He must pay the *gorjeta*."

"*Gorjeta*? What's that?"

Ferreira smiles.

"It is the tip. The gratuity. For the pleasure of doing business."

"I don't think Trimmingham got that much pleasure out of it," I say. "But I tell you what. I'll pay you the seventy thousand. Plus ten percent interest. That makes seventy-seven. And because you're such a nice guy, what the hell, I'll round it up to an even eighty."

The smile leaves Ferreira's face. He glares at me.

"You have no room to bargain here. I am doing you a favor just to talk."

"And I'm doing you a favor by offering to settle Trimmingham's debt. You aren't going to get anything from him. He's tapped out."

Ferreira puts the cigar in his mouth. He chews on it, spits out a piece of tobacco.

"We have other ways to settle his debt."

"Fine," I say. "Have it your way. Get rid of Trimmingham. It saves me eighty grand."

I turn to go. Boggy follows me.

Just as we reach the door, Ferreira says, "One hundred thousand. Even."

We stop.

"Sixty-five," I say.

"Sixty-five? But you just offered eighty."

"Yeah, I know. But if you're lowering your offer then so am I."

Ferreira starts to say something, stops. He throws up his hands.

"That is not the way to bargain."

"It's the way I bargain."

"Then you are a fool."

"Heard that before."

I reach for the doorknob.

"OK, then," says Ferreira. "Eighty thousand dollars."

I walk to Ferreira's desk, stick out my hand.

"Deal," I say.

Ferreira stands. His grip is firm. As we shake, he says, "You will pay the money now."

"No, I will not."

Ferreira releases my hand.

"What do you mean, you will not?"

"I mean, I will pay you the money as soon as I can."

Ferreira shakes his head.

"No, this will not work. You walk in here, you say you are paying another man's debt to me, I want the money now."

I pick up the record album from his desk, hand it to Ferreira.

"You need to put this back on, get in the *saudade* mood," I say. "Because you are wanting something that is still way out of reach."

Ferreira snatches the album away from me.

"One day," he says. "That's what I am giving you."

"And then what?"

"Then, my people, I send them to see you."

"Didn't work out real well for them the last time you did that."

Ferreira puts the cigar in his mouth, sucks on it, but it has lost its fire. He flicks a hand to the door.

"Get out," he says.

57

It takes an hour chugging on *Miss Peg* to reach a site far enough offshore to commend Ned McHugh to the sea. It's a full boat, with Bill Belleville and a bunch of folks from Deep Water Discoveries aboard, too.

Polly has brought along a CD player. Ben Harper's "In the Lord's Arms" plays as the funeral director and an assistant lift the canvas-shrouded body to the gunwales.

Fiona breaks out a bottle of champagne. She pours it around and raises her glass.

"To Ned," she says. "I know you would have preferred a pint of Victoria Bitter, but I'll buy one for you when we meet on the other side."

Belleville and some of Ned's diving buddies make toasts. And Polly says simply: "I love you. I miss you. May you know eternal peace. *Namaste.*"

She folds her hands by her heart and bows her head.

Fiona gives the funeral director a nod and Ned's body is slowly lowered into the water. It sinks in an instant and is gone.

Aunt Trula has had her florist prepare a wreath—leatherleaf fern, red and white roses. She hands it to Fiona, gives her a hug. Fiona reaches over the gunwale and rests the wreath on the water. It bobs over waves, drifting slowly away.

Teddy cranks the engine on *Miss Peg* and we head back to shore.

I sit on a bench near the transom, between Fiona and Barbara. Everyone is quiet, the drone of the engine filling the void better than conversation.

Then, as we pull around Daniel's Head and make a line for Mangrove Bay, Fiona leans to me and says: "I've decided to wait until everyone else is gone."

"To talk to Teddy you mean?"

She nods.

I say, "So how do you plan on broaching the subject?"

"Head on," she says. "I'm just going to ask him why he never mentioned that he had met with my brother."

"It does seem curious."

"Damn curious," Fiona says. "He's hiding something."

"Be interesting to hear what he has to say."

But it never comes to that.

As we near Teddy's house, I spot three figures on the dock—Chief Inspector Worley and two patrolmen.

Bill Belleville sees them, too. He edges back to the transom alongside me.

"Is that the cops, man?"

"Appears to be," I say.

Worley and the patrolmen hop aboard *Miss Peg* before we even have a chance to tie off. The patrolmen head straight for Teddy. One of them takes him by the arm.

"We need you to come with us, Sir Teddy," Worley says.

"Whatever for?" Teddy says. "What is this all about?"

"Please, just come with us."

Teddy jerks away from the patrolman.

"I demand an explanation." He looks toward the boathouse. Other policemen step in and out of it. "They have no right to go in there. This is an outrage."

"We have a warrant, signed by the magistrate."

"What for?"

Worley doesn't reply. He gives the patrolmen a nod. And they usher Teddy off the boat.

58

Two hours later, we are sitting in the parlor at Cutfoot Estate, listening to Daniel Denton speak with one of his associates on the phone. The associate is doing most of the talking. Denton hangs up, his face grim.

"Officially, he is being held as a person of interest. No charges have been filed," says Denton. "But they appear to be imminent."

"Charges?" says Aunt Trula. "Charges for what?"

Denton looks at Fiona. She sits ramrod straight in a ladderback chair, hands folded in her lap, jaw set.

"For the murder of Miss McHugh's brother," Denton says.

Aunt Trula's face registers the shock. She tries to speak, no words emerge.

Fiona takes the news impassively, as if it came as no great surprise.

"The police have seventy-two hours in which to formalize the charges," Denton says. "Until then Sir Teddy can be detained without bail."

Aunt Trula shakes her head in disbelief.

"There must be some mistake," she says. "This can't be happening."

She slumps back in the sofa, plainly stricken by what we've all just heard. She closes her eyes, puts her face in her hands. Barbara drapes an arm around her, pulls her close.

I look at Denton.

"Has your associate spoken with Teddy?"

"No, apparently the police are still questioning him."

"Doesn't he have the right to an attorney?"

"Yes, but apparently Sir Teddy waived that right. He agreed to the questioning before my associate arrived and is cooperating with the police."

"Well, of course he is cooperating," says Aunt Trula. "Because he has nothing to hide!"

I don't say anything. Neither does anyone else.

Aunt Trula shoots a look at Fiona.

"Surely you don't believe this, do you? Teddy did not murder your brother. That dear, dear man is not capable of such a thing."

Fiona takes a breath, measures her words.

"I can imagine how difficult this must be for you, Mrs. Ambister," she says, getting up from her chair. "But, right now, I'm afraid you must excuse me. I have some calls to make back home."

As she steps out of the parlor, one of the butlers appears in the doorway.

"Beg pardon, Mrs. Ambister."

Aunt Trula looks up.

"Yes, Fredrick, what is it?"

"The caterer is on the phone," he says. "A question about the canapés."

59

T hat evening I sit on the terrace, no glass of rum in my hand. I've been wanting a drink for hours, but I keep thinking we might get a call to visit Teddy Schwartz. Better that I remain sober for that.

Barbara returns from checking on Aunt Trula.

"She won't come out of her room," Barbara says.

"What about the party?"

"She won't talk about it. But I'm proceeding as if it is still on. At this point, it would be far more difficult to notify all the guests and cancel with the vendors. I've OK'd the canapés, upped the number of cases of white wine for the bar, and signed off on the playlist for the band."

"Did you request 'Jailhouse Rock'?"

Barbara looks at me.

"Not funny," she says. "You want a drink?"

"Yes, I do. But no, I won't."

"Well, I'm having one," Barbara says.

She steps inside, comes back with a gin and tonic. She sits down beside me. She takes a sip of her drink. Then another one.

"So," she says, "what's your take on all this?"

"Same as everyone else. I'm floored."

"You think he did it?"

"Killed Ned McHugh?"

Barbara nods.

"No," I say. "I don't."

"Then what could possibly lead the police to believe that he did it?"

"Because they know something we don't," I say.

"Thanks for sharing, Sherlock."

"Plus, there's the fact that Teddy knew Ned McHugh, but never saw fit to mention it—not to Aunt Trula, not to Fiona, not to anyone. He even went by Ned's house looking for him on the day Ned was murdered. He's obviously trying to hide something."

"What?"

"Don't have a clue, but if I were a betting man . . ."

"Which you are."

". . . I would wager that there is something inside that boathouse of his."

"Like what?"

"Again, no clue. All I know is that Teddy didn't like it that Boggy and I walked in there on the morning we went out on his boat. And when I dropped by yesterday with Fiona, he made sure we didn't get a glimpse of what he was working on inside."

"What do you think he might have been working on?"

I shrug.

"Beats heck out of me. I mean, I saw him at his workbench wearing one of those jeweler's loupes. So it's close, detailed work of some kind. He's got all kinds of lumber and woodworking equipment in there, too."

"Which he used when he was working to rebuild the roof at the chapel in Graydon Reserve."

"See, that's just it. Teddy's a good man. He's got a good heart. You know from the moment you meet him that he's a decent guy. And that's what it all comes down to: I just know in my gut that he didn't do it."

There's a footfall behind us.

"If it helps any, I don't think he did it either."

We turn around. Fiona stands in the doorway to the terrace. She's holding her suitcase.

I get up from my chair. So does Barbara.

"Please, stay where you are," Fiona says. "I just wanted to tell you that I am leaving."

"Leaving?" I say. "You don't mean back to Australia, do you?"

"No, no. I'm checking into a guesthouse. I found one in downtown Hamilton with a vacancy, sounds nice enough. I mean, it's no Cutfoot Estate, but . . ." She stops, smiles. "Look, with everything that happened this afternoon, it's better that I leave. My being here creates an awkward situation all around."

Barbara says, "I'm sure Aunt Trula would not . . ."

Fiona puts up a hand.

"Please, I've made up my mind. But I thank you just the same," she says. "Now, all I have to do is call for a taxi."

"Forget that," I say. "I'll drive you."

"No, Zack, thanks for the offer, but . . ."

"Please, I've made up *my* mind," I say. "I signed up for the job, if you remember. Plus, I'd like to think there's a good reason why I'm still on the wagon after a day like today."

60

"So what did you tell your parents?" I ask Fiona on the drive to Hamilton.

"I told them exactly what happened," she says. "That the police have detained Teddy Schwartz as a person of interest."

"And did you tell them that you have your doubts that Teddy killed your brother?"

She shakes her head.

"No, I didn't. It would just confuse things for them. They need some closure, even if it's only for the short-term."

"So why don't you think Teddy did it?"

She shrugs.

"For all the same reasons you mentioned. Gut feeling. A cop's instinct. He's just not a killer. He's not someone who could torture someone like my brother was tortured."

"OK, but if not Teddy, then who?"

"That's where I draw a blank," she says. "But that Belleville bloke might deserve a look."

"Yeah, he might. He came on all buddy-buddy with me last night."

"I noticed."

I look at her.

"Like hell you did. You only had eyes for Michael Frazer."

She smiles.

"Well, he is pretty easy on them," she says. "Matter of fact, Michael called this evening. Asked me to have lunch with him tomorrow."

"Oh, really."

"Uh-huh."

"Aha!" I say.

"Aha? Aha what?"

"Aha, so that's why you're checking into your own digs, so you can have a little love nest all your own."

Fiona makes a face, takes a swat at me.

"Let's get back to Belleville," she says. "Did I overhear you asking him where he got that gash on his face?"

"You did. But he didn't give up much in the way of details. Just said something about how he had done something stupid, a hazard of the trade."

"Could be anything."

"Could be."

"But my brother was not a lightweight. If someone tried to take him down, he'd give them a fight."

"Maybe take a poke at them, give them a gash on the face?"

"No maybe about it," Fiona says. "Plus, there's that whole thing with Belleville and Polly, how he asked her out and she turned him down."

"Yeah," I say. "There's that."

"But it's a long way from that to murder," she says.

"Yeah," I say. "It is."

We whip through a roundabout and take the road into downtown Hamilton.

"It's the Oxford House, on Woodbourne Avenue," she says. "Shouldn't be too hard to find."

Her cell phone rings. She takes the call.

"Why thanks, I appreciate that," I hear her say. "Zack is with me, that OK?"

She listens, smiles, cuts her eyes my way.

"Yes, he's that, all right. See you in a few . . ."

She flips the phone shut.

"Let me guess," I say. "Michael Frazer?"

"No, it was Worley. Says he'd like a few minutes with me."

"So it's to the police station then?"

"If you don't mind."

I pull onto Front Street, looking for Parliament Street.

"What did Worley say about me anyway?"

"Why, what makes you think he said something about you?"

"Because he did. You told him I was with you. Then you listened and you smiled and you said, 'Yeah, he's that, all right.' The 'he' you were talking about was me. What did Worley say?"

Fiona smiles.

"He said, 'That Chasteen. He's a hard man to shake.' And I agreed, that's all."

"Well, you know what I've always said."

"What's that?"

"A hard man to shake is good thing to find."

She looks at me.

"Is that supposed to make sense?"

"Try not to overthink it," I say.

61

Policemen are milling around in Worley's office when we arrive. Worley shoos them away and closes his door.

He looks at Fiona.

"I don't want to be accused of leaving you out of the loop," he says.

"I appreciate that, Inspector."

He looks at me.

"Although I've got some serious reservations about including you," he says.

"Why's that?"

"You complicate things, Chasteen."

"But, Inspector, I am just a simple man."

Worley lets it roll, carries on.

"On the one hand, you are assisting Miss McHugh in seeing to it that her brother's murderer is brought to justice . . ."

"In a purely unofficial capacity."

". . . and on the other, I would suspect that you might also be looking after the best interests of Teddy Schwartz."

"Why would you suspect that?"

"Because your girlfriend is the niece of the woman who is sleeping with him."

"If you don't mind, Inspector, that's really not an image that I like to conjure up."

"But you can understand why I have my reservations when it comes to speaking frankly about this case with you."

"Then we're even," I say. "Because I have some reservations, too."

"Reservations about what?"

"About exactly how good a case you've got."

Worley makes a temple out of his hands, rests it under his chin.

"It's a good case," he says.

"That right?"

"Oh yeah, matter of fact, it's about as good a case as you can get." Worley gives it a beat. "Found the murder weapon in the suspect's boathouse. At the bottom of a pile of towels, sitting just inside the door."

I lean back in my chair, let out some air. Wasn't expecting that. Neither, it appears, was Fiona. She's speechless.

"Ice pick," Worley says. "A blood match with your brother's, Miss McHugh. Found some needle nose pliers, too. In the same pile of towels. Another match on them."

He doesn't find it necessary to mention what the pliers were used for. Thoughtful of him.

"Questions, comments, observations?" he says.

"It just doesn't make sense," Fiona says.

"Now why is that, Miss McHugh?"

There's a tinge of facetiousness in Worley's voice, as if he is playing us. Matter of fact, I'm pretty sure he's playing us.

"It doesn't make sense that Teddy Schwartz would kill my brother, dump his body in the ocean, and not get rid of the murder weapons while he was at it. It's counterintuitive."

"Hmm. Interesting observation." Worley looks at me. He seems to be enjoying himself. "How about you, Mr. Chasteen? Anything you'd like to know?"

"Yeah. Why did you decide to search Teddy Schwartz's boathouse in the first place?"

"A very astute question, Mr. Chasteen. One I hoped you might ask. The answer—we got a phone call."

"Let me guess," I say. "Anonymous?"

"But of course," Worley says. "Desk officer said the caller was a male. Beyond that, nothing."

I say, "Someone could have planted the ice pick, the pliers."

Worley raises his eyebrows.

"You think?" he says.

"I was in Schwartz's boathouse the other day."

"Sir Teddy mentioned that. And you know what my first reaction was to that, Mr. Chasteen?"

"You thought maybe I planted the murder weapon?"

Worley smiles.

"I must tell you—yes, the thought did cross my mind. But only for a brief moment. Then it occurred to me that, based upon the coroner's estimate, you would still have been in Florida at the time of Ned McHugh's death. You couldn't possibly have done it."

"I'll consider that a vote of confidence."

"Don't get too carried away," Worley says.

"Teddy Schwartz did seem surprised that I was in his boathouse. Angered and surprised, actually. I remember him checking the doorknob, the lock, as if the place might have been broken into."

"You are full of interesting observations, Mr. Chasteen. As it turns out, Mr. Schwartz remembers exactly the same thing. It is his contention that his boathouse was indeed broken in to," Worley says. "One problem—he didn't report it at the time. Plus, if you are found to be hiding murder weapons in your boathouse then the most expedient response would be to . . . ?"

"Claim it had been broken in to," I say.

"Exactly. Especially if the boyfriend of your girlfriend's niece could corroborate it."

"Gnarly lineage, but I can see what you mean."

"What about the break-in at Ned's house?" Fiona breaks in. "Did you get anything from that?"

Worley shakes his head.

"Nothing, really. No physical evidence. Could have just been a neighborhood thief. About the only thing we got out of it was a supplementary statement from the young woman . . ."

"Polly? Ned's girlfriend?"

"Yes, her. She told us that Teddy Schwartz came around there looking for Ned McHugh, on the day of the murder. She hadn't seen fit to mention that before."

"She's a little flighty," I say. "Could have just forgotten about it."

"Yeah, could have."

"There's something else that's off about all this," says Fiona.

"What's that?"

"Motive."

"I'm listening," says Worley.

"Why would Teddy Schwartz want to kill my brother? And why would he have wanted to kill Richard Peach and Martin Boyd seven years ago? I mean, we are still assuming that the murders are linked, aren't we?"

"We are," says Worley. "But I don't have to provide motive to the prosecutor, only evidence. Nor must I concern myself with the previous murders when I have enough in hand to proceed with this one. A murder weapon is a compelling piece of evidence. And when a police department comes up with a compelling piece of evidence there's not a lot of internal motivation to discredit it. You understand what I'm saying? The higher-ups are ready to formalize charges."

"But you aren't?" I say.

Worley rubs his jaw, considers his response.

"Let's just say that things are a little too neat for my liking—a phone call out of the blue, the murder weapon found, a suspect now in custody. A pretty package."

"And one that could blow up in your face?"

"It could prove embarrassing at the every least."

Worley's phone rings. He answers it, listens.

"Be right there," he says.

He hangs up.

"I'm being summoned," he says.

"The higher-ups?" I ask.

He nods, stands up from his desk. We take the cue.

As we head for the door, Fiona stops, looks at Worley.

"One more question," she says.

"Ask."

"Why are you telling us all this?"

Worley smiles.

"Like I said, Miss McHugh, I just want to keep you in the loop."

Neither one of us is buying it. Worley knows it.

"Then again," he says, "seeing as how you are a police officer and seeing as how Mr. Chasteen is whatever he is, I can fully understand it if the two of you feel the need to second-guess this investigation, maybe even continue conducting an investigation of your own. If so, I would suggest that the time to do that is right now."

62

"Well, I guess Worley really can't make it much clearer than that, can he?" Fiona says as we exit police headquarters.

"You mean, short of putting us on the payroll?"

"It was decent of him."

"Yeah, but he's covering his ass, too," I say. "This way he doesn't have to buck department politics and give the appearance of torpedoing an investigation that looks as if it's locked up tight. At the same time, he's got us out here doing the legwork for him."

The parking lot has emptied out since we arrived. The Morris Minor sits all by itself at the far end, under a streetlamp. We head for it.

The air is heavy, anticipating rain. Not enough breeze to stir the palm fronds. From the bars of Front Street comes the sound of revelry. Two more cruise ships have put in along the pier.

"Ned's GPS," Fiona says. "I still need to see where it takes us."

"One problem—we no longer have a boat at our disposal."

"Did the police impound *Miss Peg*?"

"I'm guessing they did. Probably want to check it stem to stern for any physical evidence."

"I could ask Michael when we have lunch tomorrow,"

Fiona says. "I don't see why he would object to taking us out."

"Worth a shot," I say.

I unlock the Morris Minor. We get in.

"To the Oxford House, madame?"

"Yes, driver," she says. "And be quick about it. I am ready for a long, hot bath."

I turn on the ignition. It's only then that I notice the business card that has been tucked under one of the windshield wipers.

I get out and grab it. The card bears the logo of the *Royal Gazette* with Janeen Hill's name under it.

I turn it over. Written in block letters, the message reads:

I NEED TO SPEAK WITH YOU. MY PLACE. PLEASE . . .

I get in the car, hand the card to Fiona. She reads it.

"You mind postponing that hot bath?"

She shrugs, noncommittal.

"Because I could go by there by myself if you're ready to call it a night," I say. "I know how prickly it got the last time you were around her."

"What do you think?"

"I think Janeen redeemed herself, at least a little bit, by calling Worley after we left there the other day, trying to tell him what she knows. That counts for something. She's reaching out."

"Then let's go hear what she has to say."

63

I couldn't believe it when I heard they were holding Sir Teddy for questioning," Janeen Hill says. "I know damn well he didn't kill your brother, Fiona. He didn't kill Peach and Boyd either."

We sit around the table in Janeen's apartment. We've dispensed with the pleasantries and put aside recent bad history. Janeen and Fiona haven't exactly kissed and made up, but they aren't at each other's throats either.

"That's all very well and good," Fiona says, "but until we can actually prove who did commit those murders, then Sir Teddy is staying right where he is."

I look at Janeen.

"The other day, when I was getting ready to leave here, you told me there was a lot we didn't know about this Lost Cross thing."

"There is," Janeen says, "a whole lot."

"Time to educate us," I say. "I don't need the long version. It's late. I'm tired. Just tell me how you think it's related to the murders and who the hell is behind it."

"The Sangrento Mao," Janeen says.

"Sangrento what?"

"Mao," Janeen says. "Spelled just like Mao in Mao Tsetung, but no relation whatsoever. *Mao* is Portuguese for 'hand.' *Sangrento* means 'red.' The Red Hand."

"Bad guys?"

"Can be. You remember what I told you about the Fratres Crucis?"

"Yeah, yeah. The secret brotherhood. Supposedly found the last piece of the True Cross, put it in a fancy reliquary, shipped it off to the New World on some ship . . ."

"The *Santa Helena.*"

"Whatever. And it was never seen again, blah-blah-blah-blah. Does this Sangrento Mao have something to do with that?"

"They most definitely do," says Janeen. "But first, let me show you something. Just so you have a physical point of reference here, just so you know that the reliquary really did exist."

She steps over to the bookcase and returns with a copy of Richard Peach's book, *The Legend of the Lost Cross.* There's a sheet of paper stuck in it. She pulls it out, lays it on the table in front of Fiona and me.

"Behold the Reliquarium de Fratres Crucis," says Janeen. "As drawn by the unfortunate goldsmith who met his end after showing this around town."

There are two sketches on the sheet, actually. One shows a front view of the reliquary. It's shaped like a cross with arms of equal length. At its juncture there's a grating held shut by an elaborate latch.

"The design is after the *crux immissa quadrata,* also known as the Greek cross," says Janeen. "The goldsmith likely chose that design because it was more compact and stable—better suited for traveling—than the traditional Christian cross. Made out of gold and silver and studded with jewels. Probably rubies and emeralds. They were much more popular than diamonds back then."

The second drawing is a close-up. It shows the juncture of the cross with the grating open to reveal the interior of the reliquary.

"That's where the piece of the cross would have been displayed," says Janeen. "It's hard to tell from the drawing, but there was probably a layer of glass inside the grating to offer further protection. It wasn't like they had vacuum-sealing back then, you know."

I pick up the piece of paper and study the drawing more closely.

"So where did this come from?" I ask Janeen.

"The original is at the Museu de Marinha in Lisbon. But I copied it from a copy in Richard Peach's papers. According to his wife, he was considering this drawing as the cover illustration for his uncompleted book."

"Peach have a name for the book?"

Janeen nods.

"Working title was *Finding the Lost Cross*," she says. "Peach was quite optimistic regarding his search here."

"So, out of all the other possible places where the *Santa Helena* might have met its end, how did Peach settle on looking for the reliquary in Bermuda?"

"It was thanks to a bit of serendipity, actually," says Janeen. "Shortly after his first book came out, Peach was planning to focus his search along the coast of North Florida. But first, he and his wife traveled here for vacation. Like everyone else who comes to Bermuda, he was just looking for some R and R. And then, just by chance, he visited Spanish Rock."

"Spanish Rock. I think I remember seeing a sign for that when I was riding around with Barbara the other day."

"Yes, it's a part of Spittal Pond Nature Preserve. A big rock on a bluff overlooking the ocean. There's a bronze casting of a curious inscription that was found carved into the rock. The original has long since been removed."

"What do you mean by curious?"

"Well, the inscription is hard to make out. It's very worn. The earliest theories were that it read 'TCF—1543.' Alongside it was a crude carving of a cross. It was attributed to a Spanish explorer, Theodore Fernando Camelo. Hence the name Spanish Rock," says Janeen. "But it was later suggested that the inscription was made by Portuguese sailors who were shipwrecked here and the initials they carved were actually 'RP' for 'rex portugaliae," king of Portugal. When Richard Peach visited Spanish Rock, he looked at that inscription, along with the carving of the cross, and saw something else—RFC."

"For Reliquarium Fratres Crucis," says Fiona.

"Exactly," Janeen says.

"But what about the date—1543? That doesn't jibe with when the *Santa Helena* left Portugal," I say. "That was 1499, wasn't it?"

"It was. But Peach had proof that the Fratres Crucis launched another ship to search for the *Santa Helena* around that time. It was his theory that it, too, wrecked in Bermuda and that survivors etched those initials in the rock," Janeen says. "He planned to lay out all the evidence in *Finding the Lost Cross*. After, of course, he found it."

Fiona asks, "Is that what you're calling the book you're working on, too?"

"No, not unless by some miracle the cross is actually found. I don't really have a name for my book yet." She gives Fiona a sad smile. "Look, I apologize again for the way I handled the whole book thing the other day. I'm sorry."

"We're past that," Fiona says. "Let's move on."

"Yeah, let's talk about this Sangrento Mao outfit," I say. "How do they fit into things?"

"Well, as you might imagine," says Janeen, "when the *Santa Helena* was lost, and the reliquary with it, it dealt a devastating blow to the Fratres Crucis. They sank a lot of money into funding search expeditions for the *Santa Helena*. And faced with financial difficulties, the brotherhood eventually began to abandon its spiritual quest in favor of, shall we say, more secular pursuits. It leveraged its sizable following and secretive methods into a natural venue—extortion, gambling, whatever illegal activities presented themselves. In short, by the early 1800s Fratres Crucis had morphed into the Portuguese version of the Mafia. It became known as Sangrento Mao, the Red Hand."

"So named, I'm guessing, for its bloody way of doing business?" Fiona asks.

"You got it. And to this day it controls organized crime in Portugal, the Azores, Macao, Brazil, wherever Portuguese colonization made a notable footprint," Janeen says.

"But that doesn't include Bermuda, does it?" Fiona says. "This was never a Portuguese colony."

"No, it wasn't," Janeen says. "But shortly after the Sangrento Mao began flexing its muscles, the first wave of immigrants from Portugal started arriving in Bermuda. Over the years the Portuguese community has grown to the point that it now represents nearly twenty percent of the population. There's a Portuguese cable TV channel and a radio station that plays Portuguese music. And, yes, the Sangrento Mao has a presence here as well."

I'm hearing the sound of fado, smelling a cigar smoked by an old man with a leathery face.

"It's run by a fellow named Papi Ferreira."

64

laugh. Technically, I suppose, it's more of a guffaw. Whatever it is, I do it again.

"Well, kiss my ass and call me cutie-pie," I say.

Janeen and Fiona look at me.

"It's true, Zack," Janeen says. "I'm not just making this up."

"Oh, it's not that I don't believe you," I say.

"What is it then?" Janeen says.

"Let me tell you a little story," I say. "It's not an especially funny story. Still, you might get a kick out of it."

And so I share the whole thing with them. Or most of it anyway. I don't go into the specific details of exactly how much money is at stake—that's my business, not theirs—but I tell them about how I tracked down Brewster Trimmingham and how that ultimately led me to Papi Ferreira. I leave out the part about Boggy and me whupping up on Ferreira's minions. No need to appear boastful or anything like that.

"Inspector Worley told me Ferreira was a bad guy," I say. "Didn't mention that he ran an organized crime ring."

"Not something the Bermuda Police Service likes to acknowledge," Janeen says. "I've knocked heads with them over the years when I've broached the subject in stories. But I was never really encouraged to pursue it by the paper.

Organized crime in Bermuda is not something the *Royal Gazette* likes to acknowledge, either."

Janeen gets up from the table, puts water on to boil, gets out cups.

"I'll pass on the tea," I tell her. "You got any beer?"

She shakes her head, no.

"Rum?"

"Sorry," she says, "all I have is vodka."

"That'll work," I say. "Just pour it in a glass and float some ice in with it."

She does that. I drink some.

"I'm still not getting the connection between Ferreira's bunch, the Sangrento Mao, and the murders," I say. "What am I missing here?"

"You mean, besides the most obvious connection—the ritualistic removal of their victims' eyes?"

"Yeah, besides that."

"Well, despite the fact that they devolved into what they are today, the Sangrento Mao never completely abandoned its hopes of one day finding the Reliquarium de Fratres Crucis. The reliquary is still part of its internal lore, its myth," Janeen says. "So, seven years ago, when Ferreira got wind of what Richard Peach and Martin Boyd were up to . . ."

"Wait a minute," Fiona says. "I thought Peach and Boyd came here under the radar, that no one knew what they were looking for."

"That's right. At least, no one knew what they were looking for until Martin Boyd let it slip to one of his lady friends."

Janeen steps to the table with cups of tea for herself and Fiona. She sits down.

"Worley mentioned something about Boyd when Fiona and I met with him the other day," I say. "Something about Boyd getting involved with someone's wife while he was here in Bermuda."

"That someone was Cristina Ferreira." She lets the name sink in. "Papi Ferreira's daughter-in-law. Married to Papi's only son, Antoni."

"Bad choice of bed partners," I say. "So your theory is

that Papi went after Boyd for cuckolding his son and
Richard Peach was just collateral damage?"

"Not exactly. I think they wound up putting Peach in their
sights, too," says Janeen. "What I heard, from a fairly reli-
able source with ties to the Sangrento Mao, is that after Antoni discovered his wife was having an affair, he was all for
getting rid of both her and Boyd. But she managed to bargain her way out of it."

"How did she do that?"

"She was on the inside of the Sangrento Mao. She knew
its history, its origins. She knew how important the Reliquarium de Fratres Crucis was to them. She offered information about where Peach and Boyd were searching for it in
exchange for her life. She's living in L.A. now. Sells real estate. Antoni died five years ago while visiting Portugal. Automobile accident."

I sip more of the vodka. It's not awful. No taste. Just
burn. But the burn is what I want, that and the boost that
comes afterward.

"When we spoke to Worley, he never mentioned Antoni
Ferreira by name, just that he'd ruled him out as a suspect,"
I say. "Said he was in Miami when the murders were com-
mitted."

"Doesn't mean that Papi, wanting to provide his son with
an alibi, couldn't have arranged to have Peach and Boyd
killed while Antoni was out of town," Janeen says.

"After they'd led Ferreira's outfit to where they thought
the wreck of the *Santa Helena* might be found."

"Something like that," Janeen says. "I haven't worked out
all the details. All I know is that Peach and Boyd must have
been killed before they pinpointed the exact location."

"Why's that?"

"Because in the years since their deaths—again, this is
from my source—Ferreira and crew have been looking for
the wreck on their own."

"What do you mean?"

"I mean, the Sangrento Mao were underwriting a small-
scale salvaging project that was searching for the wreck of

the *Santa Helena*. It hit a bump last year when a few of their guys got hauled in for disturbing a wreck site without a permit."

Fiona perks up when she hears that.

"You mean, Michael Frazer caught and arrested them?" she says.

"Yes, it made headlines for a while. Of course, there was no official connection with the Sangrento Mao, but anyone who knows anything about Bermuda recognized who was involved and connected the dots."

"Sounds like a gutsy move on Frazer's part," I say.

"Yeah, he's pretty devoted to protecting all the wrecks out there, making sure that any salvaging that takes place is done only under his authorization and supervision."

I finish off the vodka. Janeen doesn't ask if I'd like another. So much for the lost art of hospitality.

"Was Frazer on the job when Peach and Boyd were killed?" I ask Janeen.

"Yes, I think he'd been here for a couple of years at that point," she says. "Why?"

"I don't know. Guess I'm wondering why Peach, being the good academic and all, someone who planned to publish his research and hold it out for public scrutiny, didn't get a salvage permit from Frazer's office."

"I've often wondered about that myself," Janeen says. "Best explanation I can come up with is that Peach and Boyd might still have been prospecting potential sites when they were killed. The permit requires the applicant to list a relatively specific location and maybe they just didn't have that yet. They were waiting until they knew for sure.

"I do know that Peach met with Michael Frazer on a couple of occasions while he was here. Frazer told me about it. Turns out, Frazer was a graduate student under Richard Peach when he was at Leeds University."

It piques Fiona's interest.

"Oh, really?" she says. "Michael didn't mention anything about that when we spoke the other night."

"Yes, Frazer even helped Peach with some of the research on the first book," Janeen says, reaching for the copy of *The Legend of the Lost Cross* that sits on the table. She opens the book, flips to the acknowledgments page, and reads from it. "The author is particularly indebted to the contributions of his graduate assistant, Michael Frazer, who labored long hours for little reward on the author's behalf."

"Funny," I say, "when we spoke to Worley the other day, he said one reason why he didn't believe the *Santa Helena* story was that Michael Frazer had pretty much debunked the whole thing."

"Yeah, I spoke with Frazer about that, too, when I started putting Peach's notes together and trying to get some momentum going on the book. Frazer was dismissive of the notion that the *Santa Helena* ever made it to Bermuda," Janeen says. "He claims that much of the work he did for Peach was inconclusive in its findings and that Peach skewed it to support his own research."

"Did Frazer bear a grudge because of it?" I ask.

"Didn't appear to. I mean, you've met him. He's a professional. Does he seem like someone who would obsess over something like that?"

"Not at all," Fiona answers quickly.

"Besides," Janeen says, "it's hardly unusual for a professor to co-opt a graduate assistant's work and use it to whatever end he pleases. Happens all the time."

Janeen clears away the teacups, takes my empty glass. I find myself fighting off a yawn. Fiona notices. She stands up from the table.

"I'm for calling it a night," she says. "You've given us a lot to sleep on, Janeen."

"Well, here's something else to sleep on," Janeen says. "If you're up to it, I'd like to interview you about your brother. Get into some of his personal background, what his childhood was like. His hopes and dreams, that sort of thing."

"Is this for your book?" Fiona says.

"Yes, it is," Janeen says. "I'm going forward with it no matter what. But I would like to have your backing."

Fiona doesn't have to think about it long.

"You've got it," she says.

65

By ten o'clock the next morning, the seventh and next-to-last Bismarck is in the ground. The party is scheduled for tomorrow evening and we've got one palm to go. Things are looking good.

There's no doubt that there will be a party. Aunt Trula has rebounded in fine fashion. If anything, she seems even more driven to perfection for her big to-do. She's overseeing a small army of landscapers who are edging and clipping and planting and trimming, making sure everything is just so.

"She steadfastly refuses to discuss the subject of Teddy," Barbara says as we watch her from the terrace. "But if that's her way of dealing with it, then so be it."

"Any word from the attorney?"

"Not yet. Mr. Denton instructed Teddy to ask the police if Titi could visit for just a few minutes this afternoon. We'll see what happens. In the meantime, how do you rate your chances of coming up with something that will put Sir Teddy in the clear?"

"The odds are decent enough, I suppose. Depending on the police department's willingness to go after Papi Ferreira."

"And it's up to you to give them a reason for doing that?"

"Yep. And sooner or later, between Fiona and me, we'll get something. I just can't promise it will be in time for Teddy to attend the party tomorrow night."

"Something tells me he won't complain about missing a silly little birthday bash if it ultimately leads to his exoneration."

"Better watch out," I say. "If Aunt Trula hears you calling her gala event a silly little birthday bash she might disown you."

"I don't care. I am ready for this whole thing to be over. I'm exhausted, just worn out. I could crawl back into bed right now I'm so tired," says Barbara. She drapes her arms around my neck, leans her head against my chest. "Care to crawl back into bed with me?"

"Save that thought," I say, kissing the top of her head, pulling away. "I've got some errands to run."

"What kind of errands?"

"The kind that I'm making up as I go along."

She looks at me.

"Be careful," she says.

66

It has been a couple of days since I checked in on Brewster Trimmingham, so I swing by King Edward Hospital to see how he's getting along.

I'm hoping that Trimmingham's doctor is close to giving him his walking papers. Because I could use Trimmingham's help. My idea is to put him to work—contacting clients, making cold calls, yanking people off the street, doing whatever it takes to sell the six units at Governor's Pointe.

I'm even willing to throw a commission his way. At this point, I don't even mind absorbing a loss just to clean the table of the whole affair.

When I get to Trimmingham's room it's empty. The bed is neatly made. It doesn't look as if anyone has been in it for a while.

I stop a young nurse's assistant in the hall.

"I'm here to visit Brewster Trimmingham," I tell her. "Is he still in this room? Or has he been transferred again?"

"Let me check, sir. Be right back."

I wait in the hallway. I watch an orderly mop up something on the floor. The face he's making tells me I don't want to know what the something is. I watch an old woman being wheeled past me on a stretcher, her eyes already fixed on the great beyond. I watch busy nurses with clipboards and weary

doctors with charts and anxious family members huddled in
the waiting room across the hall.

I watch the young nurse's assistant heading my way, a
stern-faced older woman with her.

"This is the gentleman," the nurse's assistant says and
then steps away.

"You were inquiring about Mr. Trimmingham?" the
stern-faced woman says.

"I was. I'd like to see him if that's possible."

"Are you a family member?"

"No, a business associate," I say. "Where's Trimmingham?"

The woman takes a breath.

"I'm afraid we don't know where he is."

I don't say anything.

The woman says, "According to the night nurse, he was
in bed at eleven P.M. and received his medication. But when
she stopped in at two A.M. he was gone. No one has seen him
since."

67

I go to Trimmingham's office. It looks the same as when Boggy and I left it a couple days earlier.

I open a filing cabinet, find the folder I'm looking for, the one with Trimmingham's personal information in it. Flip through papers—old VISA statements, bills for the ex-wife in Charlottesville, membership dues for the Somerset Yacht Club. Find a recent utilities bill—2200 Water Avenue, Apt. A-2.

As I'm leaving, the door opens across the hall. The man inside the office pokes his head out.

"Your friends were just here," he says.

"Friends?"

"The three who were here the other day."

"Oh, you mean the day you called the cops?"

He doesn't respond to that.

"How long ago did they leave?" I ask him.

"I don't know. Fifteen minutes maybe."

I say, "Have you seen Trimmingham?"

He shakes his head.

"I heard he was in the hospital."

"You heard right."

"Is he going to be all right?"

"Too soon to tell," I say.

68

I find Water Avenue and follow it to 2200—a quadruplex squeezed between two other quadruplexes. I park the Morris Minor on the street out front.

A-2 is first floor on the right. I knock on the door. No answer. I knock again. No answer again.

There's a window. I look through it. Nothing much to see—crummy furniture in the front room, the kind you buy at the thrift store. Darkness beyond that.

I consider breaking the window, kicking in the door. Don't really have the motivation. Not yet, anyway. Maybe later, if it comes to that.

I turn to go, see the gray van parked behind the Morris Minor.

Paul Andrade gets out of the passenger side. I can see two other guys in the van—Barros behind the wheel, Moraes in the back seat.

I walk up to the van. Andrade slides open the side door, nods me to get inside.

"Papi wants to see you," he says.

"That's nice," I say.

"Get in."

I don't move.

"Where's Brewster Trimmingham?"

Andrade shrugs.

"Get in the van," he says.

I'm standing three steps away from Andrade. For a small, wiry guy you'd think he might have quick reflexes. Turns out, they aren't quick enough. Either that or I'm getting faster in my old age. Doubtful.

I knee Andrade in the nuts. He doubles over and I flip him around, get him in a headlock. I squeeze, lean back. His feet leave the ground. He kicks, grabs at my arm, coughing, fighting for air.

Barros sits frozen in the driver's seat, but Moraes makes a move, lunging through the open door.

I drag Andrade back with me, one arm locked around his throat. I wrap the other arm around the top of his head, get a grip just under his jaw, twist.

"One more step, I break his neck," I say.

Sounds bad-ass anyway.

Moraes stops.

"Get back in the van," I say.

He does it.

"Now close the door."

He does that, too.

I remove my arm from the top of Andrade's head, reach behind his back. The pistol is stuck in his waistband. I pull it out, hold it up for Barros and Moraes to see.

"You're going to drive. I'm going to follow," I say.

"What about him?" Barros says, nodding at Andrade.

"He's riding with me," I say. "Don't do anything stupid."

I let go of Andrade, point him to the Morris Minor. We get in and follow the gray van. I keep his pistol on my lap.

"Now let me ask you again," I say to Andrade. "Where's Brewster Trimmingham?"

He glares at me.

"How the fuck should I know? Papi says he wants to see the both of you. We go looking for Trimmingham, we find you. That's all I know."

We keep driving. Leaving Pembroke Parish, we cross a bridge. I take the pistol from my lap, make a hook shot over the car. I don't see it hit the water, but it's a high-percentage shot.

And the look on Andrade's face tells me all I need to know.

"That was brand new, I just got it."

"Yeah, I know."

"So, why?"

"Don't like guns," I say.

69

After we reach Flatts Village and Ferreira Grocery, I follow Barros, Moraes, and Andrade to the back of the store. There's someone leaving the back room—the young man I saw outside, playing dominoes, on my first visit here, the one who works with Michael Frazer. He eyes me. I eye him. Neither one of us says anything as we pass each other in the aisle.

We step inside the back room. Papi Ferreira sits behind his desk, eating from a big white bowl. The smell of garlic mixes with old cigar smoke. It is not unpleasant.

Andrade speaks, says something in Portuguese. Ferreira barks a response. Andrade stammers a meek reply. Ferreira grunts something. Then Andrade, Barros, and Moraes step out of the room and leave me with Ferreira.

Ferreira ignores me, goes in with his spoon for another slurp of soup.

I feel too much like a supplicant, standing up as I am. I sit down in a chair by the desk.

Ferreira watches me, slurps more soup.

"Smells good," I say. "What is it?"

"*Sopa alentejana*," Ferreira says. "My wife, she makes."

"What's she put in it?"

He shrugs.

"The garlic, the chicken broth, a piece of toast, some cilantro, and two eggs."

"Eggs, huh? They get stirred around like egg-drop soup?"

"No, no stir. See?"

He tilts the bowl so I can see inside. There's one egg left in the yellow broth.

"Oh, like a poached egg."

"Yes, poached," he says. "Is good for breakfast."

"I'll have to try that sometime."

Ferreira dabs his lips with a napkin, pushes the bowl aside. He swallows a burp. He looks at me.

"Where is my money?"

"Where is Brewster Trimmingham?"

Ferreira shrugs.

"That I cannot tell you," he says.

"Can't tell me, or won't tell me? Where is he?"

Ferreira turns up his hands.

"I cannot tell you because I do not know. I send out those three *babacas* to find you and Trimmingham, and they come back just with you. I know they are not telling me everything," he says. "I think maybe you knock them around again some, eh?"

"Didn't take much knocking around," I say.

Ferreira studies me.

"So, Trimmingham. You cannot find him?"

"No, I can't. He's not at the hospital. Not at his office, not at his home."

Ferreira shrugs.

"So, he is missing," Ferreira says. "But you see, this is not my problem. You are my problem. Where is my money?"

"You'll get it."

"When?"

"When I get it."

Ferreira shakes his head.

"This is not the way I do business."

"I know the way you do business," I say. "You pull out people's eyes."

Ferreira doesn't react. He settles back in his chair. He says nothing.

"That's the way it works, isn't it? Someone crosses you,

you pull out their eyes, and then stick an ice pick in their ear."

Ferreira chews his lip. Then he opens his desk drawer. He pulls out a pistol. He puts it down on the desk in front of him, keeps his hand on top of it.

"You hear too many stories," he says. "It is much easier with a gun."

"So why didn't you just shoot Richard Peach and Martin Boyd?"

Ferreira closes his eyes, shakes his head. Then he looks at me again.

"You think it was me who killed them?"

"You or someone in your organization."

"My organization?"

"The Sangrento Mao."

Ferreira's lips narrow. It might almost be a smile.

"I am just a grocer," he says.

"Play it however you want."

He picks up the gun, moves it to his other hand.

"Maybe I want to shoot you right now."

"You don't want to shoot me."

"Why not?"

"Because it will cost you eighty thousand dollars. You'd rather have the money."

Ferreira holds my gaze. He puts the pistol back down on the desk. He settles back in his chair.

I say, "I can think of two reasons why you might have killed Peach and Boyd."

"But I tell you, I did not kill them," Ferreira says. "The one, Boyd, I thought about killing him, yes. But Cristina, my son's wife, she was not worth the blood. Antoni, though, he very much wanted to kill Boyd. That is why I sent him away. To Miami."

"OK. That takes care of one reason. But what about the wreck of the *Santa Helena*?"

Ferreira stares at me, says nothing.

"The Reliquarium de Fratres Crucis. Is that worth killing for?"

Ferreira sighs. He seems suddenly weary.

He says, "These are just stories. Old stories. Like stories of the Sangrento Mao. They are stories that people want to believe. Seven years ago, the police they came and asked questions. And I tell them the same I tell you. I did not kill those men."

"Have the police come asking questions lately?"

"No. What questions would they ask?"

"About the death of Ned McHugh."

Ferreira furrows his brow.

"Yes, I hear about him. In the same way of the others, eh?"

"Yes," I say. "Exactly the same way."

"Is very unfortunate."

"I tell you something else that's unfortunate." I look at Ferreira. He waits. "Teddy Schwartz is in jail for it."

"Yes, I hear that, too," he says. "I am very much surprised by this. Sir Teddy, he is a good man."

"I want him out of jail."

Ferreira shrugs.

"About this," he says, "there is nothing I can do."

"But see, Papi, here's the deal. I'm not real good at multitasking."

"Multitasking? What is?"

"I work better when I can concentrate on one thing at a time. You understand?" Ferreira nods. "Right now I'm concentrating on getting Teddy Schwartz out of jail. You know what that means?"

"Tell me."

"It means until I get him out of jail, then I can't concentrate on getting my money. Which means I sure as hell can't concentrate on getting your money." I stand up from the chair, put my hands on the desk, look Ferreira in the eye. "So if you want to get paid any time soon, then you better figure a way to help me out."

70

I pull up in front of the Oxford House just as Fiona McHugh and Michael Frazer are walking out the front door.

Fiona spots me and waves. I get out of the car and wait for them by the curb.

Fiona sports a yellow sundress, lace at the hem. She looks quite fetching in it.

"Well, hello there," she says. "Michael and I were just heading out to lunch."

"Sorry," I say. "I'd forgotten about that."

"Why don't you join us?" Fiona says. "You don't mind do you, Michael?"

"Oh no, not at all," Frazer says. "Thought we'd hit the Whaler Inn. Great view."

"Thanks, but no," I say. I look at Fiona. "Just wondering if you had mentioned anything to Michael about him taking us out in his boat, see if we could get that GPS to show us anything worth looking at."

"She did," Michael answers for her. "But I can't. Not this afternoon, anyway. I have a couple of meetings I can't afford to miss. Perhaps tomorrow, eh?"

He seems anxious to go. Can't say that I blame him. A pretty girl in a yellow sundress, heading to lunch on a gorgeous afternoon. Ah, the possibilities.

"You heard anything from Worley?" I ask Fiona.

"Not a peep," she says. "What have you been up to?"

"Been an interesting morning. Had a little face time with Papi Ferreira."

It gets a reaction from both of them.

"Grabbing the bull by the horns, eh?" says Fiona.

"Not the part of the bull I was grabbing for, actually."

I give them a brief rundown of my conversation with Ferreira.

"You asked him straight on if he did it?" Fiona asks. "Now that took some spine."

"Don't tap-dance on the line of scrimmage," I say. It gets blank looks from both of them. "Football talk. Something a coach of mine used to say."

"So what did Ferreira tell you?" Fiona asks.

"He said he didn't do it."

"And you believe him?"

"Let's just say I'm leaning in that direction."

"Plenty of people have taken Papi Ferreira at his word and regretted it later," Frazer says.

"That's why I'm only leaning. I haven't fallen head over heels in love with the guy."

Frazer checks his watch.

"Reservations are for noon," he says. "We best be off."

"I'll check in with you later, Zack," Fiona says. "Where will you be?"

"Thought I'd drop by Teddy Schwartz's place."

She seems surprised. So does Frazer.

"What for?" asks Fiona.

"Don't know yet," I say.

71

A police van and two cars occupy the driveway at Teddy Schwartz's house when I arrive. I park down the street and walk back to the house.

The front door is open and I can see a group of policemen sitting around the dining room table, eating food out of Styrofoam containers. Looks like a lunch break.

I step around to the back of the house. *Miss Peg* is moored at the dock, just as we left her the day before, except for the yellow crime-scene tape that runs between the mooring pilings.

There's tape along the walkway to the boathouse, too. I've never understood the whole crime-scene tape thing. Seems like if cops really wanted to keep people away from crime scenes, they'd figure out a way to electrify the tape. Or do something to make it a little more daunting. Like run razor-wire along the edges. Or lace it with anthrax. Otherwise it just looks like a bad job of gift wrapping.

I duck under the tape and step inside the boathouse. I look around. It's as if the place got hit by its own private tornado.

Stacks of lumber lay scattered like a game of giant pickup sticks. The diving equipment is strewn all about. Boxes have been ripped open, their contents in heaps.

I don't know what I'm looking for. I'm just looking.

I step over power tools—drills and saws. I edge around

an acetylene torch and the tanks that go with it, banging a shin against a small anvil in the process.

I finally make my way to the workbench in the center of the room. The blue tarp that once covered it lies on the floor. Gone is the carpenter's box that once sat atop the workbench, along with the tools that were in it. Gone, too, are the small jars filled with pieces of jewelry and bric-a-brac.

The books that held down the tarp have been knocked to the floor. I kneel and sort through them. Glossy picture books from museums, catalogs from auction houses.

At the bottom of the pile, lie several sheets of paper. I pick them up, flip through them.

And suddenly I am looking at something I recognize: a sketch of the Reliquarium de Fratres Crucis.

72

The paper I'm holding contains a copy of the same drawing that Janeen Hill showed Fiona and me the night before at her house, the one made by the goldsmith who designed the reliquary.

Some notes are scribbled in pencil, with lines drawn to different parts of the reliquary. I can make out some of them—".925 silver (French)," "I.G. copper 60%." Others are indecipherable.

I fold the paper, stick it in a pants pocket. I'm still nosing around the books, seeing if anything else jumps out to surprise me, when I hear a voice: "Can I help you?"

I stand, see a young police officer in the doorway of the boathouse. He takes a step my way, suspicious.

I say, "Is Inspector Worley around?"

I know good and well that he's not. But it never hurts to drop a name. And since that's the only cop name I know . . .

"No, Worley's not here," says the cop.

"What time is it?"

The cop looks at his watch.

"Almost two thirty," he says.

"Dammit, where is he then? He was supposed to meet me here at two."

The cop sputters for words.

"I don't know, sir. I . . ."

"Look, I don't have time for this. I've got things to do," I say, moving past him toward the door. "When Worley finally decides to show up tell him Zack Chasteen was here."

And in a full-blown, self-righteous huff, I head out the door.

Then the cop says, "Hey, wait a minute."

I stop. The cop already has his cell phone out and is punching buttons.

"I can get Worley for you right now," he says.

"No, that's all right, you don't have to."

"No problem, sir, I'm happy to." And then I hear him speaking into the phone: "Yes, Inspector, this is Officer Dodwell at the Schwartz house. There's a gentleman here, a Mr. Chasteen . . ."

He listens, cut his eyes my way. He turns, so I can't hear what he's saying. He listens some more. Then he hands me the phone.

"Hello, Inspector," I say. "I hope you have a good excuse for standing me up."

"Just what the hell do you think you're doing in that boathouse, Chasteen?"

"Why, yes, Inspector, I suppose I could reschedule our appointment if you like."

A pause on Worley's end. When he speaks, he speaks low.

"Anything I need to know?"

"Maybe," I say. "When is good for you?"

"I've been trying to find you, Chasteen. I've arranged a few minutes for you with Sir Teddy this afternoon."

"Yes, I think that will work for me."

"It better. I've had to pull a few strings, go behind a few people's backs to make this happen. Situations like this, no one gets in to see a suspect except the attorney. And even then, perhaps only for a single visit. I don't want this to come back and bite me."

"So what time then?"

"Five o'clock," says Worley.

"Fine," I say, "I'll have my secretary call to confirm."

"Yeah, you do that," Worley says.

And the line goes dead.

73

I've got time to kill and, as long as I'm in the neighborhood, I drive down Bedon's Alley and stop at Ned McHugh's house. There's a pickup truck in the driveway. It bears the logo of Deep Water Discoveries.

Polly is on the front porch with a broom, sweeping. She stops when she sees me get out of the car. She turns toward the door, says something. By the time I near the house, Bill Belleville is stepping onto the porch.

"Hey, man," Belleville says. "Good to see you again."

Polly smiles.

"I was just getting the place cleaned up," she says.

"Have you moved back in?" I ask.

She shakes her head.

"No, I'm still too weirded-out by everything to do that. I'm just getting it fixed up again so I can get the deposit back from the landlord. He's got someone else who's ready to rent it."

"Where you going to live?"

"Well . . ." She looks at Belleville.

"I've got a spare bedroom at my place," he says. "I made her a good deal on it."

"It's just for the time being," Polly says. "Bill is helping me move a few things over there."

Belleville unfolds a chaise lounge, moves it alongside a rickety Adirondack chair.

"Here, man, sit. You want a beer? I've got some in a cooler. I was having one."

"No, I'm fine, thanks. But go ahead."

I take a seat. Belleville grabs his beer from inside and joins me.

I peek inside the house. The mess of a few days earlier is gone. Boxes are stacked in the living room. The refrigerator door is open so it can air out.

"Looks like you've about got everything shipshape," I say.

"I've been working like crazy since the service yesterday," Polly says. "Came back here and just dived into it. Think I was getting rid of nervous energy, know what I mean?"

"I'm told housecleaning can be therapeutic," I say. "Can't speak to it firsthand."

Belleville laughs.

"Me neither, man." He looks at Polly. "Although I might have to change my ways now that I'm getting a housemate."

Polly smiles, starts in with the broom again, working her way down the porch steps.

"So how did you like playing for Don Shula?" Belleville asks.

I get asked that a lot, so I've got my standard spiel: Shula was a class act all the way. One of the greats. Then I tell a Shula story or two.

Polly finishes sweeping.

"I almost forgot," she says. "I did find something else missing from the break-in the other day. Ned's box is gone."

"Ned's box?" I say. "What's that?"

"It was this box he picked up in Thailand. It was nice, hand carved and everything. He hid it under the bed. I didn't see it all that often, so I didn't think of it at first. Ned kept stuff in it."

"What kind of stuff?"

"Little odds and ends. Things he'd picked up in his travels. He had all this leftover money in there, from Thailand and Indonesia and other places he'd visited. It might have looked like a lot of money, but it really wasn't worth much. Just mementos from the road. Whoever took the box might have thought they were getting something, but it was just a bunch of foreign money and some of Ned's papers."

"What kind of papers, Polly?"

"His passport, his work visa. That sort of thing. And the papers for that salvage permit he was working on."

"The one he was getting ready to turn in to the curator of wrecks office?"

"Yeah, that. He was all done with it, I think. He was excited about finally being able to file it and everything."

Polly leans the broom against the porch rail, picks up the doormat, gives it a shake.

Belleville says: "You sure I can't get you a beer or something, Zack? I've got plenty more."

He gets up from his chair.

"No, really, I need to be going."

I get up, step off the porch.

"Thanks for stopping by," Polly says. "If you hear anything . . ." She grabs a Post-it pad from a table by the door, scribbles phone numbers on it. "Here's where you can find me."

Belleville says, "Hey, man, what are you doing tomorrow night?"

I blank for a moment. Then I remember—Aunt Trula's party.

"There's this birthday party I'm going to."

"Too bad. I was gonna say, you could join us for a night dive out at Fish Rock like I was telling you about. Got a couple of spaces left," Belleville says. "Maybe another time, huh?"

"Yeah," I say. "Maybe another time."

74

I t's still only four o'clock by the time I make it back to
Hamilton, so I pay Daniel Denton a surprise visit.

If Denton is pleased to see me, then he does a dandy
job of not showing it. And when I tell him I'm on my way to
visit Teddy Schwartz, he bags all pretense.

"Really, Mr. Chasteen, your involvement in this matter
cannot in any way advance Sir Teddy's cause. Our firm is
presently assembling the best defense team available in
Bermuda, or anywhere for that matter, and the last thing we
need is you blustering your way into things."

"Blustering?"

"Yes, I've seen the way you do business—heavy-handed,
full of swagger, bull in a china shop."

"Gosh, that hurts. Does this mean you no longer want to
be my attorney?"

"Believe me, Mr. Chasteen, had you not invoked Mrs. Ambister's good name and bludgeoned me into doing that nasty
bit of work involving Mr. Trimmingham, then I never would
have agreed to represent you in the first place. As it is, I performed my services, you paid me, our account is clear and I
am free of you. I do hope you didn't come here in hopes of re-
taining this firm for another of your misbegotten schemes."

"Wow, misbegotten. That sounds almost biblical. But no,
that's not why I'm here," I say. "I was just wondering—who
is Sir Teddy's attorney?"

"That would be Russell Urban; he heads our criminal division. You won't find a better trial lawyer."

"Then I'd like a word with Mr. Urban."

Denton thinks it over.

"Certainly, why not? I'm sure Mr. Urban would like to weigh in on this as well."

He picks up his phone, makes the call, and Russell Urban soon joins us. He's a big, good-looking guy, prematurely gray in a way that probably serves him well. He exudes fatherly authority. A high degree of pomposity, too, but that goes with the turf.

Denton says, "As I was just explaining to Mr. Chasteen, we are looking after Sir Teddy's best interests and, to employ terminology he might understand, he should remain on the sidelines."

Urban nods, fixes a look of deep seriousness on his face.

"Yes, by all means. We have our game plan . . ." He flashes Denton a grin to show he's hip to the metaphor. ". . . and you are not a part of it, Mr. Chasteen."

"So what's the game plan?"

"Well, in the event that charges are filed against Sir Teddy, which does seem rather likely at this point, considering the evidence at hand and the ticking of the clock, we intend to attack the prosecution's case on all fronts. I have no doubt that should the case come to trial, which, I'm afraid, might also be rather likely, then I have every confidence that we will gather sufficient evidence of our own, along with testimony, that will acquit Sir Teddy."

"As far as gathering evidence, what have you done on that front so far?"

"Our firm does not employ full-time investigators. We have contacted an agency that we've done business with in the past—a very reputable agency, I might point out—and I would anticipate that we would formally retain their services within the next few days."

Just a lawyerly way of saying they haven't done jack-shit.

Denton says, "So do we understand each other here, Mr. Chasteen?"

He rises behind his desk. Urban stands. I get up, too.

"Sure, I understand. But as long as we're tossing around football terms, here's one you might add to your list: 'You don't drop back and punt when it's only first down.' "

"What's that supposed to mean?" Urban says.

"It means, you boys follow your game plan, I'll follow mine."

75

The police are keeping Teddy Schwartz at Westgate Prison, just outside of Hamilton. Worley isn't there when I arrive.

"He just called. Won't be able to make it. Tied up in a meeting," a woman working the reception desk tells me when I sign in. "But he did make arrangements for you to visit briefly with Mr. Schwartz."

A few minutes later, I'm sitting in a dingy, overlit room with a metal table and four chairs. And a few minutes after that, Teddy Schwartz is escorted in by two guards. As soon as Teddy is seated, the guards step outside.

Teddy wears the same thing he wore on *Miss Peg* for Ned McHugh's memorial service—khakis, a navy blue shirt, and boat shoes. His eyes are puffy and he looks a little tired, but, all things considered, he's bearing up well.

"Sorry to get you sucked into all this," Teddy says.

"Don't worry about it. Besides, I sort of sucked myself in."

"And I appreciate that," Teddy says. "How's Trula?"

"OK, I guess. But this has thrown her for a loop."

"Yes, I would imagine."

"She's forging ahead," I say. "Don't get your feelings hurt, but she hasn't pulled the plug on her party simply on your account."

"Nor should she," Teddy says. "I'll be out of here by then."

I look at him.

"You know something I don't know?"

"What do you mean?"

"I mean, the police have the murder weapon. They found it in your boathouse. And they are hell-bent on formalizing the charges against you just as soon as they can," I say.

"My attorney assures me that he has everything under control."

"You ever met an attorney who wouldn't tell a client that? I just came from talking to your attorney, Teddy. And, as far as I can tell, he's in no great rush to discredit the evidence or offer a plausible explanation for how it might have wound up in your possession. Meaning, unless we figure out something in a hurry, you're going to be charged with Ned McHugh's murder. Forget going to the damn birthday party. You might not even be going home."

"But it's a setup. I didn't do it."

"OK, then, let's start with the easy question: Who did?"

Teddy shakes his head.

"That's what I've been trying to get a handle on. I can't think of anyone who would do this to me."

"No enemies out there, no one with an old score to settle?"

"Why sure, I've run up against a few people over the years. But no one who would commit a murder and try to pin it on me."

"Three murders, counting Peach and Boyd," I say. "But there's nothing tying you to that. Not yet anyway."

The words sting him.

"What's that supposed to mean?"

"It means, you are a man of constant surprises, Teddy Schwartz."

"How so?"

"Well, for starters, I was surprised to learn that you knew Ned McHugh. Not only did you know him, but you apparently met with him on several occasions, loaned him books, even came by his house on the day that he died," I say. "Only you didn't see fit to mention that to his sister. Or to anyone else as far as I know. I had to learn it from his girlfriend. Just like the cops did."

Teddy looks away, doesn't say anything.

"For all I know, it was even you who broke into Ned's house . . ."

Teddy slams a hand on the table.

"I didn't do that!" he says.

"OK, I'm listening. Why didn't you tell anyone about Ned McHugh?"

He takes a moment to answer, says: "Because I felt guilty."

"Guilty?"

"Yes, guilty," Teddy says. He looks across the table at me, pain in his eyes. "I didn't kill Ned McHugh."

"I know that, Teddy."

"But I let him get killed."

76

The room is quiet, except for the hum of the air conditioner. I settle back in my chair. The ball is clearly in Teddy's court.

"Ned sought me out not long after he arrived in Bermuda. Bright young man, clearly meant for big things. What he lacked in experience, he more than made up for in enthusiasm and a thirst for knowledge.

"I'm getting to be an old man, you know? No children of my own. Still, I'd like to think that I had passed along a little wisdom to someone. That someone was Ned. I was flattered that he wanted to spend time with me, listen to my stories, learn from me.

"Then one day he came to visit and I could see it written all over his face. I recognized the look. It's the same look I used to get whenever I came upon something out there. It just fills you up inside and you can't hold it back.

"Ned didn't come right out and say what it was he'd come across. No, he was circumspect about it, cautious. Which, if you're a treasure salvor, is not a bad thing to be. He just stuck out his hand and said, 'Look what I found.' And there in his hand he was holding a soul-saver, a red one. You know what a soul-saver is?"

I nod.

"The old-time sailors used to carry them," I say. "Polly, Ned's girlfriend, she wears one around her neck."

"Likely the same one Ned showed me that day. And the moment I laid eyes on that thing, I knew what he'd found. Oh yes, I knew. Couldn't be but one thing."

"What's that?"

Teddy looks at me.

"The *Santa Helena*," he says. "You've heard tell of her?"

I nod.

"So, there really was such a ship."

"Oh yeah, there really was. And if anyone should know then it's me."

"Why's that?"

He looks at me, a grin emerging on his face, like he's filled up inside and can't hold it back.

"Because I found her, that's why. Well on twenty-five years ago." He slams the table again, only this time it's in exultation. "Now how's that for a surprise from Teddy Schwartz, eh?"

He slides his chair out from the table, gets up, paces around the room. It's as if a giant burden has been lifted, energizing him. He puts his hands on the table, looks across it at me.

"I've been waiting to tell someone I'd found that ship for all these long years," he says. "And, I've got to say, it feels good to finally let it out."

"You never mentioned it to anyone?"

"Just one person," he says. "Peg."

"Your wife."

"Yes, dear, dear Peg. I told her. It was near her final days when I found the *Santa Helena*. Stumbled across it really, just like Ned did. That's the way it is with salvaging. Sometimes you see this one little something, doesn't look like it could be much of anything. But you go after it. And it turns into something big."

"What was the little something you saw?"

"A soul-saver, like the one Ned found, only this one it was green. Peg's favorite color. I took it as a sign from above. Not that I'm one to believe in such things. But Peg was. Oh, she was a believer, a believer in all things great and good. I took it right home and gave it to her. Two months later, she was holding it when she died."

Teddy reaches in a pocket, pulls out his hand, opens it. A green piece of glass in the shape of a beetle rests in his palm.

"I'm never without it," he says.

There are tears in his eyes. I give him a moment, then I say: "So you knew right away it was the *Santa Helena* that you'd found?"

"Had a pretty good idea. The vast majority of wrecks in these waters came after the mid-seventeenth century. But finding a soul-saver? That marked it as something else, something else entirely. Late 1400s or thereabouts. Took a couple weeks for me to get the proof that finally nailed it." He thinks about it, chuckles. "Funny choice of words that was."

"The reliquary?"

"Yes," he says. "The Reliquarium de Fratres Crucis. There wasn't much else left of the *Santa Helena*. The ship's timber and whatnot, it was scattered all about. She'd been covered up by another wreck, one that came along about three hundred fifty years later. So what little that was left of her was well camouflaged, almost indistinguishable from the ship atop her, which had all sorts of boilers and engines and metalwork. Big worthless stuff that no treasure salvor, not even a desperate one, would go to all the trouble of looking under for what most likely was naught.

"I got lucky. A tropical storm had come through just a couple of weeks earlier, must have shifted things around some. It popped out that soul-saver, a couple of other things, too. Made it almost easy to find the reliquary. It was shining up at me, out of the sand. Battered it was, crumpled and worn, pieces of it stripped away, some of it ate up by critters and time. But the heart of it, yeah, that was still there."

"The piece of the True Cross, you mean, it was still inside?"

He looks at me.

"I'll not pass judgment on what it was or what it wasn't. I'm not a believer, you know. That's where Peg and me differed. She was a churchgoer, a godly woman through and through. Worshipped Jesus Christ as her lord and savior. Me, I've got religion, but that's a thing between my god and me."

"Still, you understood the significance of the reliquary, knew the lore that surrounded it."

"Oh, yeah, I'd studied it in and out. I'd read stories about the *Santa Helena,* researched the possibilities. Had dozens of books that referenced her as bona fide and just as many that said she never existed. Had my mind mostly made up that it was all just fibbery and sham. And then . . ." He stops, a faraway look on his face. "Got the reliquary up on the boat, wasn't expecting to find anything but mud and rot inside, torn up as it was. Surprised me, it did. But the water, it's cold down there. Things hold up better than you might think. And the wood it was well sealed in glass. About yea big," he says, making the shape with his hands. "About the size of a roof shingle, not even that."

"So, what did you do with it?"

"Ah, the question of all questions," Teddy says.

"I have to ask."

"Yeah, you do. And if I were in your shoes, then I'd ask, too. Let's just say that we talked about it, Peg and me. We talked about it long and hard. In the end, I did what she asked me to do."

I wait for him to tell me more. He smiles.

"That's all you'll get from me on that. I did what Peg asked me to do," he says. "End of story."

77

Teddy sits down, folds his hands on the table.

He says, "But I suspect you have other questions . . ."

I reach into a pocket, pull out the sketch of the reliquary that I took from Teddy's boathouse. I unfold it and place it on the table in front of him.

He looks at it, then at me.

"Appears as if you've done a bit of salvaging yourself," he says.

"I just want to know what's going on."

He leans back in his chair, folds his arms across his chest.

"What do you think is going on, Zack?"

"I'm not sure, but that boathouse of yours . . ."

"Interesting place that boathouse, isn't it? All sorts of things in there to catch a person's attention. What caught yours?" He flips a hand at the sketch. "Besides this, I mean."

"Your workbench, mainly. It was covered with a tarp the first time I walked in there, the day we went out on your boat."

"The same day I should have known that something was up. I'd left the boathouse locked, always do. That's why it threw me off to find you in there. But I was in a hurry to get out on the water, do what I had to do, and so I didn't pursue it."

"You went straight to the workbench and looked under the tarp to see if something was missing. What was that something, Teddy?"

He answers by pointing at the sketch on the table.

"The reliquary?" I say.

"No, not the real one, not the one I found," he says. "But a damn fine imitation, if I don't say so myself."

I think about: the precision tools, the books about metalwork and silversmithing, the jeweler's loupe Teddy was wearing the day that Fiona and I dropped by to visit unannounced.

"You were making a replica of the reliquary?"

"I'd already finished it, actually."

"A hobby of yours or something?"

Teddy smiles.

"Started off as a hobby. The odd piece of jewelry, gifts for Peg. Became something of a necessity though, especially after Betty's bat got stolen."

The scepter, Schwartz's Scepter, the gem-laden treasure that had been on display in his museum.

I say, "Rumor always has been that the scepter wasn't really stolen, that you'd sold it to a rich collector and substituted a fake for it."

"I much prefer the word 'replica' to 'fake,' if you don't mind. But, point of fact, the scepter really was stolen. By whom, I have no clue. A damn clever somebody, that's all I know," he says. "It grieved me, yes, but mostly it embarrassed me. Humiliated me. Here I'd fought the government for years, saying that the scepter was best left with he who found it, that I and only I could guarantee its safekeeping. And then I let it get snatched away.

"I didn't report the theft. Again, the humiliation. But I immediately shut down the museum, under the pretext that I was remodeling, making some improvements. Ha! The only thing that improved was my skills as a goldsmith. Took me nearly a year to craft a replica of the scepter. Was right proud of it, too." He sighs. "Sadly, it didn't fool the experts. In the end, I suffered the humiliation of losing the scepter anyway."

"So why make a replica of the Reliquarium de Fratres Crucis?"

"Because the original, shall we say, looks nothing like it once did. And I wanted to put an end to it once and for all."

"Put an end to what?"

"People getting killed over the damn thing." He shakes his head. "It's my fault, all my fault. Had I only made public that I'd found the *Santa Helena* back when I found it, then none of this would have happened."

"Why didn't you make it public?"

He looks at me.

"Have you not been listening to me? It was our secret, me and Peg's. Something twixt the two of us. Something as close to holy as I ever expect to know. And when she died, it was a secret that I did not wish to share." He closes his eyes, lets out air. "Then came those first two, Peach and Boyd. I kept an eye on them out there. They knew what they were doing, all right. They were getting close, right close. And then . . ."

He stops, shakes his head.

"After their murders, that's when I started to work on the replica of the reliquary. It was difficult, finding French silver from that era, finding the right grade of copper and all, the same materials that they would have used back then. I worked on it in fits and starts, got her almost done. But the steam, it went out of me. Until Ned arrived, that is."

"So Ned knew that he had found the *Santa Helena*?"

"No, I don't think so. He just knew the wreck was old, older than anything that had ever been found in these waters," Teddy says. "I liked Ned. He was a fine one. I figured he was due his glory, that he would wear it well, go on to greater things. So, I finished making the replica, had it looking more or less the same way it was when I pulled it from the water, right down to that tiny piece of wood at the heart of it. I was planning to salt the wreck with it. But then . . ."

He looks at me, tormented and torn.

"He died. He died because of me."

"No," I say. "He died because someone killed him. You can't blame yourself for that."

He sloughs it off, won't hear it.

"That night at dinner, at the Mid Ocean Club, when you told me the way he died, about his eyes, same as the others, I decided right then that I could wait no longer, that if someone wanted that reliquary so badly that they would kill for it, over and again, that I would give it to them. Or at least trick them into thinking they had what they were looking for.

"And then, after I got it set in place at the wreck site, my intent was to keep a vigil on *Miss Peg,* at safe distance, of course, monitor who came and went from the spot where I had put it until . . ."

"Hold on," I say. "You're telling me that you took the replica out there to the wreck site?"

Teddy looks at me.

"You can be a thick one sometimes," he says. "I didn't really care to go out there alone, thought there might be safety in numbers. It was good to have you and Boggy with me that morning at Sock 'Em Dog. And why else do you think I suited up and saw to it that you lagged so far behind me?"

"Your dive bag," I say. "You had the replica in it. That's when you put it out there."

Teddy smiles, nods.

"Yeah, put it right where I found the original. Near the hub of the *Victory*'s paddle wheel."

Before I can muster a reply, the door swings open, the two guards come in. One of them takes Teddy by the arm.

"Time's up," the other one says.

They start to lead him away.

"Wait," I say. "Just a few more minutes."

"Sorry, sir. Superintendent's orders," says the guard. "This is all for today."

78

All hell breaks loose bright and early the next morning at Cutfoot Estate.

I'm out with Boggy and the gardening crew, preparing the hole for the final Bismarck, when the auger seizes up in the limestone. The backhoe operator tries to free it and succeeds not only in snapping the bit, but rupturing a hydraulic hose. It flails like some furious serpent, spewing fluid in every direction, coating the lawn in an oily sheen.

A perfect time for Aunt Trula to step down from the terrace to investigate the commotion. She strides onto a slick spot and spills ass over teakettle onto the grass.

The only thing hurt is pride, which in her case is a whole lot of hurt.

"Where is Barbara?" she demands as I help her to her feet. "I need her out here this instant!"

"I'll find her," I say. "By the way . . ."

"What?" Aunt Trula snaps.

"Happy birthday."

Turns out, Barbara is still in bed, where I'd left her a couple of hours earlier. Not like her, not like her at all. I give her a kiss and rouse her awake.

"You OK?" I ask as she stretches and yawns.

"Oh, fine, just fine." She smiles. "Just needed to catch up on my sleep, that's all, get ready for the big day."

A few minutes later we are standing on the terrace, surveying the scene, plotting damage control.

"We'll get bags of white sand, spread it in the grass," Barbara says. "That should solve the problem of people slipping or tracking oil on their shoes."

"I suppose, but I am more concerned with that thing," says Aunt Trula, nodding at the auger. "We can't very well have a giant metal rod poking out of the ground like that."

"We could always get some brightly colored streamers, have the guests make a circle and pretend it's a maypole," I say.

Aunt Trula and Barbara look at me. They don't say anything. They don't need to.

"I'll get to work on it," I say.

"You absolutely must get that last palm tree planted," Aunt Trula calls after me. "Four on one side, three on the other. That simply will not do. There must be symmetry!"

I walk to the scene of the disaster. I'm thinking that from this day forward, whenever I'm off-center and seeking balance in my life, I shall rally myself by hearkening the words of dear Aunt Trula: "There must be symmetry!"

Boggy and Cedric have rounded up a sledgehammer and chisel. The hole is only big enough for one person at a time, and so we take turns, pounding away at the limestone. It is slow, slow going.

By early afternoon, the tent people have arrived and are putting tables and chairs in place. The caterer has brought three trucks and a troupe of chefs has taken over the kitchen. The floral designer and a half-dozen assistants are fretting over bouquets and wreaths and table arrangements.

I take my turn in the hole. I put chisel in place, pick up the sledgehammer, and swing. Chips of limestone fly every which way. The auger remains locked in rock. I reset the chisel and pound it again. And again and again.

It's hot in the hole. I'm sweating. The work is mindless. Still, vagrant thoughts fall into place, of salvage permits and sunken ships, ancient glass gewgaws in the shapes of beetles . . .

I swing the sledgehammer, hit home, and the auger is free. I help the backhoe operator reset the bit.

And then I crawl out of the hole.

"I'll be right back," I tell Boggy.

I hurry up to the bedroom, find the sheet of paper that Polly gave me, the one with her phone numbers on it. I call the first number, Deep Water Discoveries, and she answers. I ask her a few questions, and she tells me what I need to know.

I call the Oxford House and ask for Fiona McHugh.

"I'm sorry," says the desk clerk. "But Miss McHugh just stepped out."

"Did she say where she was going?"

"No, but the same gentleman who called on her yesterday arrived here again to pick her up. The way they were dressed it appeared as if they might be going boating."

I call Westgate Prison and ask for the superintendent's office. I get his secretary and after a few minutes of wrangling I get the superintendent himself.

"There is absolutely no way that I can allow you to speak with Mr. Schwartz," the superintendent says.

"But it's urgent. I have to . . ."

"Then take it up with Mr. Schwartz's attorney. He found out about your coming here yesterday and demanded that I not let it happen again. So I suggest . . ."

I hang up the phone. I call Inspector Worley's office. He's not there.

"He accompanied the commissioner to a subcommittee meeting at Parliament regarding the police service budget," says a secretary. "I expect he will be tied up the rest of the afternoon."

There's no one left to call.

I hurry to the backyard. The auger is out of the hole. Cedric and Boggy are putting a sling around the eighth and last Bismarck so it can be set in place.

I pull Boggy aside.

"Come with me," I say.

79

As we wait for a gap in traffic so we can pull out of Cut-foot Estate, I spot a blue Toyota parked near the entry gate of the place next door. I can't tell how many people are in it. Too far away.

I turn onto the road, heading for Somerset and Teddy Schwartz's house. The blue Toyota zips into traffic a few cars behind us.

I tell Boggy where we're going and why we're going there. I tell him about the phone calls, what I learned and what I didn't learn and what I think it all means. It only takes a few minutes. By the time I'm done, the Toyota has moved up a slot or two.

I see a sign for Heron Loop Road. It's a scenic detour that reconnects with the main road about a mile ahead. Barbara and I drove it on our moped outing.

I whip onto Heron Loop Road. I've only gone fifty yards or so when I see the blue Toyota in my rearview mirror.

"Looks like we've got a friend," I say.

Boggy adjusts the side mirror. He looks in it, says: "It is only one person."

"Can you make out who it is?"

"No, too far."

The Toyota keeps its distance as we follow Heron Loop Road back to the main road. It hangs back even as we stop and wait to turn. Once we're about a quarter mile down the main road, I spot it again in the rearview mirror.

I slow down. Cars pass me. Soon the Toyota is the only car behind me, but still it hangs back.

I pass the driveway to Teddy Schwartz's house. I go a hundred yards or so, then veer onto the shoulder. The crunch of gravel, a storm of dust. The blue Toyota keeps going past us, its driver looking straight ahead.

I say, "You see who it was?"

Boggy nods.

"Yes, the one who works with Michael Frazer," he says.

"That's what I thought, too. The same one we keep seeing at Papi Ferreira's house."

We talk about what it could mean as I turn us around and park in the driveway at Teddy Schwartz's house. As we get out, the Toyota passes slowly on the road. The driver sees us. I give him a big friendly wave. He keeps going.

The same police crew from the day before is back at it again at Teddy's place. They've apparently committed themselves to scouring every inch of the grounds to find anything else that might seal the case against Teddy.

Boggy heads straight for the dock, begins untying the lines on *Miss Peg*. I step into the boathouse. Three cops, including the young guy who found me snooping around the day before, are sifting through the pile of lumber that sits at the far end of the room.

I give them a nod, say: "How you doing?"

Then I reach for the key rack. There are at least a dozen key chains hanging from it, and I can't remember which one Teddy used on our previous trips. But four of them are the kind you buy at nautical stores, with foam floats attached. I grab all four of them and head out the door.

Behind me, I hear the young cop saying: "He was here yesterday. Knows the Chief Inspector."

I hop on *Miss Peg* and Boggy pushes us off from the dock. Not standard boating procedure—you always wait until the engine starts, just in case it doesn't—but the cops are hurrying out of the boathouse.

"Hold it right there!" shouts one of them.

I try the first key. Doesn't work. Try the second. It doesn't work either.

The cops are on the dock.

"Where do you think you're going?" says the one who seems to be in charge.

"Just out for a little boat ride," I say, as I fiddle with the third key. It doesn't work.

The cop reaches for a cell phone.

"I need to clear that," he says.

The fourth key works. The engine fires. I throttle up and we pull away.

I point *Miss Peg* out to open water, then let Boggy take the wheel while I busy myself with the GPS.

It's not one of the newer models and, even if it were, I am no great hand with electronic gizmos. The GPS flashes on, gives our present coordinates. I punch buttons, see if I can luck out and punch up something that might be a log of previously visited sites, then figure out which one of them might be Sock 'Em Dog. But nothing works.

I open a compartment in the console, find the weathered logbook that Teddy had consulted the day we went to Sock 'Em Dog. I flip through pages. There are dozens of coordinates. And, as I feared, they are listed by Teddy's private code rather than any common name that I can recognize. At any rate, there's nothing in the book that says Sock 'Em Dog.

I sling the logbook back into the compartment and slam it shut.

Boggy looks at me.

"What is it, Zachary?"

"We're screwed. I can't locate the coordinates, either on the GPS or in Teddy's logbook."

"They are the same as the numbers on the GPS that Fiona had?"

"Yes, probably the same. Near enough anyway. But we don't have that GPS either."

Boggy reaches for the GPS on the console. He punches in the coordinates: N32° 18.024/W064° 52.622.

I look at him.

"Where did you pull that from?"

"You forget, Zachary. I fixed Fiona's GPS. I found that number for her."

"And you remember it?"

Boggy shrugs.

"Just a number," he says.

80

An hour later . . .

  The wind has come up from the southeast and a rising swell, straight out of Africa, churns the water as we near Sock 'Em Dog. Things are getting knocked all around in the cabin. I go below and stow fallen gear in its racks. The fire extinguisher rolls on the floor. I put it back in its holder. I try my best to fasten down everything that needs fastening down.

When I come back out, I can see a boat just ahead of us, cresting and falling with the waves. Sleek profile, red hull—Michael Frazer's boat.

We draw closer. There's no one on it.

We put out bumpers and tie off *Miss Peg* alongside the other boat. I find a full tank, suit up. There's a mesh dive bag in one of the gear lockers. I tie its drawstrings to an eyelet on my vest and shuffle to the transom.

On the ride out, Boggy and I talked over how this whole thing might go down. Lots of variables. A shitstorm waiting to happen.

Not to worry. We've come up with a plan. Or what might pass for a plan if it didn't have so many goddamn holes in it.

But there's no way to fix it now. And not much that needs saying.

"See you when I see you," I tell Boggy.

"And you, Zachary," he says.

Then I take a giant stride and hit the water.

Maybe it's the adrenaline of the moment. Or maybe Boggy slipped some of his pig's bile tea into my coffee at breakfast. In any event, I don't have my typical difficulty equalizing the pressure on my ears. I drop down, down, down.

And as I drop, I angle toward the seamount, that predatory spire of rock and coral with the benign face of a friendly dog.

I check my gauges—60 feet, 2,800 psi in the tank.

I swim over the first scattering of wreckage. It's the bow of the *Victory,* I'm assuming, since the paddlewheel, attached to its stern, went down on the other side of the seamount.

I wonder: How did the *Santa Helena* meet its end? Did it crash into the rock and rebuff itself, only for brutal waves to drive it into the seamount again and again? Or was it impaled atop the spire, a mighty hole that sent it quickly to the bottom, alone there for some 350 years, until the *Victory*'s doomed visitation?

Again, I offer silent tribute to those who met their fate here, then fin onward to whatever fate lies waiting for me.

I round the seamount, swim toward the ledge under which the paddle wheel rests. Fifty feet below me, two dark figures poke around in the timbers that lie on the seafloor— Fiona McHugh and Michael Frazer. They don't see me.

I swim over the ledge and down to the sandy lip of the cavern. The rising sea has created a considerable surge. It intensifies as I near the ghostly remains of the paddle wheel. Tiny cyclones of sand and sediment swirl around the broken spokes. Purple sea fans sway back and forth with the upwellings. Broken bits of this and that flutter about like flakes in a snowdome.

I head toward the hub of the paddle wheel, grab hold of a spoke to fight off the outflow, gather new purchase as the surge flows in. I reach under the rusty nexus, fumble around with a hand, find nothing. The seaflow sucks me out. I hold on and wait. And when it sends me back in again, I reach behind the hub, put my hand on something made of metal. I root blindly, pry it loose and pull it free.

Had Teddy Schwartz not told me it was a replica, placed there only a few days earlier, I most surely would have believed I was holding something ancient. The silver reliquary in my hands is a ringer for the one in the sketch, its imperfections making it even more authentic. One arm of the Greek cross is broken off near the juncture. Another is badly battered. The whole piece is worn in a way that could only come from more than five hundred years under the sea. Or so it would appear to anyone who didn't know better.

I open the dive bag, stuff the faux reliquary inside. I swim out to the lip of the cavern and look down.

Fiona and Frazer have left the wreckage on the bottom and are finning upward, not twenty feet away. The sight of me startles both of them. Fiona grabs Frazer's arm. He windmills backward in alarm.

I see wide eyes behind their masks. I raise a hand, give them the OK sign. They recognize me and relax.

Frazer holds back while Fiona kicks and heads my way. She turns up her hands, questioning me. It's a "What the fuck?" moment.

I give her another OK sign, hold up the dive bag, and point to it. She reaches for it, wants to look inside. But I pull the bag away.

I make the hatchet sign: Back to the boat.

I roll away, kick, and angle upward. The two of them fall in behind.

81

I surface a few yards astern of *Miss Peg*. I look for Boggy on the boat. I don't see him. That's OK—part of our plan.

But now I recognize a gaping hole in that plan: I forgot to hang a ladder off *Miss Peg* so we could climb aboard.

For everything to fall into place, we all need to be on *Miss Peg*. That way, Boggy and I will have a slightly better chance of controlling the situation. But the sea is so rough, there's no way I can scramble over *Miss Peg*'s transom without getting beat all to hell.

A ladder hangs down from Frazer's boat. I paddle to it. I take off my fins, sling them onto the boat, then climb up the ladder. I slip out of my vest and rest it on the floor with the tank still attached.

Fiona is next up. I take her fins, give her a hand. As she reaches the top rung, a swell lifts the boat. She loses her grip and tumbles backward, narrowly missing Frazer on the way down.

"You OK?" I yell to her. Frazer climbs up the ladder and moves past me onto the boat, shrugging off gear as he goes.

Fiona coughs. She's swallowed water, but she's all right. She makes her way back to the ladder.

Frazer says, "You scared the hell out of us down there, you know that?"

He's smiling, playing it loose and easy. He moves to the

console. He finds his keys, unlocks a compartment, rummages around inside. Then he grabs a towel and starts drying off.

I don't say anything. I turn back to Fiona. She struggles to get a grip on the ladder, but it is banging against the transom, hard to hold. I lean down, try to give her a hand. Too far to reach.

I turn and look at Frazer. He watches me. The towel is draped over a hand now.

He says, "So what did you find down there?"

"See for yourself," I say.

I look down at Fiona. She's still having a hard time with the ladder.

I tell her, "Take off your vest, hand it up to me. That'll make it easier for you to climb."

Frazer puts down the towel and opens the dive bag. He pulls out the reliquary. He turns it over, admiring it, carefully, gently.

I say, "Is that what you've been looking for, Frazer?"

He doesn't say anything. He sets down the reliquary and picks up the towel. There's a gun underneath. He levels it at me.

He says, "How did you know where to find it?"

"Had a little inside information," I say.

"From who?"

"Teddy Schwartz. He's the one who made it."

"Made it? What are you talking about?"

"It's a fake."

Frazer looks at the reliquary, then back at me.

"I don't believe you," he says.

I shrug.

"Suit yourself. But if you'd looked around his boathouse a little more closely when you broke in, you'd have seen it on his workbench. You must have been in a big hurry, huh? You put the ice pick and the pliers in that pile of rags by the door. And then you got out of there."

Behind Frazer, I see movement in *Miss Peg*'s cabin. OK, Boggy. Now's the time. Frazer has laid down his hand. It's what we were waiting for. Rush him from behind.

But my glance gives it away. Frazer takes a step back from me, shoots a look at *Miss Peg*.

He says, "Who's with you?"

I don't answer him.

"Is there anyone else on that boat?"

"Yeah, Boggy is on it. He's got a rifle trained on you right now. Put down the gun."

Frazer shoots another look at *Miss Peg*.

"Yeah, right. I don't believe that either."

Still, he moves to the other side of his boat, all the better for keeping an eye on me and *Miss Peg* at the same time.

Down in the water, Fiona can't see what's going on.

She calls up, "Zack, are you going to come get my vest or what?"

I look at Frazer.

"I'm going to help her up, OK?"

He nods.

I turn my back to him as I move to the ladder, burn an image in my mind of exactly where he is—about fifteen feet away, a bit forward, near the port gunwale. I look down the ladder. Fiona holds the vest up to me. I reach for the steel tank that is strapped on the back, grab it by the K-valve on top. I adjust the weight in my hand, all forty pounds of it.

I raise up slowly, and then I pivot, grabbing the tank with both hands and hurling it across the boat at Frazer. It's a lousy shot, high and to the side. Frazer deflects it into the water.

And as I charge, I see him raise the pistol, fire . . .

82

've never been shot before, never even come close. And all I can think as the bullet strikes my left thigh and sends me spinning is: Thought it would hurt more than that.

I land facedown by the hatchway and as I roll onto my back I see Fiona come up the ladder. Frazer is on her in an instant, yanking her onto the boat, then shoving her toward me, keeping his gun trained on us.

"On the floor, next to him!" he shouts at Fiona.

Fiona looks down at me. A hand goes to her mouth.

"Omigod!"

She reaches for a towel, kneels beside me, and applies pressure to the wound. It's on the outside of my thigh, about halfway between my knee and hipbone. A small hole in the front, a bigger hole in the back. And a lot of ripped flesh in between. I don't think it got the bone. But blood, lots of blood. And now the hurt sets in.

Frazer looks down at us, smirks.

"It's not going to make any difference," he says. "A few minutes and you'll both be dead."

Fiona looks at me.

"He killed Ned?"

I nod.

She doesn't react. She ties off the towel around my thigh. Then finds another towel, hands it to me.

"Keep applying pressure," she says.

I take the towel from her, and as I do, she lunges for Frazer, going in low toward his knees. He steps back, kicks, and catches her in the jaw. She falls back, beside me.

Frazer waves the gun at Fiona.

"I want you to reach up under the console, get the roll of duct tape," he says.

Fiona doesn't move.

"Do it, bitch!"

Fiona moves to the console, finds the duct tape. Frazer waves the gun at me.

"Now help him get up on his feet," he says.

Fiona gets an arm around me, helps me stand. And now the pain in my thigh really sets in, throbbing, throbbing.

Frazer steps to the console, turns the key. The engines rumble and catch. He lets it run in neutral.

"Now get on the other boat," Frazer says.

"What for?"

"Just do it," he says.

He moves close to us now, prods the pistol into my back as Fiona helps me hobble toward the gunwales where the boats are lashed together. She steps onto *Miss Peg* first, then helps me aboard.

Frazer steps on behind us.

"Now sit him down in the captain's chair," Frazer says. "Lash the tape around him. Make it tight. Put it over his mouth, too."

Fiona does as she's told. As she does, I look in the cabin. No sign of Boggy.

When Fiona's done, Frazer checks the tape, makes sure it's tight, says: "OK, now you get in the other chair."

Fiona sits down. Frazer peels off some tape with his teeth. He slaps it onto her mouth and begins wrapping it around her with one hand, keeping the other on the gun.

When he's finished lashing her to the chair, Frazer looks at what's left of the duct tape. Not much. He tosses it into the cabin and backs toward the transom.

And as he does, the roll of duct tape sails out of the cabin, hits the floor, and skids to a stop at Frazer's feet.

Frazer looks at it in disbelief. He looks at the cabin.

"Who's in there?"

No answer.

"Come out. Now!"

No answer. No movement in the cabin.

Frazer takes a step toward the cabin. Then another, holding the gun with both hands in front of him.

As he nears the cabin—a gusher of white foam shoots out, spraying Frazer across the face. He lurches back and out comes Boggy, ramming forward with the fire extinguisher, knocking Frazer back.

I strain to see what's going on, but can't turn in the chair. Neither can Fiona.

They struggle at the aft of the boat, body crashing against body.

Then a shot. And another.

A splash—the sound of someone going into water.

Then three more shots.

A long moment.

Then Frazer's voice: "I got the son of a bitch."

83

Frazer moves within my line of vision. He stands by the gunwale, pistol aimed at the water. Then he moves aft again, to a point where I can't see him.

I look ahead. No other boats on the horizon.

We are pointing west. The sun is low now. No more than an hour until dark.

Three or four minutes go by. I hear Frazer pacing around the boat, presume he is looking for Boggy.

And then he says: "Well, I guess that's that, eh?"

I hear him rustling around in the transom. And then I smell the gas.

I don't have to see him to know what he's doing: The auxiliary motor's gas can. He's emptying it onto the boat.

Frazer steps forward. He looks at Fiona and me.

"Don't want it to go up in flames all at once," he says. "I need a few minutes running room."

He steps back aboard his boat, unlashes the lines. He reaches under the console, pulls out an emergency kit. He steps to the side of his boat, a flare gun in hand.

"At least you'll go out with a bang," he says.

Frazer aims the flare gun, fires. A small thud as the ball of sparks hits *Miss Peg*'s transom. And then a frightening whoosh as the gas ignites.

I feel the heat. The fire sizzles and feeds off itself. This is not going to take nearly as long as Frazer thought.

And sensing the same thing, Frazer guns the engines, throwing up a rooster-tail of water as his boat speeds away.

I turn, look at Fiona. I see terror in her eyes, the same terror I'm sure she sees in mine.

The heat grows more intense and I can see flames reflected by the windshield in front of me, a deadly orange dance that seems to have already consumed *Miss Peg*'s rear quarter. The air is heavy with the sickening smell of molten fiberglass.

I struggle against the duct tape and can see that Fiona is doing the same thing. But every move unleashes a new wave of pain from my thigh. I think: Maybe as the flames move closer they will catch the duct tape around my feet on fire and I can kick free . . .

Then I think: You'll be a crispy critter by the time that happens.

I look at Fiona. She struggles against her bindings, in full panic mode now. And just as I am ready to yield myself to the inevitable, the boat lists to port and I see Boggy pulling himself aboard near the bow.

He runs our way, one arm limp at his side, a bloody wound in the shoulder. And then he's beside us, yanking out drawers, finding a knife.

He cuts Fiona free first, shouts: "Grab the bench cushions. Jump!"

She leaps up and darts away.

As Boggy moves toward me, there's a new blast of heat from the rear of the boat. Above me, the cockpit roof begins to smolder. Along the gunwales, the stanchion lines are aflame.

The knife is dull. It catches and snags. Boggy throws it aside, ripping at the tape around my legs, pulling me free of the chair. My torso is still wrapped in tape as he lifts me onto his good shoulder and stumbles to the side of the boat.

The flames are everywhere, the heat so intense that it burns my eyes. We fall overboard. Boggy kicks us away from the boat, speaks to me: "It's OK, Zachary. Hold on. It's OK."

I begin to lose consciousness. Just as I give in to the blackness, there comes a final violent roar, and *Miss Peg* is no more.

84

Voices draw me out of the deep.

Fiona: "It's bleeding again. I can't seem to stop it."

Boggy: "Zachary is strong. He has much blood in him."

Fiona: "What about you?"

Boggy: "I am OK."

Fiona: "Here, let me see your shoulder."

Boggy: "It is OK, I am telling you."

Fiona: "Let me see."

I open my eyes. I am lying on a boat cushion atop a piece of *Miss Peg*'s transom. I can see the lettering under my arm. Boggy and Fiona are in the water, holding on.

I try to sit up.

"Easy," Fiona says. "Lie back down."

I lie down.

I say, "How long?"

"How long were you out?"

I nod.

"I don't know. Fifteen minutes maybe. Not long."

I turn my head. The sea is swallowing the last sliver of sun. The sky is tinged with streaks of red and purple.

"Oh, boy," I say. "Maybe we'll see the flash of green."

"No such thing," Fiona says.

"Like hell there's not," I say. "I've seen it twice. Once in

Grenada, once in Boca Grande. You were there both times, Boggy. You saw it. Tell her."

"Yes, Zachary. I saw it."

"It's real," I say. "Lights up the sky. When you see it, you know it."

We watch the sun. It disappears. We wait. No flash of green.

"Maybe another day," I say.

"I'll settle for that," Fiona says.

I shiver.

"It's cold," I say. "Really cold."

I catch the look between Boggy and Fiona.

"You think I'm dying," I say. "Don't you?"

"No, Guamikeni, you are not dying."

"You bet your ass I'm not."

I reach out for Boggy. He offers his hand.

"Thanks," I say.

He nods, says nothing.

"But let me ask you one thing." Boggy looks at me. "What the hell took you so long?"

Boggy starts to speak, but I cut him off.

"I mean, you could have done something sooner. Like right after Frazer pulled the gun. You could have done something then. He'd already revealed himself. We had him."

"But, Zachary, I thought he would shoot you."

"He did shoot me, dammit! And then, when we were getting on *Miss Peg,* before he wrapped us up in that goddamn duct tape, that would have been a perfectly good time to come barreling out of the cabin. Between the three of us, we could have taken him."

"His gun, it was aimed at Fiona. I thought maybe . . ."

"But no, you waited."

"I got shot, too, Zachary."

"I got shot worse," I say.

Fiona slams a hand on the float.

"Stop it, the two of you!" she says. "I think I see a boat."

Sure enough, there is a light to the west, moving across the water. Still far away, too far away to give any real hope.

We wait. I'm getting colder. I try not to shiver.

Fiona looks at me, says: "How did you know?"

"You mean about Frazer?" She nods. I say, "He was the point where all the lines came together. He knew Peach. He knew your brother. I figure he ambushed Ned while he was diving here. Frazer had spoken to him enough to know what Ned might find at Sock 'Em Dog, even if Ned didn't know that himself. But what cinched it was the soul-saver."

"How's that?"

"Polly was wearing it the day she and Ned went to Frazer's office to get the papers. I called her this afternoon and she told me about it. Said Frazer noticed the soul-saver, commented on it, and Polly told him that Ned had found it and given it to her. That's all Frazer really needed to know to give him an idea what Ned had found."

The boat is getting closer, still on course for us. We all watch it, none of us say anything. Might jinx it.

Fiona says, "And Frazer broke into Ned's house afterward?"

"Yeah. He tried to make it look like a burglary. Took all kinds of other things, but he was after the papers. Ned had filled them out, put the coordinates down. Frazer couldn't risk the papers falling into anyone else's hands, especially not until he'd had a chance to dive the site himself."

"He did a pretty good job of setting up Teddy Schwartz."

"And the Sangrento Mao, too. It was a double setup, really. Even if Teddy was able to clear himself, the police could still point a finger at Papi Ferreira and his bunch," I say. "Frazer thought he was well removed from any suspicion."

"So that day, when you came by the Oxford House, when Frazer and I were on our way to lunch, and we started talking about everything in front of him . . ."

"Saying that I didn't think Teddy did it. Or Ferreira either."

"Frazer panicked. Figured he had to make a move."

"That's what I'm thinking."

Fiona shakes her head.

"When he came by to get me this afternoon to go out in his boat, I told him we needed to call you, that you should go out with us. But he said he'd already called, said you were busy getting ready for that party."

"I never spoke to him."

"No kidding," Fiona says. "I was stupid, so stupid."

We are quiet for a moment. I am cold, really cold.

Boggy says, "The boat, it is coming."

A Q-beam sweeps the water, lights up the floating remains of *Miss Peg*. Boggy and Fiona wave and holler. The beam sweeps our way, locks on us, and holds.

The boat closes in. On the bow, I can see Bill Belleville holding the light.

"We're heading out for a night dive at Fish Rock . . ."

I can hear Belleville shouting orders to others on his boat. He kneels on the bow, shines the light on us.

"Shit, man," he says. "What happened to you?"

85

The next forty-eight hours are an opiate fog, voices drifting in and out, people coming and going, my mind unable to grasp what is real and what is not. It's a hazy netherworld, a crazy composite of flotsam and jetsam, random bits and pieces.

I dream that I am on a ship, a ship from long-gone days, with two tall masts and great billowy sails, a ship like the *Santa Helena*. Brewster Trimmingham is at the helm. He's dressed in full admiral's regalia—blue waistcoat, a sword in its sheath, the ridiculous sideways hat, and everything. Papi Ferreira is at his side, scanning the waters ahead with a spyglass. I'm on the bridge, too, and I keep telling them that we are on the wrong course, that we are headed straight to Sock 'Em Dog. They laugh me off, tell me to leave the navigation to them.

I go looking for Barbara. And suddenly I am on a fancy cruise ship and I need to find Barbara so I can get her off the ship before we crash into Sock 'Em Dog. I unfasten a lifeboat, lower it to the water. Aunt Trula and Polly, wearing white terrycloth robes, watch me from teak deck chairs. I tell them to get into the lifeboat. Aunt Trula looks at her watch.

"Not quite yet," she says. "Almost time for tea."

I run through the ship, looking for Barbara. Worley and Teddy Schwartz play blackjack in the casino. They are winning big. Fiona McHugh wears a glittery showgirl costume and is dancing on a stage. Janeen Hill applauds from her seat in the audience.

I head to my cabin, hoping to find Barbara there. Instead, there's a man sitting on our bed, a man with long gray hair and a scraggly beard. I cannot see his face, but in his hands he holds the Reliquarium de Fratres Crucis, shining and unblemished. He lifts it up and as he does I see that the man has no eyes.

"In Lisbon," he says. "I once was a goldsmith."

I leave the cabin, and there is Barbara watching me from the end of a long hall. She waves to me, calls out. I run to her. But no matter how fast I run, I cannot reach her. I yell to her: "Get to the lifeboat! Get to the lifeboat!"

And she is calling to me, calling to me . . .

"Zack. It's OK, Zack. I'm here."

I open my eyes. And Barbara is there. This is real. This is all so sweet and real.

She gives me water. I drink it.

"Just rest," she says. "I'm not going anywhere."

I drift off again. I sleep a deep and dreamless sleep. And when I wake up, Barbara is sitting in a chair by the hospital bed, a hand on my arm. Her eyes are closed.

I say, "Hey, baby."

She opens her eyes, blinks.

"Hey," she says. She squeezes my arm, then kisses my forehead. "Good to see you again."

I look out the window. It's dark outside.

"How long?"

"Two days," Barbara says. "You lost a lot of blood, Zack. An hour longer and you wouldn't have made it."

I try to sit up, reach for my leg. It's a mound of gauze with plastic tubes hooked up to it.

"Don't," Barbara says, easing me back. "It's going to be OK. They think they've stopped the infection."

"What about Boggy?"

Barbara smiles.

"They released him this afternoon. He's back at Aunt Trula's. He's fine."

I lay there, trying to reassemble the pieces, moving backward: Belleville's boat, floating in the water, *Miss Peg* going down in flames . . .

I say, "What about Michael Frazer?"

Barbara shakes her head.

"The police have yet to find him," she says. "Inspector Worley has been calling, wanting to see you. I told him maybe tomorrow."

"Yes," I say. "Maybe tomorrow."

And then I'm asleep again.

86

We're baffled, totally baffled. We don't know where Frazer is."

Inspector Worley sits by my bed. Barbara is in the room with us. I'm feeling pretty good. There are fewer tubes running in and out of my leg.

I say, "Did you find his boat?"

"Oh yeah, we found it. Tied up at the marina he uses. His car was still parked in the parking lot. It's like he just vanished."

"Could he have flown out of here before you threw out the net for him?"

Worley shakes his head.

"Not a chance. By the time he reached shore, it would have been seven P.M. at the earliest. There wasn't another flight until ten P.M. and we had everything locked down by then. We've checked the private carriers. Nothing there, either."

"Boats?"

"We thought maybe he could have snuck onto one of the cruise ships, but there wasn't a departure until yesterday and he definitely wasn't on it. We swept it, had every passenger out on the deck," Worley says. "Checked the commercial ships, too. Nothing."

"Think he might have someone helping him? Someone who's hiding him here in Bermuda?"

"That's what we're working on at this point. His face is all over the newspapers, on TV. There's a hundred-thousand-dollar reward for information leading to his arrest. If he's still here, we'll shake him loose," Worley says. "We've questioned everyone he's known to have associated with, including his coworkers."

I tell Worley about the young man I'd seen on Frazer's boat, the one who followed Boggy and me in the blue Toyota.

"We talked to him," Worley says. "Nestor Ferreira. He came up clean."

Worley sees the look on my face.

"Yeah, as in Papi Ferreira," Worley says. "Nestor is Papi's grandson. Antoni Ferreira, Papi's only child, that was Nestor's dad."

I don't say anything.

Worley says, "You say it was Nestor Ferreira who was following you?"

"I think so. Sure looked like him."

Worley makes a note on a pad.

"We'll talk to him again. See what he has to say about that." Worley studies me. "By the way, that business you had with Papi Ferreira, you never told me what it was."

I look at Barbara.

I say, "Aunt Trula's party the other night—how did it turn out?"

Barbara looks at Worley, then back to me. She knows I'm dodging his question.

"Why, it turned out just fine, Zack, everything considered. I mean, I was a perfect mess, not knowing where you were. But the food, the music, the company—everything was splendid. And the palm trees looked magnificent. Everyone commented on them. It went on and on and on, with people standing up and offering toasts to Titi. And then when Sir Teddy showed up . . ."

"Teddy made it to the party?"

"Why, yes," Barbara says. "He arrived there shortly before midnight."

She cuts her eyes at Worley.

Worley says, "The only reason he made it there was because I drove him there. Fiona McHugh called the moment she got ashore, told me what had happened. And I had Sir Teddy released then and there. He was insistent upon going to that party. So I drove him."

Worley looks at me.

He says, "It was a nice party, Chasteen. A very nice party. I even drank some champagne. I never drink champagne." He stops. "What's your business with Ferreira, Chasteen?"

"It's got nothing to do with Frazer."

"You sure of that?"

"Yeah, I'm sure."

"This business, you done with it?"

"Almost," I say. "Still some loose ends to wrap up."

"You plan on wrapping them up pretty damn soon?"

I nod.

"I could use your help," I say.

"Oh, really? You want me to help you with some business, only you won't tell me what that business is? And it involves Papi Ferreira and we all know what business he is in."

"Yeah, that's pretty much it," I say.

"And I should do this, why?" says Worley.

"Because that's just the kind of guy you are. Helpful."

"Fuck you," says Worley. He looks at Barbara. "Excuse me."

She waves it off.

I say, "I need you to help me find someone."

"Who would that be?" says Worley.

"A guy named Brewster Trimmingham."

87

By the next day, I'm able to maneuver to the bathroom all on my own. The day after that, I'm navigating the halls of King Edward Hospital, making a complete nuisance of myself. And the day after that, they set me free.

Back at Cutfoot Estate, Aunt Trula instructs her staff that my every wish is their command. After almost a week in the hospital, I'm fairly ravenous. Still, I try not to take advantage of Aunt Trula's hospitality. I limit myself to four meals a day. No cocktails until five.

People come to see me. And, considering the alternative, it's nice to be seen.

Fiona McHugh drops by on the morning she is to fly home to Australia. She has spent the previous few days being interviewed by Janeen Hill.

"She's going forward with the book?"

"So it appears," Fiona says. "Her agent is even more keen on it now than before. He says that with Michael Frazer still missing and an international search for him now under way, it gives the story legs."

"Legs, huh?"

"Janeen's words, not mine," says Fiona. "Where do you think Frazer is, Zack?"

I don't say anything. She looks at me, says: "Do you know something you aren't telling me?"

"Not yet," I say.

"What's that supposed to mean?"

"It means, if I find out something, then you will know it, too."

"Fair enough," she says.

She gives me a kiss and says good-bye.

Aunt Trula and Teddy Schwartz join me for lunch. I've asked the kitchen staff to re-create the Onion's version of fish stew. They manage to do it even better.

"I'm sorry about *Miss Peg*," I tell Teddy. "I know how much she meant to you."

"Hard means to a good end," he says. "I'm forever in your debt."

"Yeah, you are. Big time." I smile. "That's why I have a proposition for you."

"What's that?" asks Teddy.

I look at Aunt Trula.

"Would you mind?" I say.

She responds with more graciousness than I would have expected.

"No, not at all," she says, getting up from the table. "I'll leave you to your men's talk."

When she's gone, I lay out my proposition.

Teddy's eyes light up. He says, "I'd be delighted, consider it an honor."

"How long do you think it will take?"

"A month maybe, certainly no longer."

"Perfect," I say.

Inspector Worley shows up while I'm having a midafternoon snack: Fish-and-chips and a Heineken. I can't talk him into food, but he sits down to drink a beer with me.

"That fellow you were looking for . . ."

"Brewster Trimmingham?"

"Yeah," Worley says. "He turned up."

I wait. Worley looks at his notepad.

"After leaving King Edward Hospital nine days ago, he took a cab to Bermuda International. He boarded U.S. Airways Flight eight thirteen for Washington, D.C., arriving at ten fifteen A.M. He then took Piedmont Airlines Flight ten twenty-four for Charlottesville, Virginia, arriving at . . ."

"He went to see his wife."

"Whatever you say." Worley rips a sheet off the notepad, hands it to me. "That's the address and the phone number."

"Thanks," I say.

"You owe me."

I don't say anything.

Worley says, "Finally talked to Nestor Ferreira. Turns out he went down to Miami for a few days. Just got back."

"What did Nestor have to say?"

"He said you must have been mistaken. It wasn't him in that blue Toyota. Says he was out fishing with his uncle that day."

"Well, then, I must have been mistaken."

Worley looks at me. I look at him. He gets up.

"You heading home soon?" he asks.

"Day after tomorrow," I say.

"Plan on coming back?"

"I'd say there's a very high probability of that."

He sticks out a hand. I shake it.

"Give me some warning," he says.

88

At fiveish, Barbara joins me on the terrace. I'm sipping a glass of Gosling's neat. She opens a bottled water.

"You've had a busy day," she says.

"Not over yet. Daniel Denton called to say he needed to speak with me. He should have been here already."

"What's he need to speak with you about?"

"No idea," I say. "It seemed urgent. But then, he's a lawyer. Everything they do is urgent. To them."

Fifteen minutes later, Denton shows up. I ask him if he wants a drink.

"I think not," he says.

He has brought along a manila folder. It sits on the table in front of him. He looks at it. Then he looks at Barbara.

"If you don't mind, Ms. Pickering, I have a matter I'd like to discuss with Mr. Chasteen," he says. "A business matter."

Barbara starts to get up from her chair. I stop her.

"She knows my business, Denton," I say. "Start talking."

Denton swallows. He opens the folder, then closes it. He gives me a smile. His face does not wear it well.

"Well, I suppose I should first begin by offering my most sincere and deepest apologies, along with those of my associate, Mr. Urban, for the reception we gave you when you visited our office the other day. We acted rudely and ungentlemanly, and for that . . ."

"Sugar kisses on a cow's ass," I interrupt.

"Excuse me?"

"Something my grandfather used to say. You're just sweet-talking me to set me up for something else. You didn't come here to apologize."

"Why, Mr. Chasteen, I . . ."

"What's in the folder?" I say.

Denton takes a deep breath.

He says, "A certain client of ours, who wishes to remain anonymous, has authorized us to make an offer on his behalf for your holdings at Governor's Pointe."

"What's his offer?"

Denton slides the folder to me. I open it, look at the numbers.

"That's exactly what Brewster Trimmingham paid for those units," I say.

"Yes, we thought it was a fair offer, considering . . ."

"Considering what?"

"Considering the manner in which you obtained the property."

I turn to Barbara.

"Would you mind doing me a favor?"

"I'd be delighted. What is it?"

"Go find a phone book."

"A phone book?"

"Yes, I want to look up the number of the Bermuda Bar Association. I need to make a call."

"Now, listen here," Denton sputters.

"No, you listen, Denton. I'm no legal eagle, but something tells me it's not exactly kosher for an attorney to represent a client in one matter and then use information obtained through that representation to leverage against the same client in another matter. Am I wrong?"

Denton glares at me.

"I am authorized to negotiate," he says.

"Negotiate away," I say.

Denton pulls a pen from his pocket, takes back the folder. He scribbles something on the papers, then pushes the folder back to me. I look at it.

"That's a little better," I say.

"No, that is considerably better, Mr. Chasteen. I would urge you to . . ."

"I'll think about it," I say. "Thanks for dropping by. I'll get back to you in a couple of weeks."

"Really, Mr. Chasteen. I would urge you to take the offer that is on the table. My client has given us an extremely tight timetable under which to . . ."

"Anxious, is he?"

"Yes, quite."

"In that case, may I?" I say, pointing to his pen. He hands it to me.

I scribble some numbers of my own. I pass the folder back to him. He looks at it. His mouth drops.

"Let me think out loud here while you're digesting those numbers, Denton. See, I'm thinking that your law firm, while highly reputable and certainly beyond reproach, is, after all, a Bermuda law firm and, therefore, from time to time, does represent certain clients who need to move large amounts of money in very hasty fashion with not a lot of questions asked. That's OK. Comes with the turf. And, you know, I don't really have a problem with that.

"What I do have a problem with, is you coming here with your apologies and your slick smile, thinking that you can lowball me based on knowledge obtained by our previous relationship, then turn around and flip those properties at Governor's Pointe for a hell of a lot more than you are offering to pay me."

Denton doesn't say anything.

I say, "Look at those numbers again, Denton. And tell me the truth, is this client of yours prepared to pay you more than that for those goddamn condos?"

Denton doesn't say anything.

I turn to Barbara.

"I think there's a phone book on that stand in the kitchen," I say.

"No, wait," Denton says. He looks at me. "I think we have some wiggle room."

"Well, wiggle away, Denton. Those are the numbers. Take them or leave them."

I grab the folder. I flip through the papers. I find the bottom line. I hand Denton his pen.

I say, "You need to sign right there."

89

We've booked a late afternoon flight back to Florida. It gives me plenty of time to do what I need to do.

Boggy goes with me. Barbara doesn't really like the idea of me driving the Morris Minor, but I tell her that working the clutch will be good therapy. I'm going to miss that car.

We go to Richfield Bank. I meet with Mr. Bunson and Mr. Highsmith.

"The funds have arrived from Mr. Denton," Mr. Bunson says.

"Very good," I say. "There will be more after the closing."

"We have done as you instructed," says Mr. Highsmith.

He hands me a cloth money bag. It's pretty hefty. I look inside. I don't bother to count it. I get up.

"Pleasure doing business with you," I say.

Boggy and I don't talk much on the drive to Flatts Village. When we get to Ferreira Grocery, we park near the tree where men play dominoes. Paul Andrade is there. So are some of the others.

Andrade gets up when he sees us.

"Don't bother," I say. "We know the way."

Andrade sits backs down.

We walk into the store. The same middle-aged woman sits behind the counter reading a magazine. She barely gives us a glance.

I knock on the door to the back room, hear Papi Ferreira say: "Yes, come in."

We step inside. Ferreira sits behind his desk, smoking a cigar. Nestor Ferreira sits in a chair across from him. There are plates on the desk, remains of a recent meal. Music plays from the old stereo—fado.

Ferreira opens his arms in greeting, smiles.

"My grandson and I were enjoying a late breakfast together," he says. He looks at Nestor. "The music."

Nestor steps to the stereo, switches it off.

"Please, sit," says Ferreira. There are only two chairs. Boggy and I take them.

Nestor leans against the wall, watching us. He's a good-looking guy, no more than twenty-four or twenty-five. Sad brown eyes, long dark hair.

I take the money bag, put it down in the middle of Ferreira's desk.

"That's yours," I say. "Eighty thousand dollars."

Ferreira looks at it. He leans back in his chair, smokes his cigar. He looks at me.

"You are an honorable man," he says.

"I have my moments," I say.

Ferreira smiles.

"I, too, am an honorable man," Ferreira says. He reaches for the money bag, pushes it across the table to me. "That is why I cannot accept this."

"Why not?"

Ferreira shrugs.

"You have paid your debt to me," he says.

I look at Nestor. His face shows nothing. I look at Ferreira.

"Tell me how it happened," I say.

"It is not necessary," Ferreira says.

"Yeah, it is. It is something I need to know." I look at Nestor. "That was you in the Toyota, wasn't it?"

Nestor says nothing. He looks at his grandfather.

Ferreira says, "When you came here before, you said that if I wanted my money then I should help you. So, I asked

Nestor to keep an eye on you, should you require my assistance."

"Go on," I say.

"Nestor is good at keeping an eye on people," Ferreira says.

"Did he keep an eye on Michael Frazer?"

Ferreira puffs on his cigar, flicks ashes on the floor.

"I thought it would be a good job for him, yes. I talked to some people. He got the job." Ferreira looks at Nestor. "You liked that job, didn't you?"

Nestor nods.

Ferreira says, "Nestor, he grew suspicious that morning. Frazer called him very early, told him that he could take off the next few days. A free vacation. That was very much not like Frazer. So Nestor, he followed Frazer. Saw him get the woman . . ."

"Fiona McHugh."

"Saw him take her to the boat. And that is when he decided to follow you," Ferreira says. "He saw you go to Teddy Schwartz's house. Saw you leave on his boat."

"And that is when the two of you decided to go fishing?"

"There were many of us who went fishing that day. The sea it is big. Many boats were needed," says Ferreira. "I must apologize to you."

"Why is that?"

"We saw the explosion, the fire that took the boat of Teddy Schwartz. We were not far away. We could have come to help you. But instead . . ."

"You went after Michael Frazer."

Ferreira nods.

"We were three boats. Three good, fast boats. He had little chance."

I think about it.

I say, "But how did you know?"

"Know what?"

"Know that Frazer was after the reliquary?"

Ferreira looks at his grandson, nods.

Nestor says: "Frazer was a man obsessed. His books, his

papers—they were all about the Reliquarium de Fratres Crucis. He was writing his own book. I saw the pages in his desk. And that day when the young man and his girlfriend came into the office . . ."

"Ned McHugh?"

"Yes, the one who died," says Nestor. "After they left, Frazer was very agitated. The paperwork, he made it very difficult for Ned McHugh. The young man, he kept coming back and each time Frazer would tell him: 'You must be more precise. You must tell where this site is exactly.' And that is how I knew. There is nothing else that would have made him like that."

There is a long silence. Then Ferreira says: "When finally we caught him on his boat, when finally we saw the blessed reliquary, he tried to tell us it was not real. He said it was a fake." Ferreira stubs out his cigar. "It was over soon after that. Nestor returned his boat to the marina."

"And the reliquary?" I ask. "What will happen to it?"

Ferreira smiles.

"It will go home, to Portugal, to a place of honor. Finally, after all these years."

90

It's a fine May morning and I'm standing on the dock behind my house in LaDonna, cast net poised and ready to sling. Mullet are schooling with the flood tide. I've every intention of filling my smoker with a goodly number of them.

About forty feet out, dorsal fins slice Vs in the water. It's well beyond my net-throwing range.

I wait.

A mosquito lands on my ankle. I shake my leg. It flies away.

The mullet move in—thirty feet and closing.

The boathouse phone rings.

I finger the monofilament, adjust the balance of weight on my shoulder. These mullet are skittish. As soon as the net touches water they'll scatter. It will take a good spread to haul them in.

The phone rings.

More mosquitoes find me. I shake both legs, do a little dance. Can't set down the net to slap them.

The phone rings.

Twenty-five feet . . . twenty feet . . . come to Poppa, come to Poppa. I can see their big googly-eyed, silver heads now, swimming right at the surface, just where you want them to be.

I rear back, get ready to let it fly . . .

"Yo, Zachary!"

Stutter-step . . . lead weights snag on my shirtsleeve, the net collapses in midarc, goes kerplunk in the water.

I turn around. Boggy stands in the door of my office. He holds up the phone.

"For you," he says.

I haul in the net. Nothing to offer but oyster shells. I leave it in a heap and walk to the boathouse.

Boggy holds out the phone.

I say, "You couldn't just let it ring like we usually do?"

Boggy shrugs.

"The phone," he says, "it told me to answer."

"Get a grip."

I grab the phone.

"Zack Chasteen."

A man's voice: "Who is Fiona McHugh?"

"What? Who is this?"

"I said, who the hell is Fiona McHugh?"

As I try to place the voice, Boggy walks out to the end of the dock. He picks up the net, shakes loose the oyster shells.

And then it clicks.

"That you, Trimmingham?"

"Yes, it's me. And I am sitting here in my office looking at a thank-you note from someone by the name of Fiona McHugh."

"You back in Bermuda?"

"I am." A cough on his end. "We got back together, my wife and I."

"Nice to hear."

"Yeah," he says. "So who is Fiona McHugh? I got this thank-you note from her. The letterhead says 'Ned McHugh Memorial Foundation.' The trustees are listed in the margin. I saw you were one of them."

So I tell him the story of Ned McHugh. And I tell him how Fiona started a foundation to honor her brother.

"It awards scholarships to students who want to study marine archaeology," I say. "I made a donation in your name."

"Oh, really? How much?"

"Forty thousand dollars."

Silence from Trimmingham's end.

On the dock, Boggy ties the cast-net line to his wrist. He lifts the net, folds the top half over his shoulder, studies the water.

I say, "If it helps, I gave forty thousand dollars, too. Eighty thousand dollars total. What we owed Papi Ferreira. I paid him off in trade."

Trimmingham doesn't ask for details, not that I'd tell him.

He says, "The condos. At Governor's Pointe. You sold them?"

"I did."

"I don't want to know how much you got for them, do I?"

"No, Brewster, you really don't."

Another long pause on his end.

Boggy tosses the cast net—a perfect spread. He hauls it in, shakes it open. A dozen mullet flop around on the dock.

"You know," says Trimmingham, "I was lying there in that hospital bed and thought: OK, this is it. Now or never, you've got to pull it together. So I got out of there, got back with Sally. I'm making a clean start of things."

"Clean starts are good."

"Yeah, they are," he says. "And I was going to thank you for it, but jeez, forty thousand dollars? That stings."

"What about your car?"

"What about it?"

"I washed it, waxed it, left it with a full tank of gas."

A pause on his end, then: "Thanks, Chasteen."

91

By the time Barbara gets home that evening it's eight o'clock and I've got everything ready. Table set, candles lit, Andrea Bocelli on the stereo. A tad hokey, but romantic as all get-out. The steaks are warming to room temperature, au poivre in waiting.

We start with appetizers on the front porch—smoked mullet dip, Ritz crackers. A bottle of Schramsberg in the ice bucket.

Barbara scoops up dip while I pop the champagne.

"Just the tiniest bit for me," she says.

"But it's a special occasion."

"I know."

I look at her.

"What do you mean you know? It was supposed to be a surprise."

"It was." She smiles. She raises her glass. "I'm pregnant."

Five minutes later, we've calmed down. Hugs and kisses and tears . . .

And more champagne. For me anyway. After a tiny sip to toast, Barbara switches to bottled water. Men definitely get the better end of the whole pregnancy deal. Maybe that's why women get to live longer.

"So how far along?"

"About a month," she says.

"That would have made it . . ."

"I'm thinking the night we had dinner at Mid Ocean Club."

"A nice night."

"Yes," she says. "It was."

"So that would make it . . ."

"January," she says. "A January baby."

"Super Bowl Sunday."

"Not if I have anything to do with it."

"I'll settle for the AFC championship," I say. "And if by some miracle the Fish are in it, I'll take it as a sign."

"Speaking of signs . . ." Barbara shakes her head. "This is rather spooky."

"What is?"

"Boggy," she says. "I started thinking about it after I left the doctor's office this afternoon. Remember when we flew into Bermuda, how he went into one of his trances there on the tarmac? You remember what he said?"

"Something about the palm trees, wasn't it?"

"That's what we thought at the time. I mean, it certainly seemed like it. He said: 'That which is planted here will grow strong.'"

I look at her. She looks at me.

We sit back on the couch, lean on each other. I finish my champagne, pour a little more.

A few minutes later . . .

"Girls' names," says Barbara.

"Agnes, Chloe, and Gert."

She looks at me.

"You will have no input on names," she says.

"Boys'—Hansel, Ike, and Mort."

"Nor will you come anywhere near the birth certificate."

She scoops up more mullet dip.

"I'm hungry," she says.

"That's my line."

She laughs, gives me a kiss.

"We have so much to talk about," she says.

"You only know the half of it."

I reach for my pocket. The ring arrived earlier in the day. Wrapped in bubble tape. Teddy Schwartz enclosed a note, apologizing for not having a proper tiny box.

I go down on a knee. I take Barbara's hand. I put the ring on her finger.

"Marry me," I say.

92

It's a June wedding. Not a lot of planning needed, not a lot of family with which to contend. Just a few friends—Stephie Plank, Barbara's right-hand woman at *Tropics* and maid of honor; Robbie Greig, my pal from Minorca Beach Marina; a couple of former Gator teammates—Mac Steen and Larry-Bud Meyer; and Boggy. He's my best man.

We descend upon Bermuda for a long and festive weekend. Aunt Trula graciously puts us up. And Teddy Schwartz happily agrees to give the bride away.

The wedding takes place in the morning at the little chapel at Graydon Reserve. Sister Kate and Sister Eunice have been working on a special arrangement of Corinthians 1:13, just for the occasion. I tell them they oughta cut a CD. They could give Andrea Bocelli a run for his money.

One of the monks, a big, bearded fellow named Boyd, appears in the doorway with bagpipes and offers a tune while we await Barbara's entrance.

The chapel is so small that, standing by the altar, I'm right next to the front pew where Aunt Trula sits. She tugs on my pant leg. I bend down.

"That song," she says. "Do you by any chance know its name?"

"Yes, Barbara and I picked it out," I say. "It's 'The Cradle Song.'"

"How lovely," Aunt Trula says.

Boyd is soon piping "The Irish Wedding Song" and Barbara enters the chapel on Teddy's arm. She's never looked more beautiful.

It's an Anglican service. No mass, just the basics. We say the vows, we exchange the rings—Teddy made them, too—and then we kiss the kiss. Eleven minutes and we're out the door as Boyd pipes "She Walks Through the Fair."

We mill around outside, enjoying the breeze off the bay. J.J. and another driver arrive with vans to take us to Mid Ocean Club for the reception.

As everyone starts to pile in, I notice that Teddy Schwartz has wandered off to the cemetery behind the chapel. I step over to join him.

He stands looking down at a granite headstone. It's inlaid with pieces of gold and silver. A glass cutout encases a worn piece of wood, no bigger than a paperback book.

The name on the headstone: "Margaret Schwartz."

Teddy looks at me. He smiles. He raises a hand—touches his forehead, his chest, left shoulder, right.

He makes the sign of the cross.

Acknowledgments

Under ideal circumstances, and with unlimited resources, I would have taken up residence in Bermuda while I wrote this book, enjoying a daily dosage of Gosling's while gazing upon the gorgeous waters. Sadly, I was limited to a brief research trip and then had to rely on a number of Bermudians to do some of my legwork for me.

I am most grateful to Rosemary Jones, acting curator of the Bermuda Maritime Museum, for her cheerful willingness to answer my out-of-the-blue questions on topics that ran the gamut from the Hamilton bar scene to local lingo. It was Rosemary who first suggested that a mystery set in Bermuda absolutely had to involve shipwrecks, and I thank her for steering me in that direction. Dr. Edward C. Harris, executive director of the maritime museum, also answered numerous inquiries.

Keith A. Forbes, the proprietor of www.bermuda-online .org, proved an invaluable resource about all things Bermudian and went out of his way in responding to my queries on everything from burials at sea to the availability of dynamite in Bermuda. His website is a treasure trove of information and much recommended to anyone seeking more background about Bermuda.

Thanks, too, to Bryan Mewett, general manager of the Mid Ocean Club, who shared the history and lore of that illustrious institution.

Even though I took two years of Latin in high school, none of it stuck, and Matt Ramsby, of the Hammond School in Columbia, South Carolina, was a translator par excellence.

And, just as he did with *Jamaica Me Dead,* forensic accountant Bill Cuthill, of Maitland, Florida, was a most astute guide through the gnarly world of offshore banking and money laundering.

To all, my deepest thanks . . .

*Keep reading for an excerpt
from Bob Morris's next mystery*

DEAD AHEAD

Coming soon in hardcover from St. Martin's Minotaur

1

**Thursday
Bon Voyage**

There's something creepy about a 75-year-old woman with a boob job."

Barbara Pickering lasered in on the bejeweled matron sitting at the table next to ours.

"It's like someone erected a pup tent on her chest," she said.

"Maybe she got them when she was 60. That would make it slightly less creepy."

"No, I'm betting those are brand new. Bought just for this cruise."

"Safety measure," I said. "The ship goes down, she can use them as flotation devices."

We were two hours out of port aboard the *Golden Seas*, chugging across the Gulf Stream, Miami just an insolent glow on the pistol butt of Florida.

It was the inaugural voyage of the *Golden Seas*, a 420-foot gem of a vessel that had been hailed as the "most exclusive cruise ship in the world." Of course, the person who had done most of the hailing was the ship's owner, Heissam Jebailey, known better as just Sam, a Florida gazillionaire who had spent a reputed $500 million building the *Golden Seas* and outfitting it in a fashion befitting the New Gilded Era.

Each plush suite was a customized vision from one of the world's top interior designers. Celebrity chefs presided over the ship's three restaurants. And passengers—only 100 at maximum occupancy, with 125 crew—enjoyed free-flowing Krug Grand Cuvee, small mountains of Persian caviar and the gracious service of private butlers.

So, yes, nabbing a spot on the guest list for the ship's maiden voyage—all Barbara's doing—was quite the coup.

The bon voyage bash was in full swing. Much popping of champagne corks, much nibbling from long silver trays offered by tuxedoed waiters, much merry buzz from the passengers gathered on the main deck.

All in all, a pretty swank crowd. Not that I was much good at recognizing A-list types. That was Barbara's job.

She pointed out an actor or two or three. A fashion model who had just married a tennis star. A film director chatting up a brand-name heiress. A famous lawyer, a famous artist, a famous somebody else. And a scattering of corporate tycoons who, even though the suggested attire for the evening was something called "casual elegant," had shown up in suits anyway. Some guys are just like that.

Pup Tent stood. She strolled past our table. Everything about her—eyes, cheekbones, boobs, butt—defied gravity.

"Really," Barbara said. "One shouldn't be terrified of a tiny bit of sag. It's only natural."

I looked at Barbara. More specifically, I looked at her breasts.

"I like natural," I said.

Barbara smiled. She sat up straight, all the better for me to admire her.

"And what is your position on sag?"

I observed her breasts some more. Lately, there had been an increasing amount of them to observe.

"With you, it is not a matter of sag."

"What would you call it then?"

"I would call it fullness. I would call it abundance. I would call it plentitude."

"And I would call you quite full of it." She stroked my cheek. "But in the best possible way."

The band was one of those cruise-ship ensembles that can play just about anything and, in the process, suck the soul right out of it. They started in on "What a Wonderful World." The lead singer was no Satchmo. Didn't really make any difference. It's one of those songs that no matter how bad the band plays it, you want to reach out and hold the one you love.

Barbara took my hand.

"Let's dance," she said.

We were the first couple on the floor. I held Barbara close. Well, as close as the situation would allow. Dancing cheek-to-cheek was out of the question. But belly-to-belly worked just fine.

Barbara flinched.

"Ooh," she said, "Did you feel Critter kick?"

"I did," I said. "Must like the oldie-goldies."

Another kick. And then another.

"Critter's dancing," said Barbara.

"A regular Rockette's chorus line."

"Which would indicate a girl."

"Not necessarily so," I said. "Boys can grow up to dance in chorus lines."

"And that wouldn't bother you?"

"What?"

"To have a son who danced in a chorus line?"

"Not in the least," I said. "However Critter comes out is fine by me."

"Me, too."

The band kept playing songs we liked, so we kept dancing. I could waltz through hell with Barbara Pickering and it would be just fine with me.

Truth was, being on a cruise ship, even the world's most luxurious one, came pretty close to my vision of hell. For Barbara, it was just another day at work. She is the owner/publisher of *Tropics*, the best travel magazine in the world. Not that I'm prejudiced in such matters. But such is her standing in the business that she was on the very short list of media types invited to join the *Golden Seas* on its maiden voyage.

I'm Barbara's husband, her chattel and helpmate. I was along for the ride.

My name is Zack Chasteen. And my resume would include abundant use of the word "former." I am a former football player (Florida Gators, Miami Dolphins, blew out a knee), a former inmate of federal prison (subsequently pardoned on all counts) and a former charter captain/fishing guide/dive-boat operator (gave it up when I decided that trying to make money on the water was ruining my love for it).

Nowadays, I am owner and head flunky of Chasteen's Palm Tree Nursery in LaDonna, Florida. I grow and sell rare specimen palms. It's a business I inherited from my grandfather, and it includes thirty-some-odd acres along Redfish Lagoon, just south of Minorca Beach, where I make my home.

Let me rephrase that. It's where Barbara and I make *our* home. I'm still enough of a newlywed that the whole collective pronoun thing throws me for a loop sometimes.

In any event, on the evening the *Golden Seas* set out from Miami, bound for ports unknown, Barbara and I were celebrating our six-month anniversary. And she was roughly eight months pregnant. If that upsets your sensibilities, I have three words: Get a grip.

The band segued into "Come Away With Me." The lead singer was no Nora Jones either. But I gave him points for singing a song that's typically sung by a woman. Like Lyle Lovett doing "Stand By Your Man."

"I'm glad we came," Barbara said.

"Me, too."

"You're just saying that. You hate the idea of being on a cruise ship."

"I don't hate the idea of being on a cruise ship with you."

"Good save," Barbara said, settling back into my arms. "Just think, we're almost parents."

"Nervous?"

"More like anxious."

"Anxious in the sense of not wanting anything to go wrong? Or just wishing Critter would hurry up and get here?"

"Mostly hurry up and get here. But some of the other, too."

"You've just got the pre-game jitters."

"Oh, do I now?"

"I used to throw up before every game. Just like being pregnant."

"Mmm, yes, just like it in every way."

"Why I always asked to be on the kickoff team. Get in a good lick, lay somebody low, and the jitters would be gone."

Barbara looked up at me.

"Are you seriously trying to draw an analogy between your experiences playing football and mine of giving birth to our child?"

"In my own feeble way."

"You used to wear a helmet, right?"

"I did."

"So try passing that."

"You're not talking forward pass here, are you?"

"No, I'm talking push-push, squeeze-squeeze, out the bottom."

"Thanks for sharing that imagery."

"What's mine is thine," said Barbara.

2

The killing started on Deck One, the lower level of the engine room, when the man the others called Trini pulled the SAR-21 from its hiding place and opened fire on the chief engineer and the junior chief as they made their evening rounds.

Trini wore protective earmuffs under his hard hat, like the rest of the engine crew. Still, the rifle shots were louder, much louder, than he'd expected.

The first five shots hit their targets. The next five went high and wide. Then Trini took a breath, lowered the rifle and triggered the last shots home.

The impact blew the chief engineer and the junior chief backward, over the catwalk rail and onto a boiler. Their bodies sizzled on the hot metal, sending up little puffs of smoke before sliding to the slick gray floor. The floor had been mopped just an hour or so before, the job completed at 8:30 p.m. to be exact. Trini knew because he had done the mopping.

Three other crewmen were on the catwalk, near the control room door, guys who worked side-by-side with Trini. They froze as Trini wheeled around on them. Nowhere they could go, nothing they could do.

One of them, Wendell, accent on the Dell, had grown up

in Port-of-Spain, just like Trini. Hard worker, Wendell. Another veteran of the cruise lines. Put in his shift in the engine room, then played steel pan in ship bands when they wanted to give it an island flair, playing crap like "Hot, Hot, Hot" and "Day-O," not soca like Wendell preferred. Wendell, a good Christian man. Had just bought a house up in the hills by Tunapuna, down the road from the monastery where the monks kept bees and sold honey from a store by their chapel. A wife and two little kids. Had just visited them before signing on with the Golden Seas. Brought Trini a jar of honey.

"A sweet taste of home," he'd said.

Trini shot Wendell first. Then he shot the other two, adrenaline pumping, pumping so hard that before Trini could back off he had emptied the 30-shot clip.

And to think he had been skeptical about the SARs, had worried they might not work, had worried over so many things.

No time for that now.

Trini stepped over the bodies, glancing into the engine control room. It was empty, the door secure. Plexiglass walls enclosed the room, and Trini could see the bank of monitors mounted near the ceiling, their screens showing nothing but fuzzy gray static.

One less thing to worry about.

Sonny had come through. Sonny, the chunky Korean kid who was the ship's entire I.T. department. He had disabled the network of closed-circuit cameras placed throughout the ship, then phoned the bridge, telling the watch officers it was just a minor glitch, something he'd fix in a hurry. No reason they wouldn't buy it. They bought everything Sonny told them.

Now Sonny was on his way to Deck Eight where he would climb a ladder to the roof above the Observation Room and disconnect the two satellite dishes, along with the backup Inmarsat system. It would cut off all communication with the Golden Seas. There were still a few VHF and short-wave radios scattered around the ship, but Sonny knew where they all were. He would take care of them.

Sonny, the pervert, the one who had put Trini's faith, his resolve, to the test. Sonny, his fat yellow cheeks, the thick black glasses slipping down his nose, his plump lips always in a pout. The way he smelled, sour cabbage and garlic and chili pepper, kimchi, the stuff he ate, seeping from his pores.

Trini shuddered, putting Sonny's vileness out of mind, focusing on matters at hand.

He removed his hard hat and earmuffs, dropped them on the floor. He grabbed his backpack, pulled out a new clip. He slapped it into the rifle.

Yes, surely, his deeds here were blessed. The hand of the Prophet guided him. Soon he would walk in glory.

He moved out of the engine room, down the hallway and up the stairs to Deck Four.

There had been no chance to test-fire the SARs. They had arrived only the night before, seven of them hidden in 55-gallon containers of E-Z Powder laundry detergent and delivered to the provisions station on Deck Two by an official, T.S.A-inspected Port of Miami supply truck loaded down with cases of liquor, dry-ice lockers filled with meat and drums of canola oil.

Arranging the buy had proven easy enough. In the long-standing tradition of the cruise industry worldwide, the tight-knit Chinese cabal that ran the laundry on the *Golden Seas* not only controlled the ship's loan-sharking enterprise but provided procurement services for everything from dope to fake passports and, in this case, assault rifles.

Yap-Yap, the laundry manager, hadn't asked any questions when Trini placed his order. He was a small man with tar-black eyes and skin so smooth and flawless it was impossible to tell his age. Maybe 30, maybe 60. All the Chinese were like that. Trini thought it must have something to do with working in the laundry. The heat, the steam. It dried them out, preserved them.

"What you want, it cost much money," Yap-Yap said.

"I've got money."

Yap-Yap studied him.

"It take long time," he said. "Weeks maybe, months."

"Bullshit, mon. This Miami. Everyone selling guns."

Yap-Yap narrowed his lips. If snakes could grin, so could he.

"You come back two days," Yap-Yap said.

When Trini returned, he could tell Yap-Yap had found a source and was ready to dicker because right off he started talking about how tricky it would be getting the rifles onboard and what would happen if they got caught, going on and on, working it, making it sound harder than it really was in order to jack up the price.

"Very dangerous, very dangerous. TSA, they watch everything. I no want go jail."

"How much?"

Yap-Yap told him. It was twice what the SARs cost on the open market, but about what Trini expected to pay. Still, they went round and round and finally settled on a number. Yap-Yap said he would need it all up front. Trini pulled out a roll of hundreds and paid him, making sure Yap-Yap saw the roll was still plenty thick when he returned it to his pocket.

On the night of the delivery, Yap-Yap was there waiting for the supply barge, along with the provisions master, a fat Belgian with big ears whose job it was to inventory everything that came aboard the *Golden Seas* and let no opportunity for personal gain go unseized. The provisions master had been more intent upon requisitioning a case of single-malt scotch and a flat of beef tenderloins than paying attention to Yap-Yap and the three other Chinese as they loaded the detergent containers on handcarts and hauled them away.

Trini met Yap-Yap just after midnight in the laundry storeroom. He brought along Pango, the Indonesian headwaiter. Pango had been Trini's original recruit, before Sonny even, the first person Trini had entrusted with his plan, or at least part of it, back when the crew of the *Golden Seas* first signed on. Trini knew Pango from other ships, knew he needed someone like Pango on his side if this was going to work.

Yap-Yap eyed Pango with suspicion, uneasy that a third party was in on the deal.

Trini counted out another thousand dollars, handed it to Yap-Yap.

"That's for the guarantee," he said.

"What guarantee? I no guarantee nothing. You pay money, I find guns, I get them on ship. That that. No guarantee, no guarantee."

Trini let Yap-Yap finish talking. When the laundry manager got wound up he really did sound like a little dog barking.

When he was done, Trini looked at him and said: "It's my guarantee."

"You guarantee? You guarantee what?"

"I guarantee you say anything I'll kill you."

Yap-Yap was quiet after that. He took the money and pointed to a corner of the storeroom. Then he walked out, leaving Trini and Pango alone with the rifles.

The SARs came bagged in plastic. So did the ammo clips. Despite that, Trini and Pango had to use hair dryers to blow out little blue balls of detergent that had slipped past the wrapping and threatened to gum up the rifles.

Having served in Tentara Nasional Indonesia, Pango had some experience with assault rifles. He claimed to have been an officer, attached to an elite guard unit at the presidential palace in Jakarta. Claimed, too, that he would have been there still had not a past election brought in a new regime.

Trini figured it was a lot of talk. He couldn't see Pango as an officer in any country's army, not even some fucked-up one like Indonesia. Still, when it came to commanding the wait staff, Pango was Patton of the dining room. Strutted like him, too. All puffed up and self-important. Trini had caught him once dabbing shoe polish on his mustache, making it look thicker than it really was.

For all his insufferableness, there was no denying that Pango enjoyed considerable influence aboard the *Golden Seas*. It extended far beyond the waiters, to the galley crew and the room stewards, most of whom were Indonesians and owed their jobs to Pango putting in a favorable word with the recruiting agents. True, he extracted a little something from their pay on a monthly basis to insure continued goodwill. That was just the way it worked.

"Like union boss," Pango had explained to Trini. "Make sure all the wheels greased. More grease, more happy."

And there was no doubt Pango knew his way with the SARs. Once they had gotten the rifles cleaned up, Pango showed Trini how to insert the clip, how to switch from single shot to full automatic, how to give the clip a sharp slap on the butt end to make sure the ammo didn't jam.

Pango assured Trini that his money had bought the real deal, that Yap-Yap hadn't cheated him.

Pango held up one of the rifles.

"You watch out this. Get hot, get hot fast," he said, tapping the muzzle. "But SAR very good. Made in Singapore. You like very, very much."

Trini edged down the hallway on Deck Four, closing in on the security office. The door was closed. Trini heard men talking behind it. He knocked on the door.

"Yes, who is it?"

Trini recognized the voice of the chief security officer, a retired sergeant from Scotland Yard with the rheumy eyes and bulbous nose of a not-so-reformed drunk.

Trini said, "Delivery, sir."

The door swung open and Trini found himself face-to-face with one of the assistant security officers, a recent departee of the Royal Thai Army. His boss sat behind a desk.

This time Trini was much more efficient with the SAR. Two quick blasts and that was that. Pango was right. Trini liked the SAR. He liked it very, very much.

He spent a few seconds poking around the bodies. Neither of the men had been armed.

That's what had amazed Trini about cruise ships, what had planted the seed of his plan. In eleven years of employment with various cruise lines, Trini had never once seen a gun onboard a ship. They were kept stashed away in secret lockers with access given only to a select few.

No one—not the captain, not the officers, not even the chief security officer—ever carried a weapon.

It was all for the benefit of the passengers. A cruise was a chance for them to escape, leave all their cares and worries behind.

And seeing a gun, well, that might upset them.